the flip side of heartbreak

meg bradley

D1714134

Copyright © 2023 by Meg Bradley

All rights reserved.

No part of this book may be reproduced in any form or by any electronic or mechanical means, including information storage and retrieval systems, without written permission from the author, except for the use of brief quotations in a book review.

"Hearts live by being wounded."
— *Oscar Wilde*

the flip side of heartbreak

What's the only logical thing to do when you find out your wife is pregnant with another guy's baby?

You buy a house—sight unseen—in a town you've never set foot in, just so you can tear the whole thing down to the studs. Seclusion and sledgehammering are my kind of post-divorce therapy.

Problem is, the feisty next-door neighbor is some best-selling romance author with a bad case of writer's block.

When she asks me to be a critique partner for her latest novel, I know I shouldn't agree to it. She needs a muse and I have ways to inspire her I don't want anyone else reading.

But I need her help, too. Demolition I can handle; it's the renovation part that isn't in my wheelhouse.

Suddenly, she's got me rebuilding more than just my fixer upper—she's working on my trust. But after being with the same woman for the past decade and then getting hurt beyond repair, I don't know how to let anyone else in. Or even if I want to.

That's the flip side of heartbreak, right? You have a say in how your heart gets pieced back together.

I came to this town to break something. I won't let it be my stupid heart again.

The Flip Side of Heartbreak is an age-gap, neighbor romance with steamy scenes and heart melting moments that will have you laugh-crying one minute and fanning yourself the next. It's the first in a series of standalones including swoon-worthy heroes and guaranteed HEA's.

1 /
nathan

EACH TIME my eyes inadvertently flick up to the rearview mirror and glimpse the assembled crib in the back of my truck, I feel the weight of my misjudgment.

I should've left it.

The only reason it's wedged between a rusted toolbox, five cardboard moving boxes, and a rolled-up, inflatable mattress is because I thought it might make my ex-wife feel something to see me pull away with it in my truck bed. A visual reminder of the path she chose to deviate from when she decided our marriage vows were optional.

That to have and to hold garbage? I can't even remember the last time I held her in my arms, let alone had any part of her.

When I told Archie and Logan that Sarah had been having an ongoing affair with her coworker over the last two years, my buddies just twirled their amber beer bottles on the bar, absorbed by the wet circles the bottoms left on the sticky surface. They couldn't look me in the eye because they already knew. We all knew, even if we never said it.

1

Logan likened the separation to watching the San Francisco Shot Clocks in the first round of the playoffs years back. We knew they didn't stand a chance—that it was miracle level luck they even made it that far in the postseason—but we still rooted for them with all we had because, as he said, "How sweet would it be if they were able to pull it off?"

Even after a decade of matrimony, Sarah and I weren't able to pull it off. Unlike NBA sports teams, we wouldn't have another season. We had failed big time and sweet redemption wasn't an option for us.

In the end, Sarah kept the house and furnishings, and I got the equivalent in our savings, which I promptly used to purchase a fixer-upper in a town I've never even been to. After all, Donovan had been staying in our house more frequently than I had lately, so I figured it already felt like home to him. That's what happened when you slept in someone's bed and ate breakfast at their table and had sex with their wife.

Being comfortable doing the wrong thing doesn't suddenly make it right.

But I'm not sure if what I'm doing is right, either. I mean, who bids on a house they've never even seen? The realtor promised it has good bones, and I've looked at comps of recently sold homes in the area. I figure I can easily net upwards of fifty grand in profit with this remodel. That is, if I can get it fixed up and on the market by fall. Once winter comes, it'll be a dead zone for sellers.

I don't plan to stick around when the snow begins to fall.

Dragging my gaze from the rearview mirror, I bump my blinker with my knuckle and when the traffic light turns green, I punch the gas and take the turn faster than I should.

Instantly, I recognize I should've spent a few more minutes strapping things down because I hear the scraping of the wooden legs as the crib shifts, teeters over the side of the truck, and then plummets to the street. My foot slams against the brake pedal. Breathing hard, I veer toward the curb before I throw the truck into *park*.

"Looks like it's still in one piece," a man who appears to be around twice my age says as he exits the car behind mine.

He must have been trailing me, just waiting for that crib to dislodge. He has a certain feel about him, the sort of guy they would cast as a friendly neighbor on a television sitcom. Neatly trimmed gray mustache with small hooks and not quite handles that bracket his smiling mouth. Eyes that disappear behind red apple cheeks. His hazard lights flash on his late model sedan and he's left his driver's side door open.

"Here buddy, let me help you with that real quick."

I huff an incredulous laugh and rub the tension cording my neck. Of course, the crib is salvageable. I don't know why that makes me feel like I have heartburn. Somehow, it would be more fitting to have it in shambles on the pavement. More expected, at least.

"You grab that end," he instructs, taking charge in a way that's expected. "I've got some rope in my trunk. I can help you get it tied securely."

We lift the crib by the rails back into the truck, and I move some boxes around before I slam the tailgate shut.

"Thanks, man, but I don't have much more to go. It should be fine. I'll just try not to take any more corners on two wheels."

"Got a little one on the way?" he infers with a grin like

this is universally good news and he should be happy for me, even though we've only just met.

"Yep," is all I say because it isn't a lie. There is a little one on the way. It just isn't mine. "Due next month."

"Good thing that crib's a sturdy one!" he hollers as he jogs backward toward his car. Before he drops into his vehicle, he flicks me a firm salute. "Congratulations, Dad!"

I'm suddenly grateful I pulled my truck off on the side of the road because I sit in the driver's seat without moving for at least a dozen light changes, that word completely immobilizing me.

Cars whir past, blurs of colored steel in my periphery. I lock in on one, but only because it appears to be slowing down behind me, its running lights growing larger and closer as it creeps my way. I don't want to make small talk. Declining the help of another well-meaning stranger isn't in my nature, so I fire up the engine and coast into the steady stream of cars until my GPS instructs me to turn off the main drag and then onto a side street.

I don't know where I'm going; this town is as foreign as the name the man just called me.

I'm not about to become a dad and hauling around a crib doesn't make me feel like that could ever be my reality.

2 /
quinn

THERE'S a crib in the gutter with a torn piece of cardboard and the word *FREE* scrawled across it in sloppy, nearly illegible handwriting.

When I'd left for my evening run just before sunset, the sidewalks were empty, save for the random newspaper that didn't get collected that morning. I had cranked up my favorite playlist and let the newest hot girl anthem set my pace.

Back in high school, I had a five-mile route I would run each morning before school. Even though it's been years since I've lived at home, my feet still have the path memorized like a choreographed routine. I can almost keep my eyes closed and make my way back in one piece, except for the fact that there's currently a crib obstructing my path.

I pace in front of it, mostly to allow my heart to decelerate at a steady rate, but also because it's an odd place for a perfectly good piece of baby furniture. My hands are planted on my hips and I'm sure I look like I'm judging this gutter crib when a man steps out from the open garage.

5

"I can help you carry it to your place if you're interested in it."

I rip my earbuds out and pause my playlist. "Are you talking to me?" I glance around.

He scans the area like I do, but his movements are exaggerated, like he is almost mocking me, really searching for something that clearly isn't there. "Unless you have some imaginary friend that I can't see, pretty sure you're the only one I could possibly be talking to."

"Do I look like I need a crib?"

Two hands fly up in surrender and he takes an overly intentional step back. "Listen, that's a trap and I know it."

"I don't mean do I look pregnant. But that's smart of you to not answer. I'm just out on a run, buddy. I don't need your crib."

"Gotcha." The guy strokes his jaw and I notice how stubbly it is, like he can't commit to growing a full beard, but isn't consistent in shaving it regularly. "I guess I'm just eager to get it off my hands. And it's not my crib."

"It's not, huh?" I deliver it as a question, but I'm sure my voice indicates my disbelief.

"It was left here by the previous owners."

I knew the previous owners. They definitely didn't have a baby on the way.

I can't sort out why this man I don't even know is blatantly lying to me, but I decide not to call him out on it. He looks tired, with dark, ashen circles under his eyes and exhaustion worn in his downturned mouth, like it takes too much effort to even smile. It's a shame because he's noticeably good looking, and I have a feeling a smile would completely transform him.

"I don't have a use for it," I say. "But I suggest putting it on social media or something rather than in the middle of the road like this. We don't really do that here."

"I'm just looking to get rid of it quickly. If it's not gone by morning, I'll move it," he states, like he's appeasing me. "And since you seem to have such a vested interest in keeping the neighborhood gutters clutter-free, I should let you know I've got a dumpster coming this week. It'll be parked in the driveway for the next two months. I hope that's not an issue."

Suddenly, I feel a twinge of guilt for giving this stranger grief about something that is entirely none of my business. I don't even technically live here, for goodness' sake. I'm just house-sitting for my mom until she gets back from her vacation next week. Nevertheless, I can't keep my mouth shut. "A dumpster?"

He crosses his arms over his chest and angles his upper half toward me. Even though we're a dozen feet apart, it weirdly feels like an invasion of my personal space. "Yes. A dumpster. It's like a really big trash can."

"I know what a dumpster is, dude." I roll my eyes at him.

"Well, if putting a disassembled crib on the sidewalk gets me this sort of negative reaction, I can't imagine a mountain of ripped out cabinets, carpet, and flooring will be any more welcome."

My brow tightens. "I'm not giving you a negative reaction—"

"You're telling me this is a positive one?"

"Neutral."

"Wow. Gotcha." He scrubs a hand down his tired face and sighs loudly. "Listen, I'm not trying to get under your skin here. I honestly just plan to keep to myself and get this house fixed up quickly so I can sell it and be on my way."

"Ah, you're flipping."

"I'm what?"

"You're flipping the house." Surely, the guy has watched a television show about contractors doing this exact thing. It isn't a foreign concept by any means. "You're fixing this house up so you can flip it. Sell it."

He shakes his head. "Sure. Yeah. But this will be my first. I guess I'm not one hundred percent up on the lingo."

I huff a laugh I probably should have worked harder to contain. "Well, this house should be more comfortable than the rock you've been living under."

The guy gives me a blank look for a beat and then barks a laugh so jarring it almost makes me jump. "Jeez, you're kinda mean."

That he's called me out so quickly makes me pause. With more decorum than earlier, I trap the other nasty comment I had readied to fire off behind a tight scowl. My shoulders drop, conceding.

"I'm sorry," I relent. "I'm not usually so rude. I'm just... dealing with a lot right now."

"Aren't we all?" he mutters, and I readily pick up on the underlying tone of dejection.

Instantly, whatever misplaced annoyance I have built up toward this stranger switches into an empathy I can't quite put a finger on. There's so much audible heartache in his words that I have to swallow past the cottony lump suddenly forming in my throat.

"Are all the neighbors so...bristly?" he asks boldly.

Even if I'd wanted to, I can't hold back my laughter this time. "Not sure, really. I don't actually live here. I'm house-sitting for my mom until next week," I clarify. "That's probably the reason for my *bristly* attitude. I really just want to get back to my real life," I offer, hoping my explanation can serve as some sort of apology without saying the actual words. "Not that it's possible to have a fake life or anything," I ramble.

"I think I disagree with you there. A fake life is entirely possible." His eyes cut into mine with an intensity that has my stomach bottoming out. They're the most captivating green I've ever seen. "Apparently, I've been living one for the last decade."

Before I can react to that very cryptic confession, he turns around and flicks a wave over his shoulder.

"Anyway," he calls out. "Enjoy the rest of your run."

"I'm actually at the tail end of it," I say, and when he rotates back around to look at me, I hook my thumb over my shoulder toward the slate gray, two-story house immediately next door. "Howdy, neighbor."

With his eyes flicked skyward, he mutters something that sounds like a curse and then says, "Unreal," under his breath. He steps forward to close the gap and offers what I figure to be an obligatory handshake. "Nathan Caldwell."

"Quinn Sampson."

His hand is rough, his grasp strong.

"I was being honest when I said I planned to keep to myself. You'll hardly know I'm here." He thinks on that for a moment and then adds, "Except for the demolition part. That's sort of noisy. And the rebuild. That's noisy, too. Hammers. Saws. Drills." He shrugs his broad shoulders to his ears. "You'll probably notice the construction, but I promise you won't notice me."

That is one thing this Nathan guy couldn't be more wrong about.

I've *definitely* already noticed him.

3 /
nathan

MY ASS IS on the floor when I wake up. So much for an inflatable mattress when it can't even do the one thing it's made for and keep me from sleeping on the ground. I laugh out loud at the fitting irony. I feel just as deflated as this junk piece of plastic around me.

I groan.

There's a mental list of the things I need to do, and they all involve phone calls. I don't particularly feel like talking to anyone. Not to the water corporation. Not to the electric company. And not to my coworker, Patrick, to see how his first day of summer school is going, even though I know he'd be the first to call me if the roles were reversed. They usually are.

I stare at my phone. It's right around first period. Normally, I'd sign up to teach during the summer months. I'm one of the few people who actually likes junior highers and doesn't need the three-month break the regular school calendar provides. Plus, I enjoy teaching math, especially to the kids who have to repeat it. It's a rewarding profession any day of the week, even more so when you have the power to help a kid move on to the next grade level. When there's a real benefit to their success.

It's not like I'm a gatekeeper—not power in that sense. But power in unlocking the potential a student might not even know is there. It's a thrill that never gets old.

But I just couldn't summon the motivation to do it this year. The halls were already buzzing at the end of the semester. Middle schoolers aren't tactful. If they have a question, they ask it outright. Which is why I shouldn't have been surprised when Kenzie Porter raised her hand on the last day of school, three minutes before the dismissal bell, and asked if I was sad that my wife was having someone else's kid.

Ex-wife, I had emphasized, but my students didn't really care about that distinguishing fact.

And yes, I was sad, I had admitted, probably sharing more than I should have with a roomful of twelve-year-olds. I figure that's why I got called into Principal Morten's office after the final bell pealed and the campus cleared out. It was discreetly couched as an opportunity for a sabbatical, but I knew he didn't think I was up for business as usual.

"You've taught summer school every year you've worked here, Nathan. I think this summer you've earned a well-deserved break. Let someone else fill in."

It still shocks me how often people use those words in the context of what I'm currently doing: *well-deserved*. Each time I share that I'm taking the summer off from teaching and will be spending some time out-of-town working on a personal project, they say I deserve it.

Deserve some *me time*. Deserve a break from my current life and situation.

But I know what they're really saying is that I didn't deserve what happened with Sarah. It's a sympathy I'm not comfortable spectating, so getting the hell out of Fairhaven was my only option.

But I'm not much more comfortable here. Not physically, at least. I sit up on the flattened mattress, my legs sticking to the material as I shimmy upright, making the hairs pull against the plastic like they're being waxed.

I'm hungry, but there's obviously nothing in the pantry. I'll need to make a trip to the grocery store, but until there's power, it doesn't make much sense to stock a lukewarm fridge. Still, a guy's gotta eat.

Getting ready without electricity or running water isn't ideal, but I do my best. I work up enough spit to do a decent job at brushing my teeth and I run a comb through my hair after tugging on my jeans and white V-neck t-shirt.

I spritz on a single pump of cologne. I need to get a new one; one that doesn't remind me of Sarah and last Christmas. Every year, she'd buy me a new scent. That should've been a red flag. I mean, who gets their spouse a different cologne year after year? I would joke that she wanted me to smell like a new person, but I think that was really it all along. She wanted someone different, down to the way I smelled.

She would absolutely hate the smell of this place.

It's got a lived-in scent, like wood polish and fabric softener. I have a feeling it was an older couple that lived here. I don't get that idea from the smell of it, but from the kitschy bear-themed wallpaper trimming the ceiling and the wainscoting in every room that screams early nineties. Plus, Quinn, the woman next door, said she was house-sitting for her mother. If the previous owners were the original buyers, then they'd probably be somewhere around her mom's age, too. That puts them in their fifties, maybe sixties, I guess.

I drag a hand down my face. None of this even matters, so I don't know why I'm using any brainpower to piece together the house's history. That's the entire point—to scrap it all and make something new.

I snag my truck keys from the counter and set out in search of a breakfast joint.

It doesn't take long before I locate a small café on what I assume is the town's equivalent of a main street, only it's called Pleasant Way. It's a cloyingly cute name and I try not to let the fact that the coffeehouse is named Pleasant Way Café get to me. If I roll my eyes at every little thing that strikes me as comical about this map-dot town, they might just tumble from my head.

There's an empty parking spot right in front. I glide my truck into it, then feed the meter with more coins than I know I'll need. It's my good deed for the day and my form of an apology for judging this town so harshly. I know I'm unusually rough around the edges lately. It's part of the reason I left Fairhaven. I don't recognize the man I've become in the last few months. Sarah would always talk about her pregnancy hormones and how they made her act like a different person, but I don't have that excuse.

I *am* a different person. Or becoming one, at least. And it isn't fair for those closest to me to be on the receiving end of my misery. Archie and Logan do a decent job convincing me it's okay to be short-tempered, but I still don't like it and they certainly don't deserve it.

Being a recluse in a new place until I get my head back

on straight is the best way to salvage the relationships I still have before I end up ruining those, too.

But the crowd in this café doesn't really allow for solitude.

It's jam-packed with athleisure-wearing bodies squished into line like they're waiting for a popular ride at an amusement park. For a second, I contemplate finding another place, but as I vacillate, three more people file in behind me. Suddenly, I feel like giving up my spot might be surrendering something coveted. I root my feet in place and decide to stick it out.

There are a few mobile orders up on a long bar, and even though the customers can't be faulted for having the forethought to order ahead of time, they're still met with judgmental glances from those of us waiting.

I scan the menu written in perfect chalk lettering. They've got creative names for their drinks, ones that make you almost embarrassed to order them.

The bell over the door chimes at my back, and another mobile order customer slips past.

It's Quinn.

At least, I think it is. All I can see is the back of her. But she's got that same long ponytail as yesterday, honey-colored hair that trails down her spine in a thick, curling wave. And those shorts, if you can call them that. The word *short* is even too long for them. They stop just below the curve of her ass, and her toned and tanned legs go on for days.

I pinch the bridge of my nose, clamping my eyes shut.

Guilt I no longer have any reason to feel slithers through my stomach. For the last ten years, I've been so good. I haven't so much as thought about checking out another woman. Seriously. It wasn't like I wasn't tempted. Of course, I was. I'm a red-blooded male. It's just that my vows meant something, and I assumed Sarah was keeping up her end of the deal, too.

It didn't help that the first dance at our wedding was to "I Only Have Eyes for You." Her song choice, just like how she selected the flavor of the cake without my input, along with the dinner menu and even my lineup of groomsmen. She called the shots from the beginning, and I let her. And that wasn't because I'm some pushover. I'm not. It's just that her happiness was all I ever wanted. Even now, I still find myself wanting that for her. I want to hate myself for it—or hate her —but that's not who I am.

Which is why I have such a hard time accepting the fact that something about seeing Quinn standing at the barista bar, her full, plump lips pressed to the lid on her cappuccino, turns me on. She's young—probably a year or two out of college—but that's right around the last time I was single.

The last time I let a woman other than Sarah make me feel like this.

I hiss out a shallow breath. The woman in front of me casts an annoyed look over her shoulder for inadvertently breathing all over her. She presses closer to the customer in front of her, needing space from me. I feel oddly scolded, like I've been caught doing something I shouldn't.

But I'm allowed to appreciate a beautiful woman. I attempt to justify my attraction, but it feels false. Just because Sarah had no problem moving on with someone else, I don't think I'm there yet. My ring finger still has an indentation on it. I mindlessly thumb the groove, but my gaze doesn't peel from Quinn.

Until she spins around and locks eyes with me.

She's flushed from the exertion of the run I have no doubt she just completed. That seems to be her thing. Her cheeks are pink, and a shimmer of perspiration collects on her collarbone right above the dip in her sports bra.

My mouth goes dry. It's a good thing I'm moving up in line because I really need something to drink.

I'm about to lift my hand in a neighborly wave, although nothing about the way I treated her yesterday was neighborly. Before I can do so, she thrusts her earbuds deep into her ears and shoulders past another patron coming to collect their mobile order.

So, this is how we're going to do things. Fair enough. I'd told her she wouldn't even notice me, so why am I bothered that that's exactly what she's doing now?

Not noticing me.

4 /
quinn

"I'M NEVER COMING HOME!" Mom croons.

I squeeze the phone between my shoulder and my cheek as I thumb through the mail, all junk except for a bill from the water company and a letter from Dad's alumni association that makes me wonder if Mom recently made another hefty donation from their estate. The bill goes onto a stack on the counter two weeks high, right next to the plant I keep forgetting to water. The envelope addressed to Dad goes straight into the trash.

"Never?"

I glance down at the trio of tabby cats staring up at me with their insistent eyes. I hope my mother's declaration is another one of her exaggerations. My allergies will be the death of me. Or her cats, whichever comes first.

"I'm staying in Florence with Libero a bit longer. I'm going to have all of that man's babies, I tell you. *All* of them."

"I'm not sure that's technically even possible at your age."

"Maybe not, but he makes me *feel* so young, Quinn." I

can hear her sigh contentedly through the phone in a rush of breathy air. "Like a teenager again. It's incredible!"

Geronimo, the biggest cat, starts doing figure eights through my ankles, tangling me as I attempt to make my way across the kitchen.

"I'm happy for you, Mom. I really am." I feign enthusiasm the best I know how. "But I honestly can't house-sit for much longer. I promised Kyle I'd be back this weekend. We've got plans with his family. His little sister's engagement party is this Saturday, remember? The thing I bought that gingham dress for? The one you said made me look like a tablecloth at a spaghetti feed?"

"Oh, Kyle will understand. He was the one who encouraged me to join all those dating sites. He'll be happy for me, just like I thought you—*my one and only daughter* —would be."

I can hear a muted rumble of a man's voice in the background uttering something in slow Italian. Mom giggles a laugh I haven't heard since back before Dad died and I want to be happy for her, but the carefree sound is a gut-wrenching déjà vu.

"I'll be home in the middle of August, sweetie. I'm confident you can hold down the fort 'til I'm stateside. The cats will be fine. I'm not worried one bit. You've got this, girl!"

"August? I can't stay here until August. This was supposed to be for three weeks. I hate to let you down, Mom, but I can't be gone that long."

"Aren't you just working on your novel?" Mom interjects. "You can do that anywhere. Your father used to write full chapters on donut shop napkins."

"Technically, I can write anywhere, but—"

"Feel free to use my computer in the office. I think the password is SassyMama1968. Or DancingQueen101. Can't recall. I had to change it a couple months back when it got that nasty virus from clicking the email about free sunglasses. Remember that tech guy who came out every day for a week trying to fix it? What was his name? Something to do with food."

I grip the phone between my fingers and fight the grimace that tugs at the corners of my lips. "I don't need to use your computer. I have my laptop. But that's really beside the point."

"Was his name Jack?" Mom suggests, her words acting as a bulldozer. "No, that's not it." She pauses, then blurts, "Colby! I was close. I knew it was cheesy."

I draw in a slow, measured breath so she can't hear it through the line. "Mom—"

"Sweetie, what day is it?" She changes the subject so fast, it practically gives my brain whiplash.

"I don't know." I scan the kitchen for a calendar but come up empty. "The fourteenth, maybe?"

"Yes! That's perfect! Casserole day! In the freezer."

"Casserole day?"

What the heck is casserole day?

Pacing across the tile floor toward the refrigerator, I tug on the freezer door handle and there, balanced on top of an open bag of frostbitten hash browns, is a Pyrex dish with what looks like lasagna layered inside. Mom's endearing attempt at a lasagna, at least.

"It's very sweet of you to make this for me, but I don't need a casserole. I'm planning to put my pajamas on, order sushi takeout, and finish M.K. Griffith's latest book. It's finally getting to the part that everyone has been talking about—"

"It's not for you. Bake it at 350 for an hour and take it to the new neighbor next door."

Him? Seriously? Just great.

I pull the lasagna from the freezer and deposit it onto the kitchen counter next to a breadbox I know Mom uses to store tiny liquor bottles rather than carbs.

"Just a little longer, Quinn. That's all I ask," Mom repeats, gearing to hang up on me, I figure. Her phone call send-offs are nothing if not grand. "After all, I carried you around for nine months. I'm only asking for two of yours in return."

———

> Kimmie: I miss your face. When are you ever coming home?

I stare at my best friend's text and frown. She doesn't know the half of it. I'd love to be back at my condo, penning my latest book on my deck as the waves continued their relentless assault on the coastline in my periphery. It's totally my happy place and Kimmie is my person.

> Me: Not anytime soon, apparently. Mom's still in Italy.

> Kimmie: Tell that woman to get her ass stateside. I need my girl back at the beach with me. Oh! Danny told me to pass along that he's going to hire a contractor to fix your balcony railing if you don't. His guy's not cheap, either.

The downside of having your best friend's older brother as a landlord.

> Me: Tell Danny I'm taking care of it.

> Kimmie: Hard to take care of it when you're two hours away.

> Me: I'll figure it out.

The oven timer goes off about a minute before I expect it and even though I know it's coming, I still startle at the trill.

> Me: Gotta run. Chat later.

> Kimmie: Love you girl!

> Me: Right back at ya.

I slip my phone into my back pocket and head to the kitchen.

Mom's casserole is done. It looks like it's a little too done, judging by the blackened cheese that encrusts the surface. My guess is that Mom hopes to make a neighborly impression with the gesture. Charred cheese won't do that. With a spatula I grab from the utensil drawer near the sink, I scrape off the burnt portion and slop it into the trash right onto the discarded piece of mail bearing my dad's name.

Fitting Mom's faded yellow oven mitts onto my hands, I use my elbow to press down on the front door handle to open it and then step onto the stoop. Muggy summer air smacks my skin like I've been hugged by a massive, sweaty man who just finished a two-hour workout. I shudder.

There's a reason I used my advance from my first novel to pay the first and last month's rent on a rental that doesn't have a window view of houses and sidewalks. Waiting two more months until I'm back at my small condo on the coast has my stomach turning over, but it might be the unappetizing meal in my grip contributing to that churning feeling. Or the thought of possibly running into Nathan again. Only that makes something low in my stomach tighten.

There's a *For Sale* sign that has been newly minted with a *SOLD* badge. Something about it feels boastful. It's not like I would have ever purchased the house. I love Mom but being her next-door-neighbor is a little too close for comfort. It's just that the previous owners, Cheryl and Tig, had such a large presence in that home, to the point that the structure itself became a personification of their very existence.

The Ainsley's were too old to be like parents and too young to be my grandparents, but they loved me and always treated me as one of their own. They passed away early last spring in a freak boating accident, and I still haven't processed what their loss looks like in my life.

Evidently, it looks like a scorched, previously frozen lasagna.

I shuffle down the sidewalk, the warmth of the glass dish spreading through the padded fabric on my hands. I'm grateful this casserole is only going next door because it's getting hotter by the second.

I avert my eyes that want to focus on the overgrown planter beds along the pathway.

Cheryl always kept her planters in meticulous shape, changing out the flower varieties with the seasons like she was a groundskeeper at a luxury resort. She took pride in the appearance of her yard and home, and the weeds that now stretch taller than the mailbox serve as a reminder that her hands will never reach into that soil again. She'll never bring flowers to life because hers is gone now, too.

That's a really morbid thought.

I shake my head, shaking off the memory like pressing the delete button on a keyboard.

I'm not sure how to proceed with this story; the one where the people I've loved have died and I didn't get the chance to say my goodbyes.

When love no longer has a place to go, it takes a bit of time to figure out where to put it. It's not like it just goes away. It has to be re-homed.

I suppose that's what Mom is doing with this tragic lasagna: transferring her love from her long-time friends to her newest neighbor in the form of food. I can't knock it because it's more than I thought to do.

I pull my phone from my back pocket with one hand and swipe up to check the date, just to be sure that it actually is the fourteenth. I've been on a writing binge all weekend and it's fair to assume that my days and dates could be off.

But it's definitely the fourteenth and this piping hot lasagna needs to get out of my hands before I drop it. There's a welcome mat right in front of the door that looks new and still rubbery. I figure the realtor placed it there to make the home feel more inviting. It's a nice, if not expected touch.

I set the casserole dish on the mat and for a moment worry that it might melt it, but that isn't my issue. I'm just the meal messenger here. Lifting my hand, I curl it into a fist and pound twice on the door, not expecting the response of footsteps because it's obvious no one is home. Still, I give it a respectable pause before I decide to leave the lasagna where it rests and return later with a note, just in case Nathan does show up and wonders why there's a mystery dinner melting his mat.

Back at the house, it takes me five minutes to scrounge up something to write on, which is odd because our home used to be covered in piles of paper, stacked like folded laundry on every flat surface.

Dad would always have several books going at a time, and he'd leave one in each room, as though physically separating them kept their plots and stories contained only within those spaces. He'd tote his typewriter around the house, settling into whatever book he felt most in touch with that day.

There's none of that now, not even a scrap of paper other than the sealed envelopes that await my mother's return. Even Mom's grocery list she wrote before she left the country is penned on a dry-erase board stuck to the refrigerator.

Finally, I locate an old receipt and write, "Welcome to the neighborhood. Here's a lasagna," because even though I'm a writer, I don't know the appropriate lingo here and it's my mother's gesture, not mine.

But when I head back over to the Ainsley house, the casserole is gone, and the lights are still out.

Mom's lasagna will have to speak for itself.

5 /
nathan

I'M STILL in the back chambers of the house when I hear what sounds like knocking. Whatever delusion I have that I'm any sort of tough guy shatters when I let out a gasp at the unexpected sound. The second, louder knock has me rallying my breath.

Someone must be at the door, but honestly, there were lots of odd noises as I explored the home. Many I couldn't make heads or tails of. I did make a mental note of each floorboard that creaked beneath my foot, though. Some I will secure and others I'll rip out, but for the most part, the home appears in decent shape.

By the time I get to the door to check, the visitor is long gone. I almost don't see it, but my shoe toes against a glass casserole dish as I step onto the porch to scope things out. It knocks the foil cover off and steam rises, along with the hearty scent of a home-cooked meal.

Man, how long has it been since I've had one of those? Too long, apparently, because my stomach growls like a feral cat that hasn't had a successful hunt in weeks. The dish is still blazing-hot to the touch, so I rush with it to the counter. Even in the dim lighting, I can tell it isn't the most presentable meal. But I'm a guy. My stomach doesn't discriminate when it comes to food. I want nothing more than to scoop a heaping portion onto a plate and dive in with a fork, but I have neither of those things.

Maybe I shouldn't have let Sarah keep everything.

Then I remember the plastic cutlery I'd tossed into my glove box the other day from the drive-thru, a place I'm ashamed to say I get most of my meals lately. After retrieving the utensils from my truck, I shovel a bite into my mouth. How the top is burnt to a crisp and the inside is still frozen is a mystery, but the fact that someone left this is endearing, and I haven't been on the receiving end of a gesture like this in a long, long time.

For a split second, I wonder if Quinn left it.

Based on her reaction—or non-reaction—to me at the café, I figure that isn't likely. I highly doubt she'd give me an entire pasta dinner when she couldn't even give me a small hint of recognition this morning.

Plus, there are other neighbors on the street. I've seen several families out riding bikes or chalking up driveways in bold, bright colors, doing the sorts of things that make a small town feel exactly that. There were parents congregating at mailboxes, old women on porch rockers sharing iced tea and gossip, dogs catching tennis balls lobbed up the street in their wet, slobbery mouths.

Any one of these families could have given me a "welcome to the neighborhood" lasagna.

I hope I'm not some part of a meal train I didn't sign up for. Until a few months ago, I'd never even heard the term, but as Sarah's due date approaches, it's all she talks about. How all areas of her life will be covered once the baby comes. Dinners. Housecleaning. Even diaper subscriptions and deliveries. Her friends and relatives will take care of everything and all she'll have to do is focus on bonding with the new baby.

I don't know why that bothers me so much. We're not even married anymore. Hell, it's not even my kid. But there's this small, permanent place inside of me that feels like it's still my role to do these things for Sarah. To take care of her.

I stuff myself with more lasagna than I'm hungry for, but it's comfort food, and I think that's exactly what I need. And maybe a drink.

I made the calls to the power and water companies this afternoon. Both will turn on in the morning, so I've only got one more night to deal with the dark. It's not so bad. The sun stays out late this time of year and despite the large two-story houses and steep rooftops that obscure the view, tonight's sunset is spectacular. All pink and orange, with hues of purple smeared across the big sky. It looks like an artist painted it.

I had enough sense earlier in the day to fill a cooler with convenience store ice, along with a six-pack of beer, some bottled waters, and salami, cheese, and grapes. It's makeshift sustenance to get me through until tomorrow, but with the lasagna, I'm not sure I'll even need it now.

Still, I take the ice chest with me outside and sit on the dropped tailgate of my truck in the driveway. Cracking open a beer, I draw in a deliberately long pull and sit there with what I can only imagine is a stupid grin on my face, just enjoying the view.

I don't have a TV right now, so this is my version of bingeing. The sky seems to change every few minutes, morphing from one colorful episode to the next. I let my mind wander, let the warmth of alcohol slide through my system, loosening my muscles and my anxieties. It's the most relaxed I've been in months.

Until a cat jumps onto my lap and its claws dig into my crotch.

"What the fuck?" I almost shout it, but then I see the group of young kids playing freeze tag in the yard across from mine and I wrangle my volume.

"What the hell, cat?" I hiss as I jump down from the tailgate and swat the furry creature from my junk. One paw remains stuck. The feline dangles from my jeans and I'm flailing and flapping while its sharp nails stab in more. When they pierce into the meaty flesh of my upper thigh, I yelp like an injured animal. That must've drawn blood.

"Geri!" I hear a woman shout, but it's all a blur because I'm full-on spinning at this point. The cat sails in circles with me like we're on some out-of-control playground merry-go-round.

"Geri!" she yells again.

It's Quinn. Of course, it is.

"Name's not Geri," I grind out. Miraculously, I've still got my beer in one hand. Apparently, the cat isn't the only one with a death grip.

"Oh, God! I'm so glad you're okay!" I appreciate her concern until I realize she's talking to the cat and not to me.

Before I can compute what she's doing, she's got a hand on my thigh for leverage while the other grabs the scruff of the cat, lifting it from my leg. But things don't go that easy because that would mean life is fair and let's face it, I already know it's not. No, the cat somehow sees this as a challenge and instead of contracting its claws like a good little kitty, it goes full-on Wolverine and spears into my leg with the full length of its talons. I know birds have talons, not cats, but this isn't your average housecat. This feline is the spawn of Satan.

"Geri, let go." Quinn's palm presses firmly onto my inner thigh. I groan, not because it hurts but because it's pathetic that this is more action than I've had in the last year, and I've got a freaking cat attached to me. "Let go!"

I down the rest of the beer and chuck the amber bottle to the patch of grass that needs to be cut as soon as I get a lawn-mower. This is going to take two hands.

Grasping the cat by its middle, I yank up and out and suddenly it's freed from my leg and I'm thrusting it in front of me like I'm the monkey holding baby cub Simba.

Quinn snatches it out of my hands before it has a chance to wriggle free. As quickly as the obscure scene unfolded, she disappears, and it's back to just me and my truck and a now almost-gone sunset.

I'm immobilized. Partly from pain, mostly from shock.

That was hands-down the weirdest thing to ever happen to me, and that's saying a lot since I spend most of my days with middle schoolers.

I'm going to need another beer.

6 /
quinn

I LAUNCH the cat as far into the house as I can throw it. The only reason I'm okay with doing that is because I know it will land on all fours. It does, and then it saunters away like sneaking out of the house and assaulting the neighbor is an everyday occurrence.

This is why I don't have a cat. They are unpredictable, cocky little creatures. And even though Mom's favorite cat, Geronimo, has no shame, I do. I can't leave Nathan like that, processing the ridiculous incident all on his own.

A little of my guilt comes from my very public snubbing of him earlier this morning. I don't know why I couldn't say hi or offer a friendly wave. I think I just wasn't prepared to have him interrupt my morning like that. Like the surprise crib in the gutter, his presence in line stood out. One of these things is not like the other.

No one around here is that good looking. That broody and alluring. Sure, there are some mildly attractive men, but they carry themselves like they know it. They're manicured and groomed, with just a bit too much muscle bulging under too-tight shirts. Like pumped up Ken dolls.

Nathan is sexy in an unassuming, down-to-earth way. Even with a cat mauling him, he was hot.

I smooth a palm down my t-shirt and suck in a breath for courage. I don't know where to start with an apology for all of this and in the time it takes me to get from my front door to his driveway, I still haven't come up with anything to alleviate the shame scrambling my stomach.

He's settled back on his tailgate, working on his second beer.

Without speaking, his hand slips into the ice chest and rustles around. He draws out another bottle and stretches it toward me.

"Thank you," I say, even though I'm the one who should be doing the whole peace offering thing. I move to stand closer to his truck. His eyes flick down to the space next to him. I assume it's an invitation and when I hike a leg to join him, I think I've read him right.

"That was a first," he utters before pressing his lips to the bottle. His gaze is still fixed forward.

"You've never been attacked by an escapee housecat before?"

"Can't say I have."

I bunch up the front of my shirt and twist off the bottle cap with the excess fabric in my grip. The satisfying hiss that follows has my taste buds perking up. "Geronimo."

His head swings my way, and that strong brow lifts just above one mossy-green eye.

"The cat," I clarify. "His name is Geronimo. Geri, for short."

"Gotcha."

I keep going. "I wasn't calling you Geri. I know your name is Nathan." I need to bury my words behind a hearty gulp of beer because they're coming out faster than my brain has time to filter them. The liquid fizzes going down, so I thrust a fist to my chest to combat the burn. "But that's about all I know about you."

"What do you want to know?"

I feel those words in my stomach, that quiver of anticipation, like he's given me the key to something I'm not sure I should open.

"What brought you to Brookhill?" It's the safest thing I can think to ask. Everything else I want to know about him feels dangerous. Like what his mouth would feel like on mine. What the weight of his body would be like on top of me.

I choke on another sip of beer.

He regards me for a second to make sure I'm okay and then says, "It's not so much that something brought me here, but that something drove me away from where I came."

I nod like I understand, but really, I'm just arranging his words into something easier to compute.

He's running from something. Maybe someone.

"What about you, Quinn?"

If I felt his earlier question in my stomach, the way he utters my name hits even lower. It's smooth and deep, with an edge of challenge, like he's testing it out to see if it's okay to be so familiar.

"I'm house-sitting for my mom," I say, but he already knows that. "For the next two months."

He stills. "I thought she was coming back next week?"

33

"So did I, but apparently she's taken an Italian lover and can't peel herself away."

He snickers a little and I'm sure it's the way I've worded it. I could've just said she's extended her stay, but no. That would be too normal, evidently something I'm not.

"I'm a romance author," I add as an explanation.

"And are your mom's Italian escapades inspiration for your next book?"

I yank my chin back and whip my head so quickly the end of my ponytail stings my cheek. "God, no. Thinking about that is enough to make me never want to write again." I shudder so fully I feel it in my toes. "But that might be my fate, anyway. My last novel wasn't the big bestseller my publisher hoped it would be. And I'm really struggling with my current book."

He offers me a sympathetic look that feels genuine even though he doesn't know me. "I'm sorry. It sucks when things don't meet your expectations."

He's speaking from experience. I can feel it in his delivery and in the way he chases it with a long drink that serves as an ellipsis. I know there's more to what he wants to say, but it just hangs there between us.

"So, you're completely renovating the place?" I tilt the neck of my beer over my shoulder toward the house.

"I am. I need to demolish something."

"And then put it back together," I fill in for him. "Because I don't know many buyers that want to purchase a destroyed house. Usually, they like things like walls and floors and doors to be intact."

Nathan rewards my humor with a slow grin. "I'll put it back together."

"What style are you going for? Farmhouse? Mid-century modern?"

It's a foreign language to him. His face is blank.

"Do you have a color scheme?" I ask. "Any ideas for fixtures and appliances?"

"I'm really just focused on the demo part right now." He finishes off his beer and then looks at the ice chest like he's contemplating another but thinks better of it. "You hungry?"

"I could eat." I've already had dinner. I'm just not ready to leave this tailgate. "What've you got?"

"I would offer you some lasagna, but there's not much of that left."

"You liked it?"

He pulls out a cluster of green grapes from the chest, plucks off a few for himself, and then passes the bunch my way. "It was from you?"

"My mom."

"I thought she was in Italy."

I pop a grape into my mouth and try not to make a face when the sour fruit tingles the back of my tongue. "She made it before she left but gave me detailed instructions to bake it and make sure it got to you on the fourteenth. She's a little eccentric, but she's a good neighbor, I promise." I tug another grape from the stem and catch myself. "But that doesn't matter because you won't be living here. Where do you plan to go?"

"I don't know." A muscle clenches near the back of his jaw. "One day at a time."

I nod. It's simple advice, but still good advice. I can't tell you how many times my editor has emphasized the same sentiment. One word at a time. Even life itself is so much easier when broken down into manageable, bite-sized pieces.

I follow Nathan's gaze and look ahead. The streetlights have flickered on, taking charge of the sun's responsibilities. It's twilight, and deep blue pulls over the sky like a sapphire blanket. The planes and angles of Nathan's features are more cutting now, his eyes bearing an intensity that wasn't there in the daylight.

"If you ever need any help...," I start to say with a noncommittal shrug. "You know, with the whole decorating thing, I'm around."

His mouth lifts in appreciation, but it's brief. "Thank you."

I nod and fidget with a grape between my fingers, rolling it around like a marble.

"If you need any help with the whole book thing..." He pauses like he's going to offer up something, but then says, "I'm not sure I can be much help."

But that's not true. Something about Nathan does inspire me, and it's an inspiration I can't wait to explore.

7 /
nathan

THE SLEDGEHAMMER LANDS right between the wallpapered bear's beady eyes. The flat metal head smashes through the sheetrock, getting stuck on shards of splintered wood from the studs when I try to tug it free. I wind up for another strike.

God, this feels good.

I probably could've left this existing wall between the kitchen and dining room, but it's not load bearing and taking it out feels like taking a load off more than just the house. It's like cheap therapy. Or maybe not so cheap since I had to buy the place.

I pummel the hammer through another section.

Electricity and plumbing kicked on this morning, but I've already flipped the breakers off in this portion of the house so I don't end up electrocuting myself. I certainly don't need any more shocks in my life.

Pushing back the protective goggles from my eyes, I drag the back of a gloved hand across my brow. The work is physically exhausting in the best sort of way. I drop the glasses back and slam the hammer into the partition again. This time, it goes all the way through and light from the dining room on the other side glints between the cracked pieces of plaster and sheetrock. I nudge my shoulder to my jaw to wipe back more sweat and wind up to swing again.

The windows are all open, plus the front door. It has created a wind tunnel that sweeps a cool breeze through the house, despite the rising temperatures outside. Free air conditioning is always a good thing.

Suddenly, a quiet, "Knock, knock," filters in with the wind. It's a voice rather than an action since the door is already open.

I think it's Quinn, but I don't know her well enough to recognize the sound of her voice yet.

"In the kitchen!" I say loudly, lowering the head of the sledgehammer to my foot. I balance a palm on the tip of the long wooden handle, take off my goggles, and wait for the mystery visitor to appear.

Yep. It is her.

She enters cautiously.

The windows let a breeze in, but they also let things out. I'm pretty positive she could hear all of my grunting and smashing and occasional swearing. There's hesitation as she steps into the kitchen, like she's worried she might interrupt something.

"Hi." Her deep brown eyes zero in on mine, then dip down to my chest which hadn't started off bare but ended up that way when my shirt got soaked with so much sweat, I looked like I'd taken a dip in a pool fully clothed. Thankfully, the pants remained in place.

Her gaze pops back up, cheeks noticeably pinker.

"Hey." I grip the sledgehammer. "What's up?"

"I really hate to do this, but I've got a favor to ask."

She's dolled up in a halter dress that looks like it was made for her. It hugs her curves in a way that only pretends to be modest with its innocent red and white gingham pattern. Nothing else about it is. She's undeniably hot, but she could wear a paper bag and I'd probably still think that.

"What kind of favor?" I hope we're not doing this whole 'can I borrow a cup of sugar' neighborly thing already because I really don't have much to offer.

"I'm heading out overnight and I need someone to look after the cats."

The sledgehammer slips and jams my big toe, eliciting a sharp grunt. "The same cat that tried to neuter me yesterday?"

"Yes, the same cat." Her mouth curls devilishly before she quickly controls her expression. She bats her eyes and adds, "Plus two more."

I move the hammer to rest against the half-demoed wall and tug my fingers from my gloves with my teeth. "Yeah, I don't really do cats." I flap the leather between my hands.

"I was worried you might say that after everything that happened last night."

"I would've said that before everything that happened last night," I correct. "I'm not really an animal person."

"Right." She looks dejected. "I was just hoping you were a good person."

She might as well have just slapped me across the face with one of my empty gloves. "I *am* a good person, Quinn."

"I'm sorry." She shakes her head with force. "I didn't mean for it to sound that way. I'm sure you are a good person.

I'm just in a bind here. I've got a commitment with my boyfriend's family that I can't really get out of. Usually, he's the one who takes care of Mom's cats when I'm not able to."

For a moment, I wonder if she's taken the sledgehammer and rammed it into my groin, because the words knock the wind out of me to the point of doubling over. Of course, she has a boyfriend. I'm not sure why I would think someone as beautiful and interesting and sexy as hell as Quinn would be single. And I *really* don't know why the revelation has me more winded than the last few hours' worth of demo work combined.

"What does it involve?" I ask.

She rolls her eyes. "Oh, you know. Feigning interest while Kyle drones on and on about crypto currency while I also pretend to like his sister's fiancé even though the guy is a total douchebag and is only marrying Kristy because their family has money."

"I meant what does taking care of the cats involve?"

The pallor of Quinn's face completely drains. "Oh. Right." She shifts from one foot to the other. "Just feeding them dinner tonight and breakfast in the morning. And maybe watering a couple of ferns if it's not too much trouble."

"Cats and ferns. I think I can handle that."

She clasps her hands in front of her chest, pressing her breasts together, which I'm positive isn't to purposefully turn me on, but it can't be helped. "Seriously? You can?"

"Yeah, I can do that."

"You are a lifesaver, Nathan." She takes a step forward like she's going to hug me but retracts. "I'll leave a key under the mat. The cats can eat any time between six and seven tonight, and then again tomorrow morning before nine. I should be home by noon, so if for some reason you're not able to do the morning feeding, I can always do it when I get back."

"I can do both feedings," I say. She's got my word.

"Honestly, this means so much. You have no idea."

"It's no big deal."

"But it is. I really appreciate it. I'll make it up to you."

"That's not necessary," I say, but suddenly I'm wondering what sort of exchange might be equal to me risking life and limb to care for the very cat that tried to annihilate me the night before. I shake the thought from my mind before I'm able to fully envision what I'd like in return. "Drive safe and have fun."

She smiles, a genuine one that climbs up to those chocolate eyes. I can't tell, but I think it's the fact that I've asked her to be careful on the road that makes her look at me with this newfound affection.

But then her expression falls when she says, "Having fun isn't really an option when you're with the Vanstrouds. More like be on your best behavior and try not to do anything that will make them like you less than they already do."

"Your boyfriend and his family sound like real winners."

"They're not so bad." She wobbles her shoulders. "He's not so bad."

"He must be really great at other things, then."

She stills. "Excuse me?"

"He must have some other really great 'qualities' if you're willing to settle for someone who's not so bad." I make air quotes around the obvious innuendo. Then, when she doesn't register my meaning, I add, "The sex must be amazing."

Quinn is speechless for a breath before she says, "I'm completely satisfied in the relationship."

"I'm glad to hear he's able to satisfy you."

She looks shocked but not offended, which is good because I'm aware I'm treading into territory I have no business exploring. Maybe it's the testosterone pumping through me from smashing stuff that has me all wound up and bothered. I'm usually not this bold. I never was with Sarah.

"Yep. Totally satisfied." Her chest heaves a little, and she stuns me when she adds, "Orgasms galore."

"Galore, huh? Sounds like the guy's some sort of orgasm-giving king."

We're facing one another like a standoff, eyes locked, neither of us blinking.

"Yep. The orgasms are perfectly fine."

"If they're just fine, you're doing it wrong."

She chokes on a cough. "I'm the romance author. I do know my way around a good orgasm."

This conversation has taken a not-so-subtle, not-safe-for-work turn, but I'm not entirely sure I want to right its course. "I'm sure you do. On paper, at least. I'm just guessing this Kyle guy isn't giving you much to write about if the word you use to describe your sex life is fine."

Quinn's ruby lips press into a defiant pout. "Oh, I have *plenty* to write about."

"Good," I say with a little approving nod. "Glad to hear it."

Her eyes are wild when I suddenly step closer, my chest mere inches from hers. "Don't worry." I breach the silence. "I can take care of you."

I take a step back to see her lips part on a shaky inhale and her doe eyes widen.

"I can take care of your *cats*," I qualify, but I'm pretty sure I can take care of any other needs she has too. Better than her not-so-bad boyfriend.

"Yes. The cats." She straightens. Smooths her palms down her skirt. Gives a little shiver that swishes the fabric around her killer legs. "Thank you for your service," she says in an odd voice several octaves higher than earlier. "Not service." She pinches her eyes shut and shakes her head. "You're not servicing anyone." A hand slaps her forehead. "Oh my God. I'm just going to go."

My mouth twitches into a grin. I would see her out, but the door is already open. "Have fun with your boyfriend," I say with a wave. "I hope he gives you some good material."

8 /
quinn

KYLE IS NOT AN ORGASM-GIVING KING.
Not even a prince.

He falls somewhere in the court jester category, what with his comically short performance that leaves oh so much to be desired.

I lied to Nathan. I'm not satisfied. Not even a little. In fact, I don't think I've been satisfied in bed by Kyle once, at least not through his efforts alone. I've gotten really creative at finding ways to get off that don't involve his help. I have a few paragraphs memorized from my favorite smutty novels, so I simply insert myself into the scene and let the fantasizing do the trick.

It doesn't work this time, not that I'm surprised.

I need some new inspiration.

As usual, Kyle is off and showering before I even have a chance to verify that our romp in the sheets is, indeed, over. He's not an after-sex cuddler. Not even a wham, bam, thank you ma'am because I assure you, I've never been thanked for my contributions. And believe me, I put on a respectable show. I give it the old college try and all that by strategically alternating my moans and whimpers with *Oh God, Kyle, yes!*

I'm overworked and underappreciated.

And hungry.

I lift his cell phone from the nightstand to see if it's almost time for us to leave for his sister's engagement dinner, but the phone buzzes in my hand when it's my face and not his attempting to unlock it. Thankfully, I've got his password memorized, so I punch in the numbers to search his online calendar for the start time of the party I'm half-dreading, half-looking forward to, but only because I've been promised the food will be Michelin star status.

Kyle is one of those guys that can have over a thousand unopened emails and dozens of ignored texts without it making his teeth hurt. My molars, on the other hand, already feel like they're going to crack when I see his loaded inbox.

But it isn't his neglected email account that has something in the back of my jaw ticking. It's the lack of unread text messages. Kyle once bought an entirely new phone because he ran out of storage and didn't want to take the time to clean it up. The thought of forced organization makes the man do irrational and expensive things.

I click on the green square and expect to scroll through dozens of text threads, but there aren't any. Not even the texts I'd sent him earlier that day letting him know I was on my way over.

It's like they've completely vanished.

Or been deliberately erased.

I hear the shower shut off and the curtain scrape back on its metal rings but the out-of-tune singing still echoes against the bathroom walls as he primps for our dinner. I swear to God, the man has a longer beauty routine than I do.

There's this teeny, tiny devil on my shoulder, tempting me to dig around and find the hidden texts, but my curiosity doesn't even have the chance to get the best of me.

The incoming message from someone named Bambi answers everything I need to know.

> Still on for tonight? Your place or mine?

I don't know what my fingers are doing, but somehow, I've already typed **Mine** and clicked the send arrow.

The woman comes back with a string of phallic food emojis as her reply, some sexual fruit basket confirming her involvement in whatever debased activities they have planned.

I don't even pretend to hide the phone when Kyle finally saunters out of the bathroom with a towel wrapped so low around his waist, I worry it's going to slide right off. His dick certainly isn't big enough to keep that thing in place, which is ironic, because this whole cheating-on-his-girlfriend thing is a *colossal* dick move.

"Bambi just confirmed your scheduled intercourse for tonight. I told her it's more convenient for you to do it here. Hope that's not a problem."

He's still humming and dancing while he opens and closes his dresser drawers, and it takes a second until my words land right where they need to. His spine goes ramrod straight. The towel falls away.

He's scrambling to gather the terrycloth and hoist it up

his middle, but he's become the visual of the bumbling, fumbling idiot I've always known him to be. "What?"

"Bambi. The woman you're sleeping with." I sit up in his bed, but keep the sheet draped over me because even though he just saw me naked ten minutes ago, it's now something he'll never have the pleasure of experiencing again. "Oh, and I think she's making a grocery store run on her way over because she sent a bunch of emojis like eggplants and donuts and peaches. I think there was a banana, too. Your fridge should be fully stocked after tonight. Pretty thoughtful of her."

"Quinn." Kyle steps toward the bed but halts when I recoil. I press flush against the headboard. Ironically, it makes more noise when it hits the wall than it did during our flash in the pan sexcapade. "Quinn, it's not what it looks like."

"Sure, it is. It looks like I'm about to pass off my orgasm-faking duties to a woman who's named after a woodland creature."

"Let me explain." He has a knee to the mattress, but I've slipped out of the bed, along with the sheet that now wraps around me like a low thread count toga.

"There's nothing to explain, Kyle."

My clothes are in a pile on the ground. I unceremoni-ously shimmy and shake my way into my crumpled halter dress while keeping myself relatively covered by the stupid sheet. I jostle my boobs into place, frustrated that they look so damn great and he has the undeserved honor of seeing them. It's enough to make me pick the sheet up off the floor and use it as a makeshift shawl.

"It's not like this is a regular thing," he justifies, voice cracking like he's still going through puberty. "It's just something we do every few months when she's in town. She's an old friend from high school. And Bambi's not even her real name, just what she likes to be called during...you know..."

"Is that supposed to make me feel better?" My volume is higher than I want it to be, conveying an emotion I don't want him to detect.

Yes, Kyle is an asshole, and yes, I know I deserve better. But goddammit, this still hurts.

"She knows about you," he says, like this will somehow endear me to her. It doesn't.

"That is so, so much worse."

My keys and purse are in my hands, his bed sheet in a ball again on the floor, and with strides so deliberate I feel like I'm marching, I'm at the door to his shitty apartment, handle in my grip.

Kyle's at my back. "Don't do this, Quinnie."

I want to vomit. I always hated that nickname but put up with it because I put up with him.

Not anymore.

"Goodbye, Kyle." I shove my purse strap higher. "Tell your sister congratulations on her upcoming nuptials. I wish them a lifetime of happiness."

I don't think it's actually raining outside, but my eyes are so blurry I can barely see through the windshield. My eyelids blink like wipers to keep the deluge at bay, at least until I make it into my driveway. Then the floodgates open.

I sit with the engine off, composing a text through water-rimmed lashes.

> Me: Kyle and I are done. He's a douche nozzle.

Not even ten seconds go by before my best friend's words appear on the screen. She's a bartender at a coastal dive back home and I know she's knee deep in customers right now, but she's always lightning fast with her support when I need it. And I so need it right now.

> Kimmie: The douchiest of nozzles. Good riddance. Kyle was a tool.

I sniff around a laugh.

> Kimmie: Want me to come over and cheer you up? I'm off at two.

> Me: Which would put you here at four in the morning. I'll be fine. Promise.

> Kimmie: Seriously. Just say the word and I'm there. You're my girl.

> Me: I know. I'll be okay. Love you.

> Kimmie: Love you too.

Sniffing back any remaining sadness I have about the night, I click open the door to my sedan and make my way up the path toward Mom's house. I think most of the tears were from the whole cheating debacle, but a fair amount is over the missed meal that promised to be a culinary experience unlike anything I've ever had. For me, hunger pangs and sorrow aren't all that different. Both turn me into a blubbering, incoherent mess.

There's an unjustifiable anger coursing through me over the fact that there's not a lasagna waiting in the freezer with my name on it. Sure, the neighbor gets an entire pasta dish, but I don't even get a PB&J.

I'm resigning myself to the fact that I'll have to whip up my own mediocre meal when I realize my key isn't even necessary. The lock is already turned over.

So, this is how it ends for me.

Dumped and dead in the same night. The only saving grace is that I know I look amazing in this dress, so there's that. When I show up on one of those crime shows, they'll at least comment on my killer fashion sense.

I don't even have the energy to be scared.

There's a stranger in the house, and they've clearly just heard me enter through the front door, chuck my keys onto the counter, and toss my purse toward the table but miss.

The cats don't even come out to greet me, but I guess that's expected because they're probably dead, too. I saw on some show that serial killers start their murdery fetishes with cats, so it's fitting that we're all goners tonight.

I'm too exhausted—and deliriously hungry—to put up any fight, even when I hear heavy footfalls coming down the hall.

"Please, just make it quick," I whisper, eyes clenched, heart kicked into high gear but feet unwilling to make me flee.

"Quinn?"

I pop one eye open, but it's still fuzzy from my previous

cryfest. "Nathan?" I open the other eye. "What are you doing here?"

He's cautiously moving closer, his feet sliding forward on the tile. "I'm feeding your mom's cats. You asked me to, remember?"

Like he's Snow White beckoning birds to a window, the tabbies scurry into the kitchen, weaving in and out of his legs on cue.

"Yes. Right." I sigh, utterly defeated. "I did ask you to do that. I'm sorry. I completely forgot. I'm not in a very good headspace right now."

Nathan bends down and, I kid you not, picks up Geronimo, snuggling him to his chest. What sort of sorcery is this? The man is not a cat-person and Geronimo is not a person-cat. I shake my head.

"I thought you didn't like…?"

"We've made friends." He gives the overweight feline a scratch between the ears before returning him to the cluster of furballs at his feet. "Weren't you supposed to be at some party with your boyfriend?"

I press a hand to my forehead and shove a clump of hair from my eyes. "Yes. That. I bowed out after I found out he's been hooking up with a woman with a stripper slash caribou name."

Nathan looks at me like he doesn't fully comprehend, which is fair because the disorientation of hunger has taken full control over me. I'm not my best self.

"I need to eat something." Anything. I look at the fridge, then back at Nathan. "Have you eaten?"

"I haven't. I wanted to make sure I got these guys fed before I worried about myself."

That's nice. I smile, but it takes a lot of energy.

"I'm going to make a grilled cheese. You're not lactose intolerant, are you?"

"I'm not, which is good considering the obscene amount of mozzarella on that lasagna."

"There was even more to start with, but I had to scrape it off since it burned to a crisp."

"Good looking out," he says in a way that feels cautiously flirtatious.

I've looked at him before, but never really studied Nathan like I am now. He's older than me; quite a bit, I think. There are soft little creases in the corners of his eyes, not really crow's feet yet, but they make me think he's edging up on his mid-thirties.

"Can I get you something to drink?" I ask, forcing my gaze from his face. He knows I was staring at him, but it doesn't seem to bother him.

"I'm fine with water."

I nod toward the round table in the nook just off the kitchen. "You can have a seat and I'll get that right out to you."

I'm fully aware I sound like a waitress in a diner, but I'm not entirely sure how to entertain at Mom's place. Or entertain, period.

"Quinn, I can help you." Nathan takes a step toward me and it's then I realize his eyes haven't pulled from mine since he first came into the kitchen. He's been studying me, too.

I'm pretending this whole breakup thing isn't bothering me, but my face reads differently. There's evidence all over it and my reddened, puffy eyes are the biggest betrayer.

"Do you um...?" He can't find the words, but he makes a valiant effort. "Do you want to talk about it?"

"No," is all I say and then I'm busy at work grabbing slices of sourdough and cheddar from the fridge and assembling them on the counter. I cut a pat of butter off the half-gone stick and let it simmer over the pan, bubbling in a yellow square that slips and slides across the hot surface.

I feel like that butter—overly heated and dissolving into a puddle.

But I don't let myself. My spine pulls straight, and I flip the sandwiches when they're a perfect golden brown. It's a win I will gladly take.

Nathan took my suggestion to wait at the table, and when I arrive with two Instagram-worthy grilled cheeses, he just looks up at me, almost helpless.

"Thank you," he says quietly, like I'm so fragile that loud words might shatter me. He might be right.

"Of course." My smile is false, but it's the only type I can give right now. I sit across from him. "It's the least I can do since you took care of the cats."

He bites into a corner. A string of gooey cheese suspends between his mouth and the sandwich. When he wraps it around his finger and tugs it off slowly with his teeth, I can't feel my face. Grilled cheese sandwiches are not inherently sexy, but somehow Nathan makes eating cheese and stale bread feel almost pornographic.

"It'll get better." He lowers the slice to his paper plate and leans back. "In time."

"Are you speaking from experience?" I raise my cup of water to my lips and take a long drink. I didn't cry that much, but I feel dehydrated, completely shriveled up. Emotionally, at least.

"Not speaking from experience, but on the advice of others."

He curls another string of cheese around his finger, and I almost contemplate asking him to refrain from being so hot while eating. I can't compute what he's doing to me and reconcile that with the fact that I *really* want to hate all men right now.

He looks directly at me. "I'm working on my own heartbreak."

"Oh." My shoulders slump. "I'm sorry to hear that."

"Love can be a bitch, sometimes."

We finish our sandwiches without speaking, and I try my best not to watch him because I'm not ready to be seduced by sharp cheddar.

But that's the thing. I don't think I was ever in love with Kyle. And when I lock eyes with Nathan and see the depth of anguish in his emerald gaze, I know what I've just gone through doesn't compare. He doesn't even have to speak the words.

My heart might be cracked, but Nathan's was completely shattered.

9 /
nathan

I DON'T REALLY like grilled cheese.

Still, eating another with Quinn is all I can think about.

It's not the sandwich, obviously. It's her.

I can't get her out of my head. No amount of demolition can clear away the thoughts I have about her. How I have this strange need to make sure she's okay. This weird desire to take care of her.

I keep busy. The dumpster finally arrived yesterday, and I've already filled a third of it. There are cabinets and floorboards and broken tiles loaded into the rusty bin. Every time I gather another haul to take out to the driveway, I find myself peering over at her place, just to see if her car is parked out front.

It is. She hasn't left her house in two days.

I'm familiar with this post-breakup routine. The staying in bed and stumbling into the kitchen to make yourself eat something, only to shut yourself in the bedroom again until morning comes, and you can start the whole depressing Groundhog Day all over again.

I did that longer than I care to admit when things imploded with Sarah.

Picking up a pile of splintered two-by-fours cluttering the garage, I balance the long boards on my shoulder, readying to hoist them into the trash. I stop just shy of throwing them.

Quinn is outside.

Signs of life. That's good.

I chuck the wood into the dumpster, banging around to make a lot of noise so she sees me and I don't have to reveal that I'm the one noticing her first.

As hoped, it does the trick.

"Howdy, neighbor." She flicks a little wave that looks more like a salute. An approachable smile crinkles her eyes.

Today, she's wearing black leggings and a white crop top that barely hits below her sports bra. I wonder if she's going for a run. That would be good. Run off some of those breakup blues.

"Heading out for a jog?" I ask.

There's a low hedge that separates the houses and we both make our way toward it. It feels like a barrier, but I probably need one right now because what I really want is to take her into my arms and express my relief that she's gotten herself out of bed and out of the house. That deserves to be acknowledged.

I'm not sure why I feel like it's my job to recognize her efforts in healing. I don't even know her. But I do know what she's going through, and in some sense, that shared experience makes me feel close to her. It's irrational, sure, but most of my feelings have been lately. I'm learning to accept that.

"Not a run," she corrects. "Yoga, actually. They're starting up a new beginner's class at the community center and I thought I'd give it a go. Also thought it might be a chance for me to get to know some of the people here, since I'm sticking around longer than originally planned."

Good for her. My response was to withdraw; hers is to put herself out there. To each his own.

"You know what?" Her head cocks a little to the side and her eyes narrow, pinning me in place. "You should come with me."

"To yoga?" I bark a laugh that sounds more like a cough. "Um, thanks, but no thanks."

"What? Too manly to do some stretching?"

"Not too manly, just too busy."

She gives me a skeptical look, then glances toward the dumpster behind me. "That thing is almost full. You've been working around the clock. I've heard you. The house must be completely gutted by now."

"Nowhere near. It's going to be a long, exhausting road. I'll be here for a while."

"All the more reason to come with me so you can meet some of our neighbors. Don't you want to get to know the people around here?"

I'm about to say no, but that isn't entirely true, because there is one person I'd like to get to know very much. I don't answer, and she reads that as rejection.

"Fine," she relents. "I'll go by myself, but when I come back with three new besties, you're going to be jealous."

I've got Archie and Logan. I'm good in the friend department. But there's this look she's giving me, and the way she lingers like she's offering me time to change my mind does exactly that.

"Give me five minutes," I say. "And I'll drive."

. . .

Yoga sucks.

I've fallen over twice already, which—with my size and how quiet this whole stretching thing is—disrupts the class completely. I'm not making friends; I'm creating enemies.

We're doing some warrior pose, but I can't imagine any dude looking like this in battle. I feel ridiculous. Sweat runs down my leg and onto the rubbery mat beneath me. My feet can't get a good grip. It's like I'm on a fucking slip-and-slide.

I'm going down again and it's both in slow motion and unbelievably quick all at once.

I land with a loud *thunk* not unlike a felled tree. Even the instructor—a little old lady named Beatrice whose hair and teeth are unnaturally yellow—is getting annoyed with me. She weaves through the mats and squats next to me on little bird legs that bow out at the knees. I don't bother getting up. I know I'm going to end up back on the ground, anyway. Might as well stay here.

"Nathan, sweetie. You need to work on your balance."

No shit, Sherlock. I don't say it. She's old and it feels wrong to curse at a grandma. Still, she easily interprets my frustration. I struggle to my feet with her help.

"Quinn, dear, would you mind assisting Nathan with his posing? He needs to work on keeping that core engaged and those hips aligned."

Grandma Beatrice grabs dangerously close to my ass and jerks my hips back and forth as if she's instructing Quinn on what to do.

The little lady shuffles her way back up to the front and calls out some other pose.

"You don't have to help," I say to Quinn in a low voice. The woman on the mat next to me cuts a glare so sharp I actually flinch. She lifts a finger to her thin lips to shush me.

"Sorry," I mouth.

"Beatrice is right." Quinn has the pose down pat and flows from one graceful stance to the next without faltering. "You need to work on tightening your core."

"I don't know what my core is."

While balanced on one foot, she waves her hand over her belly. "These muscles. Engage them."

"What does engaging your muscles even mean? Flex them?"

My mat neighbor shushes me again, so loudly that she's making more noise than I am at this point, but she doesn't recognize the humor in that.

"Now everyone, down on the mat," Beatrice calls up from the front. "We're going to do the bridge pose."

Quinn leans toward me. "Engaging your core means contracting these muscles to provide your spine and pelvis support," she whispers. "You're going to need to do that for this next pose."

I am about to say that I don't understand, but then I see everyone around me already moving onto their backs with their knees bent and feet flat. Oh, and butts lifted in the air. When they dip and lift back up in an arcing backbend, I just about roll up my mat and head for the hills.

Nope. Not going to do that.

"Quinn, dear," Beatrice hollers, still unreasonably concerned with my progress or lack thereof. "Please help Nathan find his way into the bridge pose."

"We don't owe her anything," I hiss in a whisper-shout.

"She won't notice if we grab our things and go. At her age, I doubt she can even see us."

"Can't you just *try* to pretend this is good for you?" Quinn's hands land on my shoulders, leveling me onto the mat. I can't say I hate the way she's taking control, but I'm not altogether prepared for it, either. When she hoists a leg to straddle me, I'm thankful I'm already on the ground because I go lightheaded.

Without pause, she curls her hands over my hip bones and lifts them up, bringing me dangerously close to her crotch, then gently adds pressure to push me back down.

"Lift," she instructs, and I slowly hoist my hips toward her without making contact. "And now lower back down."

I shakily sink down, but I'm not engaging my core. I'm not even engaging my brain. Nothing is working right, except maybe my dick, because it's the only thing currently responding.

I let out a gusty breath.

"Lift again." Her grip lessens, encouraging me to do the work on my own. I can't take over and my backside hits the mat. "Come on, Nathan. I can't imagine this move is *completely* foreign to you."

That's it. Something about her words shifts into a challenge. I'm not about to let her think I don't know how to work this part of my body.

Still, getting an erection within the same vicinity as a dozen of my elderly neighbors isn't the way I want to spend my Monday afternoon. I try to think about really awful things like taxes and a gruesome episode of Pimple Popper that stuck with me, but Quinn's got her hands on me again, pushing and pulling my hips rhythmically up and down all while she straddles me. My teeth meet and I grind out a frustrated growl.

"Do you feel it?" Quinn's mouth drops too close to my ear.

I think she's asking if I feel my core muscles, but I feel *everything* right now. I'm like a ticking time bomb, each thrust bringing me dangerously close to a scenario that might get me banned from any future community center events.

"Alright, class, cobbler's pose!"

Thank you, sweet Jesus and his faithful servant Beatrice.

I collapse onto the mat.

Quinn slinks back over to her own mat, but I can see the cunning curl of her mouth, like she knows she's not one hundred percent innocent here. We join the others in the cobbler's pose, and although I don't need any help, my flexibility leaves much to be desired. I opt for a simple crisscross-applesauce instead.

Thankfully, neither Quinn nor Beatrice gives me grief.

———

"That wasn't so bad, was it?"

My eyes dart across the cab of my truck to see if Quinn's mocking tone matches her expression. It does. "Um, yes. It was so bad."

"You *were* a little stiff."

She doesn't know the half of it.

"Thank you for going with me, though," she says. "It was good to get out of the house."

She has her ponytail pulled around and is looking at the fringe like she's searching for split ends. Sarah used to do something similar. She even had this little pair of scissors she would keep on her vanity to trim the edges, as if anyone would even notice something that detailed.

I would never notice split ends on Quinn. Not when I could be looking at her chestnut brown eyes or her perfect mouth with its deep Cupid's bow that is so damn lickable. There are about a thousand other parts of Quinn that I would focus on before my eyes ever landed on the ends of her hair. Still, she fiddles with them and frowns.

My gaze refocuses on the road, but I say, "Next time, when you want to get to know our neighbors, can we just go to a potluck? Maybe something that doesn't involve so much bending and thrusting?"

Her laugh comes out like a snort, but it's absolutely adorable. "Fair enough. I probably shouldn't be going anywhere for a while, anyway. I'm coming up on a deadline and I've hit a wall writing-wise. I need to hunker down."

"Yeah?" I flick the blinker and roll to a stop at the left turn when the light shifts to red.

"It's hard being the daughter of a best-selling author."

I give her a look. "I thought you were a best-selling author, too." I looked her up.

Her slender shoulders waggle, but they're constricted by the seatbelt cutting over her chest. "The only reason my debut hit the charts is because of my last name. People were curious to see if my work was in line with my dad's."

"Was it?"

She sighs like she's blowing a bubble. "It's hard to compare. I write romance. Dad wrote sci-fi. Totally different genres. I think that's why my sophomore novel tanked. I haven't found my readers yet."

"So, you're working on your third book now?"

"I am, but it's been a struggle. Some reviews from that first book shook my confidence. Saying things like my characters were wooden and the scenes that were supposed to be intimate felt too clinical and forced."

"That's just one person's opinion." My foot lowers to the gas when the light changes.

"It's the majority, actually. I don't know. Maybe I'm not cut out for romance."

"You just need something to inspire you," I say because I know it's true. "Like this whole demo thing I'm doing. My divorce inspired that."

Her head swivels. "I didn't know you were divorced."

"Yeah. Finalized a couple months ago, but it was a long time coming."

"I'm sorry to hear that." There's a genuine lilt to her words, a soft understanding that makes my stomach feel warm. "Were you married long?"

"Ten years. Got married when we were twenty-four."

Even though my eyes are directed forward, I see her chest catch in my periphery.

"So young," she says, breathing through her surprise. "I can't imagine getting married a year from now."

I had my suspicions, and she just confirmed them. "You're twenty-three?"

"Just turned."

I nod. "I mean, Sarah and I were high school sweethearts. We moved in together in college and then got engaged and married shortly after I got my teaching credential. For us, it didn't feel too young."

Her head lifts up and down again. "My longest relationship was with Kyle, and that wasn't even a real relationship. We hooked up one night after our mutual friends introduced us at a pub crawl and then just kind of kept at it. At some point, the whole boyfriend-girlfriend label stuck, but I knew we'd never make it past that. The end was always inevitable."

"I felt the opposite when it came to Sarah. I thought we'd be together forever."

Our street is up ahead, but I don't take the turn for it. Either not caring or not noticing, Quinn doesn't acknowledge it.

"If you don't mind me asking, why did things end?" she asks.

"She got pregnant." The words leave a taste in my mouth that feels a lot like the sour prickle of vomit. "With another guy's baby."

This time, Quinn's breath snags audibly and her hand instinctively goes to her sternum. "Nathan. I'm so sorry."

"You have nothing to be sorry about."

"I know, but it's still awful." She's working something out, and understanding clicks together when she says, "The crib."

"Yeah. The crib."

"Makes sense that you'd want to trash it. I don't blame you."

Her approval means something, and I can't understand why. Maybe it's the fact that she's the first person since the split to show me empathy instead of just sympathy. There's a clear distinction between the two, and Quinn's understanding is like a salve that heals just a tiny section of my busted-up heart.

I owe her for that.

Taking the steering wheel in a two-handed grip, I angle the truck toward town.

She needs some inspiration, and I'm going to get that for her.

10 /
quinn

I CAN HARDLY SEE Nathan's face over the towering stack of books in his arms.

"How many are we allowed to check out?" I ask as I balance another paperback on the top. It's like a game of Jenga, and each novel added to the pile comes perilously close to toppling the whole thing over.

"Twenty each, but my arms will give out before then. They're heavier than they look."

"We're probably good," I say with a satisfied nod.

We've got it all. Regency, contemporary, paranormal, and new adult romance. Even an erotic novel about pirates thrown in for good measure. If I'm looking for inspiration when it comes to writing intimacy, it will surely be found in this teetering stack.

I feel like I owe Nathan doubly at this point. First, for enduring that geriatric yoga session, and now for helping me overcome my writer's block. Somehow, he doesn't make it seem like he expects anything in return. I'm not used to that when it comes to guys, and I'm beginning to wonder if it's a maturity thing. After all, Kyle was the furthest thing from mature. I mean, the guy legit laughed every time he farted.

It takes us a while and not without a few grimaces from the librarian, but we both open library cards and check out the monstrous heap of romance reads. Something about getting a library card makes the place feel like home again. I'm not sure why I never had one when I lived here as a kid, but I'm almost glad I didn't because it feels like a bonding experience with Nathan, and I like that we can share this moment together.

Even though I offer to carry my half, he declines and scoops them all up. It doesn't surprise me when I discover he's also the type of guy that insists on walking on the outside of the sidewalk. He wordlessly nudges me up from the curb and blocks me from the line of traffic driving down the main drag.

It's not like he's going to stop a wayward vehicle from mowing us down should it come to that, especially not with his vision obscured and hands busied with the books. But there's an inherent thoughtfulness that I don't miss.

Even when we're back at my mom's house, he carts the books in with him and helps clear a few shelves in the family room to line them up.

"Visual inspiration," he says as he pulls out several to display facing forward like they do in bookstores. He's chosen the ones with shirtless, chiseled men and women with unrealistically heaving bosoms. I can't keep from snickering at the selection.

"I hope this helps," he says. "I wish I could do more."

"You could help me with my research," I suggest. His

eyes open wider. "As in, you can help me read through them and flag any sexy-time scenes."

"I'm not a fast reader," he admits, like it's something to be embarrassed about. "I'm a teacher, but I teach math, not English. Numbers guy over here. Not so great when it comes to words."

I like that the more time I spend with Nathan, the more I get to discover the little pieces of him. I didn't peg him as a teacher, but it definitely makes sense. He's got that patient, nurturing vibe.

"We don't have to read every word," I say for clarification's sake. "Just skim for the specific scenes."

His fingers scratch the back of his neck in a move that reads as unsure. "I think I'm going to need a drink before we do that."

"How about an entire meal?" It's close to dinnertime, and I like the thought of sharing another meal with Nathan. But my cooking expertise is limited, so I suggest an alternative to suffering through another stale grilled cheese. "I'll order a pizza. What kind do you like?"

"I'm easy. Whatever you want."

Nathan just has this confident, yet casual, way about him that pulls me in. I hate that I'm even comparing him to Kyle, because the two don't line up. But even with other guys, I can't ever remember being given the green light with ordering food, let alone having free rein with pizza.

I decide to really test him when I say, "Hawaiian?"

"Yep. Sounds good."

He's either lying or has no taste buds. Hawaiian doesn't sound good to anyone. Pineapple on a pizza borders on sacrilege, but the easy way Nathan goes with my flow has my heart skipping over a beat. "Actually, what about combination instead?"

"That works, too."

I think I could fall in love with this man.

An hour later, we're five slices into a large combo pizza, halfway done with a bottle of cheap cabernet, and we each have a healthy stack of books in our laps. I'm at one end of the couch, Nathan's at the other. I found some of those tabs used for flagging in a desk drawer in the den, and I gave a handful to Nathan to mark any sex scenes he comes across in the books he's been assigned.

I should have warned him, but when he pulled the erotic novel from the shelf as his first read, something in me did a little cartwheel. This could be fun.

His fingers are furiously turning the pages, looking for anything even remotely sexy. Then suddenly, he groans, "Oh, good God!" out of nowhere, and drops the book like a hot potato. Or a bomb. The act is that dramatic.

I look up from my relatively tame historical read. All color has drained from Nathan's face, and his mouth is screwed up in an awful contortion.

"You okay?" I slip a bookmark into place.

"This woman seriously just described the guy ejaculating 'a shooting white rope of ecstasy.' Is this guy Spiderman? Is he able to sling it and swing from it?" He looks almost sick and I kind of feel bad that I'm in a fit of hysterics, his words—coupled with his horrified expression—making me absolutely lose it.

It's a challenge, but I wrangle in my laughter. "Some authors get a little creative with their descriptive language."

"Do women actually *like* this?" He picks the book back

up for another perusal, but he's flipping the pages fast and his head is turned to the side as though he can't look directly at the words.

"Some do. Personally, I like sex scenes that are more than just physical. I like the deeper feelings and emotions involved. What you're reading is erotica, and the plot is entirely sex-driven. You might want to grab a different book that's more relationship focused."

"Why didn't you warn me?" He looks wounded, but it's playful.

"I thought I'd throw you straight into the fire."

"Oh." He taps his chin as if suddenly reminded of something. "That's another thing. They described her pussy as a 'fiery ring of desire.' I'm sorry, but no guy is going to want his dick going anywhere near something that's in flames. Hard pass."

I love that until tonight, Nathan was a smutty-book virgin. I think I was around fourteen when I stumbled across one of my mom's spicy books tucked in the depths of her closet. The look on my face when I read those intimate words isn't unlike Nathan's currently shocked expression.

I move the book to the coffee table. "We can be done for the night."

"But I feel like I haven't helped much."

"You have," I assure with a nod.

His thumb finds the shallow divot on his chin again. It's something he does when he's thinking, and I like this little quirk. "Can I read yours?"

"My book? The one I'm reading, or the one I'm writing?"

"The one you're writing. Maybe if I read what you're

working on, I can get a better sense of what needs to be added in."

Suddenly, I feel more exposed than the completely undressed character I was just reading about. "I, um..." My words trail off with my breath.

He picks up on my hesitation. "It's fine. I don't want to overstep."

"No, you're not overstepping." It's actually a good idea. I move across the room to collect my laptop from the arm of the loveseat and then retake my place on the couch, but this time I sit a little closer to Nathan. "Other than my agent, I don't have a lot of people read my works in progress."

"I won't judge," he says. But there's a devilish challenge in his eyes when he adds, "Unless you make comparisons to yarn or string or any other items that can be found at a local craft store."

"No rope comparisons. Promise."

I open the computer and click around until I find my half-written novel. With my fingertip, I guide the cursor to the last scene. It's the first kiss between my two main characters, and I've been stuck on it for days.

I don't know him well, but I really do want Nathan's approval. I almost slap the laptop shut, insecure that he'll hate the whole damn thing, but he commandeers it before I have the chance.

It's silent for minutes that wear on like hours. His expression is completely void of detectable emotion, which I suppose is better than the disgust that covered it when he read that erotic novel earlier. That's got to mean something.

Once he's finished, he closes the laptop and returns it to the table.

Meg Bradley

"That was a really mechanical sounding kiss, Quinn. You *have* been kissed before, haven't you?"

Nathan looks directly at me and then slouches lower on the couch cushions, his bare feet crossing at the ankles as he props them onto the coffee table. He weaves his hands behind his head, and I have to peel my eyes from the bare patch of tanned stomach now revealed as a result.

I lift my eyes to cut him a glare. "Of course, I've been kissed. It's just really hard to get all the emotion to translate on paper. Do you think you can write a better one?"

"No." He looks over at me and squints, that tempting gaze flickering with challenge. "I didn't say that."

"Unless you're able to offer me some constructive criticism, I would appreciate it if you kept the unnecessary jabs about my make out experience to yourself."

"I said I can't *write* a better kiss." He cocks a single dark brow, then smirks. "I didn't say I couldn't give you something constructive to work with."

Oh my God. Is he going to kiss me? Because that's what his words indicate, and everything in his eyes reiterates the same. When his tongue darts out and sweeps over his full bottom lip, I almost pass out. I force myself to swallow around a lump the size of a golf ball suddenly taking up residence in my throat.

Nathan sits up straighter. The hem of his shirt falls back into place. Damn.

"Your characters are talking, and then it just says, 'He pressed his lips to hers in a kiss.' I mean, sure, that's what he physically did, but there's no build up. No anticipation." His eyes trap mine. "That's what you need to work on. The anticipation part."

I nod too rapidly. It makes the room bounce around me. Everything is dizzy, swirling chaos. I can't keep my eyes on him because it's making my armpits sweat, so I turn my head and stare at the computer. "Sure. I can add that in."

"You need some inspiration."

"The answers are probably somewhere in all of those." My hand makes this big, sweeping wave over the bookcase along the back wall. "I'll find them."

"Or I could help you," he says. "Maybe the answers are closer than we think."

I don't have time to register what's happening before Nathan's at the edge of the couch with me. I don't turn to him, and I'm not sure why. I can't move. I think he senses it.

His thumb and finger lift to gently take my chin and guide my gaze toward him.

We're face to face. We've been like this before, but always with a few feet between us. Now, there are only inches. Only breaths.

My gaze is wild, roving from his parted lips and then to his eyes. There are these little details in them I hadn't noticed before, flecks of gold that fan out within his bright green irises. I can't blink, can't look away.

He's still touching me, and then his hand slides up my jaw.

"What do you feel?"

This is where I lack words. This is my hang up. I can't put down on paper the way every piece of me trembles, like I'm so wound up I could shatter, but simultaneously held together so tightly with the hope for more. The *need* for more.

"I don't know," I say in a voice that's not my own.

He shifts and it brings his mouth closer. A single finger skims agonizingly slow down the slope of my neck, eliciting a trail of goose bumps I feel even deeper than my skin.

His eyes drop to my collarbone, and then just below.

"That did something," he says, his voice a husky whisper. "Describe what that did to you."

"I don't know..."

"Yes, you do," he insists. "You know your body, Quinn."

But he's wrong. I don't. It feels foreign, like I'm meeting it for the first time and it's introducing me to every part all at once. My breasts are heavy and my nipples pebble beneath my embarrassingly sheer top, and something low in my stomach aches like a pulse. There are all these pieces of me firing off simultaneously, and my brain can't compute anything other than that I've never been this turned on in my life and the man is barely even touching me.

"What about this?"

He lifts his hand to brush a thumb across my mouth in one long, tortuously unhurried sweep. My bottom lip pulls against the pad of his finger, parting my lips.

"What did that do?" he asks, encouraging me. "Come on, Quinn. I'm giving you some good material here. What are you feeling? What do you want?"

You is the only word that makes its way through my muddled brain. It comes close to my lips, but I don't let it out.

"I feel really warm," I say. "Everywhere."

"That's a start." His eyes lift back up, locking in. "What else?"

"I feel..."—I'm almost too embarrassed to say it—"tingly."

He chuckles softly. "Huh, yeah. That's good." His thumb pulls away. "I kind of do, too."

Something about that confession pierces straight through me, elevating my pulse, turning my breaths into shallow gasps. I draw in a shaky inhale. "I feel turned on," I say, wondering if it's too much because I know this is all a game. All for the sake of research.

His hand comes around to the back of my neck and draws me the short distance toward him. But he doesn't kiss me. With his eyes still locked in, he brings his forehead near until it touches mine. Nathan's breath hitches.

Shuddering breaths exchange between our open mouths. I could twitch and my lips would be on his. I can't keep still. Can't keep my body from vibrating with expectation.

I've had full-blown orgasms that weren't this intense.

Then, like a snap of his fingers, he draws completely back, breaking whatever connection had tethered us together.

"There." His words are feather-light on my skin but land heavily in the pit of my stomach. "That should give you something to build on."

11 /
nathan

I'M NOT TINGLY.

I'm fucking *throbbing*.

I need a cold shower and about five minutes alone.

Even after we say goodnight and I head to my place to jack myself off within an inch of my life, I don't feel satisfied.

What the hell was that back there with Quinn? Where did any of that come from? Honest to God, I never acted that way with Sarah. She cracked up once when I tried to talk dirty in the middle of a blowjob, and let me just say, no guy wants a woman laughing when she's got his cock in her mouth. No matter how big you are, it does something to your self-esteem.

But with Quinn, it was like some fiction-based foreplay, and I can't wait to do it again. Sure, it was all under the guise of research, but my dick doesn't know the difference.

I only hope that Quinn gets to the actual sex scenes in her own manuscript sooner than later, because I want to be the one testing them out to see if they read right.

Who am I kidding?

We're both on the rebound here. The last thing we should do is this little writing research play-by-play. It's dangerous. But I can't stop thinking about her and the way she makes me feel. How in those moments, it took everything in me not to kiss her for real.

I'm on my flat air mattress, staring up at the ceiling, trying to remember if this was how things felt in the beginning with Sarah. I was just a kid. She was a cute cheerleader who actually paid attention to me. That could've been because I was tutoring her in math, and her position on the squad depended on a good grade and I was the means to achieve that.

Somehow, young love turned into a committed relationship in college, and later, marriage. Like I told Quinn, it was just the natural progression of things. Point A to Point B to Point C.

But I don't know how things are supposed to progress with Quinn. There are no points. It's a squiggly mess that I don't have a fucking clue how to untangle.

Or even if it's wise to try. I'm not tutoring her, but I am helping her out and I wonder if it's not all that different. I don't want to start something because she feels indebted to me. I did that once and look how that shitshow turned out.

My night is fitful, and I don't get a lot of sleep. I feel like I should come with one of those "do not operate heavy machinery" warnings the next morning, because I'm groggy as hell. Even my muscles decide to take the next day off. I can't lift anything without it feeling ten times heavier than it should, which isn't good because today's plan involves removing the kitchen cabinetry. I need all the strength I've got to get them down in one piece. I found a nonprofit organization that will come out and pick up used cabinets to install in the tiny homes they construct for the homeless, so I hope to keep the cupboards intact, if possible.

It's a herculean effort I don't have the energy for.

I'm standing in the kitchen, wondering if there's a better way to uninstall them, when I hear Quinn's voice through the open door.

"Morning, sunshine," she says, chipper than ever. Whatever sexual frustration she had last night has been replaced with a perky, happy-go-lucky mood. I wonder if she took care of things on her end like I did. Just the thought has me getting hard.

"Hey, what's up?"

She's in athletic gear again, but this time it's black leggings and a tie-dyed sports bra with a nearly sheer, scooped neck shirt over the top. For a moment, I worry she's going to ask me to do Pilates or something equally terrible, but she just says, "I'm heading into town to get coffee and was wondering if I could pick something up for you."

It's the nicest gesture, followed by the most adorable grin.

"Yeah, actually, that would be great." Caffeine is my only hope right now. "Can you get me a triple shot Americano?" I ask, hooking my tape measure onto a belt loop. "You know what? Make that a quad."

"Are you orchestrating your own heart attack? Because that amount of caffeine just might kill you."

"Since I feel like death warmed over already, I'm hoping it has the opposite effect and brings me to life."

Her head tilts and her long ponytail swings against her back. "Rough night?"

"You could say that. My air mattress is crap. I need a new one."

There's something going on behind her eyes, like she's contemplating saying something, but then doesn't.

"Let me know what I owe you." I pull down a pencil from behind my ear.

"You don't owe me anything. I'm the one who owes you, actually. I finished that chapter late last night and I think it's actually decent."

"Actually decent, huh? Sounds like a total page turner."

"Okay, it's phenomenal," she corrects in a mocking tone. "Chart topping."

"That's more like it. You did have a pretty phenomenal teacher."

"That, I did." She looks around, her eyes meeting the opened-up walls and rafters overhead. "You've been working hard. The place is unrecognizable."

"That's the goal. It'll be completely new when all is said and done," I say. "On the inside, at least."

"Sounds like some analogy for life. How things might look the same outwardly, but inwardly, we can be completely transformed."

She's not wrong. The end goal is more than just a physical remodeling. "What a way with words, though I shouldn't be surprised. You *are* the writer."

"And right now, I'm the caffeine messenger, so I should get on it. I'll be back in a few."

"Sounds good. Thanks again."

I trail her out the door and watch as she sinks into her car before I head back inside. She's thoughtful and I like that.

But I'm going to pay her for the coffee. I don't want to get started with the whole owing thing. It complicates relationships and makes genuine gestures seem false. I helped her because I *wanted* to, plain and simple. I thought that help would be limited to checking out a few books, then maybe reading them. My intention was not to seduce her while trying to inspire, but hey, can I really be blamed?

I didn't have a whole lot of control over that part. But the coffee, I do. I already have a five-dollar bill on the counter, ready to hand her when she gets back.

Ten minutes go by, and I hear an engine cut off in the driveway. That was a quick coffee run, but I can't say I'm not happy to have the promise of caffeine within reach.

"Knock, knock," I hear from the open front door, but it's not Quinn this time.

It's a guy's voice.

Heavy footsteps echo off the subflooring as he enters. I step out from the kitchen to intercept the surprise visitor when he makes a turn down the hallway.

I'm a pretty big guy at just shy of six feet, but this dude is huge. He's easily got six inches on me. His entire stature swallows me in his shadow when he walks all the way up to where I'm standing. I'm not one to cower, but his presence feels mildly threatening. I suddenly realize I've left all my tools—a.k.a makeshift weapons—in the other room. It's a David and Goliath situation, and in this instance, David would get his ass kicked.

"Can I help you?" I clear my throat to make my voice sound deeper.

"Hey man, I'm here to collect the cabinetry for Ever After Home Design." He leans to the side to look around me. "Don't tell me those are them."

I glance at my watch. "You're a little early."

"The cabinets are still hanging, bro."

"I know." I look at the offending cabinetry and shake my head. "I thought I had more time. Couldn't get them down on my own."

"Your subs won't help you?" he asks because it's a valid question.

"I don't have any subcontractors. I'm working alone."

He turns around to take in the demolition, then brings his eyes back to me. "You're renovating an entire house by yourself?"

I just nod.

"Because you can't afford to hire help?"

"No, because it's something I want to do on my own."

"And how's that working out for you?" His eyes are back on the 1980s oak cabinetry.

"Up until this moment, it was going great."

He thrusts out a hand. "Got an extra screwdriver?"

I do, and I hand it to him, then get my own. It takes half an hour, but we get the first set of cabinets down without damaging much except the trim piece. We're just about to start on the larger hanging portion when Quinn returns from the coffee run.

"Hey there, princess," my cabinet demoing comrade blurts when Quinn comes in with a coffee cup in each hand. The bold comment makes both of us stop short.

I think about punching him for the catcall, but before I can plan out how to deck the guy without breaking my fist on his impossibly square jaw, Quinn is setting the coffee onto the sawhorse and leaping into his arms, legs wrapped and locked around his waist.

He twirls her in three nauseating turns before settling her back down.

"We've still got it, huh?" He flashes a bright white grin.

She's all bubbling laughter that I can't make any sense of. "We sure do. My goodness, Jace. How are things?"

"Can't complain." His arms bind over his chest, making his biceps bulge beneath his shirtsleeves. I'm not sure how it's possible that this guy keeps getting bigger.

"They still treating you well?"

"Pays the bills."

Clearly, the two know one another from somewhere, but unless I interrupt and ask point-blank, I don't think I'm going to get my answer.

"What about you?" Jace asks. "How's the author gig going?"

"It's going," Quinn says with a little shimmy of her shoulders. She looks past Jace and gives me a smile. "I'm just working on some research at the moment. But hey, tell the rest of the crew hi for me. I miss them."

"Sure thing," he says with a nod, then turns to me. "Hey buddy, I'm going to load up this first batch of cabinets into the trailer and take them over to the warehouse. Is it cool if I come back this afternoon for the rest? Maybe I can help with any other odds and ends you need wrapped up then, too."

"Yeah, that's no problem. Thanks again for bailing me out with this."

I'm grateful for Jace's help but could use a chance to down that coffee and hopefully get some insight from Quinn about their connection, not that she owes me any answers.

Still, I don't know why I'm so bothered that this Jace guy is obviously someone from Quinn's past. Maybe it's the fact that I never had to think of that with Sarah. We *were* each other's pasts. The only person I had to be insecure about was the younger version of myself.

When Jace leaves, Quinn collects our drinks, but a smile still lingers on her mouth, and I know she's replaying the interaction with Jace.

"Your heart attack in a cup," she says theatrically when she finally snaps from her reverie.

"Thank you." I'm about to slip the five into her hand, but she turns around to look out the front window again.

"What a trip to run into Jace after all this time." Her eyes follow his truck and trailer as it pulls off the curb.

"Yeah? You haven't seen him in a while?" I'm prying, but not outwardly.

"Not since we worked together at Ever After."

Ever After. The big amusement park about fifteen minutes from here. I remember reading online that the home design studio requesting the cabinets was some philanthropic offshoot of the organization, but I never made the connection. Still, the pieces feel jumbled.

"Sometimes I miss those princess days."

Princess? Okay, so maybe he wasn't just being a douche with the expression. "You were a character?"

"Princess Bethany of Brighton. Jace and I worked there together when I was in college. I started as a ride operator for the Storybook Streams attraction, but enough five-year-old girls commented on my uncanny resemblance to their favorite fairytale princess that after two months, I got upgraded to royal status."

I take a swig from the cup. "I don't know why, but this new information feels very fitting."

"What? That I was a princess at a second-rate amusement park?"

"No, that you've always had a soft spot for romance."

She's looking right at me when she says, "I guess you could say that." When she lifts her mocha to her lips, the cup obscures my full view of her mouth, but I think she's smiling. "Anyway, I can vouch for Jace. He's a really good guy, and it sounds like he's willing to help you out around here. You should take him up on it."

"This is kind of a solo endeavor."

"So is writing a book, but I'm letting you help me with that."

I don't want Jace's help the way I want to help Quinn, and she knows that. But she might be right. I could use an extra hand, and Jace seemed willing.

"I'll think about it."

She bounces her head once in a nod. "Good. And would you also think about coming over tonight? I want you to read my latest chapter if you're up for it."

I don't have to give that a second thought. "I'll be there. What time?"

"Eight o'clock." Her eyes drop to my mouth for a split second before popping back up. "And maybe have a drink or two first. I think this particular scene might be best if you read it a little tipsy."

I inhale sharply, and give her a nod, even though that's not something I'm going to do.

Whatever happens tonight with Quinn, I want to be one hundred percent sober.

12 /
quinn

IT'S a quarter to eight and I'm watching the clock like I'm counting down to the ball drop on New Year's Eve. I know I likely won't get the traditional kiss that goes along with it, but something about having Nathan read my latest scene has my heart pounding in hopeful expectation.

A little over an hour ago, all construction sounds ceased next door. I saw Jace's truck pull out of the driveway just a few minutes after that. Since then, I've changed my outfit five times, finally settling on a pair of sweatpants and an oversized pale blue sweatshirt that might as well be a burlap sack. I look like a potato, but I'm kind of okay with that.

Honestly, my body betrayed me on such a visceral, visual level last night that I don't want to chance that sort of embarrassment again. Even thinking about how close we came to kissing makes a wake of goosebumps break out across my skin, makes my cheeks flush with heat. Everything about Nathan creates this dichotomy within me. I'm chilled and yet fevered. Tense and yet more comfortable than I should be around a man I just met. Curious and inexplicably terrified.

I'm ready for the knock when I hear it, so I don't make him wait on the stoop. I open the door humiliatingly fast, appearing overly eager because apparently, I have no chill.

"Hi!" I yell at him. Seriously, I yell it. I can't control anything right now, even my volume.

"Hey." Of course, he's calm and steady, like a freaking lighthouse in my whirlwind storm. "Sorry, I'm a few minutes early."

I step back to let him in. "Are you? I hadn't noticed."

Right. I hadn't noticed that he was three minutes and forty-two seconds early. Not at all.

I lead us into the living room, flop down on the couch, and basically throw my computer at him. He's sitting at this point, too, so it lands squarely on his lap and there's this little wince that tugs his eyebrows, like maybe that was the equivalent of punching him in his junk.

"Oh my God. I'm sorry." I grab the offending laptop but hadn't really gauged the actual proximity of it to his dick and my hand brushes against the fly on his jeans and now I have to go fling myself off a cliff because this is starting off terribly.

"Hey, it's okay." He grips the other end of the computer and places it back onto his lap, but much more gently than I had. "You want me to just dive right in?"

"Yes." I'm confident when I say this, but it lasts a nanosecond before I vacillate. "No, actually. Let me set up the scene for you."

I spend the next few minutes telling him about my characters and giving some backstory: childhood rivals who reunite when they're unknowingly matched on an anonymous online dating app. It skews heavily toward the romantic comedy side of things, something my agent is encouraging based on current market trends. Nathan just nods along as I lay out the plot, like it's a storyline he's actually interested in, even though I'm one hundred percent sure he's not my target audience.

"So that's the gist of it," I wrap up once I realize if I keep talking, he can't start reading and if he can't start reading, then he won't be able to give me any feedback. And that's what I'm really after here: feedback.

Just feedback.

"I'll leave you to it." I get up from the couch. His hand wraps around my wrist.

"You don't need to go." He's not even looking at me. He's already scanning the chapter, his focus honed in on the manuscript. I feel like I'm a thousand degrees, like his skin burns where it touches. When he lets go, I slink back onto the sofa, but far on the other end, and hold my breath as his eyes rove over the words I'm suddenly so self-conscious to have written.

"What does this mean?" His index finger collides with the screen. "The part where it says, 'His tongue swiped against the seam of her lips, silently requesting entry.'"

"He's about to French kiss her," I don't add the word *obviously*, but it's in my tone.

"Yeah, I got that, but the whole 'requesting entry' thing is throwing me off. Like, does he need a ticket or something? This sounds weirdly formal."

"I feel like it's a common way of wording it in romance books."

"Maybe so, just giving you feedback."

Right. *Feedback.* That's what I want.

I need to let my defenses down if Nathan's going to read

this. And *why* is he reading this again? He's not my editor; he's not my target market. For heaven's sake, he teaches math, not English. Still, I feel like I owe him the chance to get a sneak peek of the scene he helped inspire. Truthfully, he's inspired *several* scenes, none that have been added to the manuscript yet, but ones that will most likely work their way into later chapters involving vibrators, the backseats of cars, maybe even a shower scene or two.

I'm not even writing out these thoughts, but just playing them in my head has the cadence of my breathing shifting into something I don't know how to control. I'm already quivering, my chest heaving beneath my (thankfully) enormous sweatshirt.

In less than five minutes, he's done. Like the night before, he moves the laptop to the coffee table and leans back. Me? I'm on bated freaking breath, just waiting to hear what he thinks.

When he says, "It's good," and only that, I think I stop breathing altogether.

"What?"

"I said, it's good."

"Good? That's it?"

A single shoulder touches his ear in a half-shrug. "I don't know. I mean, you get the point across that they're kissing."

"Sure, but I could also do that by just writing, 'They kissed,' remember? You have nothing to add?"

"I have a lot to add. I'm just not sure where to start." He looks at me in a way that isn't at all judgmental, just cautious. "I don't have any credentials in this area, Quinn."

"I mean, you do have a few years of experience on me."

It's the first time I've brought up our age difference and

I'm not sure if it's okay to do so, but it's been a quiet, polite little elephant in the room, and I feel like it finally deserves some recognition.

"Does that bother you?" The arch of his strong brow deepens. "That I'm older?"

"Why would it bother me?" I say. "Our last neighbors were *much* older than you. I don't think there's a rule when it comes to neighborhoods and age commonalities."

Something extinguishes behind his gaze, a glimmer of hope suddenly snuffed from his eyes.

I don't know why I said that. Nathan is obviously not like the Ainsleys, and our relationship, friendship—whatever the heck this is—is not just of the neighborly sort.

"I think you know what I mean," he corrects. There's a seriousness in his tone that draws up the fine hairs on the back of my neck, almost like a scolding. "I'm thirty-four, Quinn. You're twenty-three."

"Eleven years isn't that much," I say.

"It's just under half of your life."

"Math whiz." My levity isn't reciprocated in his staid expression.

"Quinn, I'm quite a bit older than you are, and if that makes you uncomfortable, we don't have to do this."

This? What *is* this thing we're doing? I want to give a voice to that burning question, but I keep it within the confines of my head for now. Maybe out of fear, maybe out of self-preservation. I'm not entirely sure.

"I'm not uncomfortable. And I do want your feedback on the scene. What do you think it needs?"

"Believability." The answer comes out lightning fast.

"It's not believable?"

"I don't get that they really even like each other."

"Well, they don't, I suppose. It's an enemies-to-lovers romance, so there's tension between them."

"Yeah, I don't get much tension. Just indifference."

"You must get *some* tension," I counter. "Sexual tension, at the very least. No?"

His head shakes. "No. There's no sexual tension in this."

"Really? None?"

"Sorry. I'm definitely not picking up on any sexual tension."

God, if this man keeps saying the words 'sexual' and 'tension,' I'm going to scream, and I don't know if it's out of frustration or fervor.

He gives me a meaningful look. "I think readers like that sort of thing, yeah?" He's sincerely asking my opinion on this. "The sexual tension stuff?"

"Yeah, for this type of story, they eat it up."

"Then you need to give it to them," he says. "In this scene, they're just talking about the winner of some spelling bee they competed in when they were kids, and then before he leaves, he says he never appropriately congratulated her. Then he just kisses her. I guess it's kind of cute, and I can see where you've taken my previous advice and added in a little anticipation where he pauses a moment before the actual kiss, but that's it."

"I'm not going for cute."

"Then you'll need to up the sexual tension."

"Oh my God!" I've finally snapped. "I get it. Sexual tension, sexual tension, *sexual tension*!"

Nathan doesn't move, just sits there taking in my mini meltdown.

"Sorry." Smoothing one hand down the front of my sweatshirt, I sit up so straight I must look like there's a rod jammed along my spine. "That was weird. Don't know what got into me with that little outburst."

There's a wicked smirk moving across his lips. "I didn't realize sexual tension was such a *sensitive* topic."

The way he utters the word has the most intimate parts of me waking up with interest. Nathan definitely knows how to use his voice to bring an edge to everything. I've never experienced that with anyone before, and I don't even know how to respond to it. Not verbally, at least. My body is quite actively reminding me of ways it can respond.

I cross my legs, attempting to bring some relief.

"You okay?" His gaze rakes up and down once, then again.

"I'm good."

"You sure about that?"

"I'll add in some sexual tension," I say, aware that these have become buzzer words in our current conversation. "Then I'll have you read it."

"I can't wait." He doesn't blink, and even when I wrench my gaze away and bring it back moments later, he's still staring at me.

And I'm suddenly aware he didn't take my advice to show up a little drunk.

He's stone-cold sober.

Something about that makes the ache intensify.

"Anything else?" I ask. I look at the computer because I think I'm referring to the manuscript. Mostly.

"I'm eager to read your edits."

We do little brainstorming after that, not relating to the

chapter at hand, at least. I ask him about the home renovation process and tell him a little more about Jace, highlighting my friend's work ethic and construction abilities. There's this look Nathan gives me—not quite jealousy—but a possessiveness in his eyes and in the way his brow tenses from some sort of attempt at restraint. Like he's aware he shouldn't feel this way but can't help it.

I love it.

He's got one arm across the back of the couch, stretched toward me so it's practically draped over my shoulder, but not quite. I would give anything to fit my body against his, but he breaks through my thoughts and says, "Did you and Jace...?"

"Ever sleep together?"

Nathan stills, eyes flashing wide. "I was going to say date. But yeah. That too."

"No. We weren't like that. We got along really well as prince and princess, and if we added anything to that, I feel like it would have messed up our work chemistry."

It's quiet for only a moment before Nathan adds, "Did you want to?"

"Strangely, no. I mean, he's a great guy who's obviously handsome, but we just didn't click in that way." I'm looking right at him when I say, "With some people you just have that immediate connection, and with others, you don't. Do you know what I mean?"

"Yeah." His voice is rough. "I do."

I could launch myself at him, and almost contemplate doing so, but he stands abruptly to his feet. "I should head out. Got an early start tomorrow morning and I know you're on a deadline."

I nod, though I don't agree that he should leave. But I

don't have the courage to ask for what I need, so I just say, "I'll see you out."

He waves me off. "Not necessary." Hovering over me, he grabs the back of the couch and bends down to leave a kiss on the crown of my hair. I melt right into the sofa. I'm an absolute puddle. "See you tomorrow, Quinn."

Even after I hear the soft snick of the front door shutting behind him, I haven't moved.

My head replays our entire evening from front to back and back to front again. Every devilish look, every flirtatious exchange, every unspoken temptation rides through my memory until my heart is thrumming so fast my ears ring.

I'm still on the couch, still in my sweats, and with no sense of inhibition, I slip my hand past my waistband. I don't even have time to get to my upstairs bedroom to grab my trusty battery-operated-boyfriend from the nightstand. I'm so close to the edge already. Just the thought of Nathan's rasping words and the image of his tongue sweeping across his lower lip like it so often does is enough to set me off.

I'm so wet. I'm surprised by that, actually. I've always needed a little help in that department when I was with Kyle. He would bury his face between my legs to get things going, but consistently stopped short of satisfying me in that way. He was a selfish lover, taking so much more than giving.

I doubt Nathan is like that.

As I visualize just how selfless I think Nathan might be in the bedroom, I find my own hands exploring my body, imagining they are his instead. One hand palms my breast beneath my shirt while the other sinks into me, swirling deep before flicking over the bundle of nerves that tingles to the point of numbness. I can't move fast enough. I groan as my fingers find a rhythm. My chest heaves wildly and my thumb brushes over my nipple while my other hand continues its relentless pursuit until I feel myself teetering close to the brink, straddling the line between desperate, primal need and the reward of sheer ecstasy.

I throw my head back against the cushions, eyes shut, open-mouthed breaths rallying toward an impending cry.

Everything's buzzing—my body, my brain, my ears—so I don't hear the door and I definitely don't register the footsteps that carry into the living room where I'm shamelessly touching myself like a woman starved.

Still, despite my blissful frenzy, I sense something—someone—but I'm so close to my release that I almost don't care. All I need is a few more seconds.

A throat clearing forces me to acknowledge what my senses already know.

Nathan's at the edge of the couch.

I yank my hand from beneath my shirt and tug the fabric down, certain my breasts were just on full display. But my other hand freezes like it's locked in place.

Slack-jawed, Nathan's shoulders broaden on a huge inhale. "Quinn."

"Oh my God." I still can't move. "I was just...I was just looking for something."

In my pants? My free hand—the one that had the good sense to stop feeling herself up—slaps my forehead, but the other is doing this whole *maybe if I don't move, he won't see me* thing. I think of playing dead.

Nathan doesn't hide the way his eyes travel to my spread-open legs and linger there. "Do you need any help?"

Even though I've got sweats on, I'm completely exposed.

That's enough to snap me back into the here and now. I jerk my hand out of my pants. "I found it, thanks."

He reaches toward the coffee table, and I see him pick up the cell phone he must have accidentally left behind.

"Have you, though?" His lip twitches. "It looked to me like you were still searching for something just out of reach."

I will the couch to swallow me whole.

My wish is not granted, just like my far-off orgasm.

And before Nathan leaves for the second time tonight, he calls over his shoulder and says, "If you ever need help looking for whatever it is you've misplaced, you know where to find me."

13 /
nathan

MY PHONE LIGHTS UP, a bright white funnel in the pitch-black room. You can't even really call it a room during this phase of construction. It's just open framing with two-by-fours that delineate different portions of the house, so I wouldn't really think of this as a proper bedroom. I don't have a bed, for starters. Just a mattress that's become more of a plastic barrier between me and the subflooring than anything.

I snatch up my cell and swipe to unlock it.

> Quinn: I'm really sorry you had to see that.

Is she kidding right now? I punch out, **I'm not**, and keep the phone in my hand when I see triplicate dots pulsing across the screen. They're there for a few seconds, then disappear.

It's eerily quiet in this place without the hum of electricity. It's on, but I don't have any appliances hooked up other than the fridge, and this is a weirdly silent one.

I hear a car alarm in the distance, followed by a barking dog that syncs up with the monotonous beeping.

The text bubbles don't reappear.

I type out **That was the hottest thing I've ever witnessed** and send it.

I'm sure she's feeling insecure about what I walked in on. That's only natural. She was in the middle of something surely not intended for my eyes. But I've never been so grateful to stumble my way into such a private moment. I'm mentally making a list of other items I can strategically leave behind at her place.

I didn't just barge in on her, either. I had knocked. Several times, actually. Based on the state I found her in, I highly doubt she heard any of them. She was somewhere else altogether, deep in the middle of a fantasy I need to be a part of.

And that's the thing. I think I *was* part of it. I had only been gone five minutes, tops. Not enough time for her to pick up a book from the shelf and immerse herself in a new story.

No, I think she was stuck in our story, the one we've been nonverbally writing together.

I don't know how we got here, but I know I don't want to leave.

Quinn? I type out, aware that she hasn't responded to my last text.

I'm here, she writes back.

I know she's referring to the text thread, but I really wish she *were* here with me right now. I'd show her just how much I liked what I saw.

I keep texting.

> Me: I'm serious. You have nothing to be ashamed of. We all do it.

Her answers come quicker now.

> Quinn: Yeah, but I'm not usually so voyeuristic.

I grin.

> Me: I think I was the voyeuristic one, because I was doing the watching. You were…just looking for something.

I think through the next words before I write them and decide not to censor myself.

> Me: Did you ever find it?

> Quinn: Nope. It's long gone.

> Me: That's sad.

I actually do feel a pang of sadness for her. It's like getting on a rollercoaster, only to have it shut down before the highest crest and freefall plummet. That's the best part.

> Quinn: Anyway, I just wanted to assure you that what you just saw will never happen again.

> Me: Are you joining a convent?

> Quinn: What?

> Me: You just said that what I caught you doing will never happen again. Is this some act of self-imposed celibacy?

> Quinn: What I mean is, you will never walk in on something like that again. I'll keep my doors locked.

> Me: I know you hide a key under the mat.

I worry I've overstepped, so I add, **But I won't use it. Next time I swing by, I'll wait for you to answer the door. Promise. Night, Quinn.**

> Quinn: Night, Nathan. Sleep well.

> Me: Not a chance with this crappy excuse for an air mattress.

> Quinn: You don't have a real bed?

> Me: No. Doesn't make much sense to have furniture when I don't plan to live here.

Those dots come up again, then vanish. This happens three more times, to where I almost put my phone back down, but then a text blips across the screen.

> Quinn: You can sleep here. There's an entire guest room not being used.

I don't know if it's the best idea.

> Me: I don't want to intrude.

> Quinn: You seriously could not intrude more than you already have. ;)

The little emoji at the end makes me laugh out loud. She's right.

> Me: Probably so. You sure you're ok with me coming over?

> Quinn: Yes. The thought of you sleeping on a deflated air mattress in an empty shell of a house is really pitiful, Nathan. I feel a little greedy over here with all of these vacant beds.

I'm not going to wait for her to change her mind because the temptation of slumbering on a surface more than an inch thick has my back screaming with relief.

> Me: Okay. I'll be over in five. And I'm going to knock REALLY loud this time.

> Quinn: I'll be waiting.

She is waiting, with the door propped open, no less.

I think any other woman would go into hiding after what we experienced earlier this evening, but whatever shame Quinn might have had is completely gone. She looks genuinely happy to see me.

"It's upstairs, just down the hall from mine," she says about the guest room as she guides me deeper into the house.

So far, I've only seen the downstairs portion of her

mom's place. The kitchen, living room, and den. I think there's a master bedroom off the back, but it's pretty far removed from the main living area and the door has remained shut.

Upstairs, there are just two rooms: Quinn's and the spare, with a large Jack-and-Jill shared bath in between.

"Sorry, it's a little outdated, but I promise the bed is comfortable and the sheets are clean."

She folds back the edge of a black-and-white checkered quilt, then fluffs a pillow before settling it back down.

"You're welcome to use the dressers, too, if you have stuff to put in them."

"Am I moving in?" I give her a look.

"Once you sleep on this cloud-like mattress, there's no way you're going to want to go back to an inflatable. But it's your call. The room is yours for as long as you need it. Until my mom comes back from Italy, I guess."

"Quinn, what if I'm an axe-murderer?"

"Is that even a thing? I mean, how often do you honestly hear of murderers using axes? That would leave a huge mess."

Not the response I was expecting, and I'm positive my expression reiterates that. This woman sure is something else.

"I looked you up," she continues, head cocked to the side. "Your record is clean. Plus, you teach junior high. I figure there's a whole screening process in order to work with youth. I'm not afraid of you, Nathan."

I don't know why, but the curl of her mouth when she says that hints at something more. Like maybe she is a little afraid. Not of me, necessarily, but of us.

I know I am.

"So, we've established that I'm not an axe-murderer," I say. "But the verdict's still out on you, huh?"

"All I'm going to say is don't go snooping around my internet search history. As an author, I've had to look up some pretty surreal stuff. Might give you the wrong idea that I lead an exciting, possibly even dangerous, life. I assure you, I'm woefully boring."

I sit at the end of the bed. "I don't find you boring at all."

"Nathan, I'm a struggling author with few friends, I'm recently single, and I currently live with three cats in my mom's house. On paper, I'm a total dud."

"On paper I'm a guy in my mid-thirties whose wife just left him to have someone else's baby. I don't sound like a real winner, either."

She's standing in front of me, and I don't know why, but I reach out for her, my hands settling gently on the curve of her hips to guide her. She lets me slide her in close, and I move my legs apart to fit her between them.

"None of this makes sense," she says faintly, looking down at me as I crane my neck to glimpse the concern crowding into her gorgeous brown eyes. The room is dim, the shadows painting the walls like dark brush strokes of night. "On paper, things don't make any sense."

"I don't think life can be reduced to moments on paper. It's meant to be lived fully, each minute. Every breath."

Her arms slink around my neck.

I don't know how I went from being flat out on a piece of plywood to having Quinn in my arms at the foot of a bed, but at this particular place in time, I'm not going to question the way the universe works.

Maybe there are stars aligning overhead. Maybe it's fate —kismet—whatever you want to call it.

Or maybe it's just that our hearts hurt in unison, and they want to be healed in the same way.

I know I just said I didn't put much stock in how things look on paper, but I will admit that I think we're on the same page.

I'm not about to take a chance that we're not, so when I slide my hand around the back of her neck and bring her forehead down to mine, I still ask, "Can I kiss you?" My mouth is only an inch from hers. "Please tell me I can kiss you."

She hesitates to give an answer, and I get that. I don't know if we should be doing this, either. And it's not lost on me that she will only be the second woman I've ever kissed. I'm thirty-four and I'm more inexperienced than most teenagers.

But Sarah got ahold of me all those years ago and caged me in. Trapped me like a pet she eventually lost interest in.

Meeting Quinn—*kissing* Quinn—feels like an opportunity to finally break free.

"Nathan." My name is a muted groan between her lips. It's the best fucking sound I've ever heard.

But I don't know if it's her way to pause and give herself time to second guess where this is headed.

When she pulls back, all my fears become reality, and the avalanche of emotion in her troubled gaze heaps me under a pile of instant regret.

I think she wants to hit the brakes.

Her hand is on my chest, right above my heart that's beating furiously, like it's trying to bust through my ribcage. I don't know if she means to, but she pushes me back a little.

Quinn's eyes dart between mine. She's going to put an end to this thing we've started. It's written in the deep pinch of her brows and in the way she swallows so thickly, I see her throat move.

I've pushed too far.

14 /
quinn

"NATHAN, please tell me you want me as much as I want you," I say.

"I don't think I can say that."

There's that dreaded feeling of getting it all wrong and it crashes over me, stealing the air from my lungs. It's shame and disappointment—laced with humiliation—and it's enough to make the backs of my eyes sting with tears.

I blink down at him.

"There's no way you want me anywhere near as much as I want you right now, Quinn. I don't think you have even the slightest idea what I want to do to you."

My breathing is nothing more than a tremor, my heartbeat a wild vibration.

His arms slip around my waist but it's rough when he yanks me flush with him. With how I'm standing, his chin hits right above my breasts and he's looking up at me with the hungriest, most feral eyes I've ever seen.

"God, Quinn." His eyelids fall shut for a beat. There's pain in the way his jaw clenches as the muscle at the back ticks. Instinctively, my hands move to cup his face. "I want to flip you onto this mattress and take you in every way imaginable."

I'm about to tell him to do it, but his eyes flutter open, dark lashes lifting. "I'm just not sure I'll know how to stop with you."

You won't have to.

He shakes his head at his own words. "I want to kiss you. I want to fuck you. I want it all, and I don't know if that's okay."

I want it all, too, but I don't have the discipline Nathan is currently exercising. For heaven's sake, I felt myself up with his image burned in my brain. I want everything he's saying. I want him. All of him.

"Can I just kiss you?" He's pleading, this struggle with his own self-restraint almost a losing battle. "I don't know if I'm ready for more than that. I don't want to hurt you, Quinn. And I don't want to get hurt."

"I won't hurt you."

He's helpless, sighing, like I've just made a promise I won't be able to keep.

But then he suddenly stops hesitating and he makes good on his quest to get me onto the mattress. Only he doesn't throw me. He doesn't even flip me. Like I'm breakable, he slowly draws me onto his lap, then lays back, pulling me down with him.

I want to feel him—feel the solid weight of his body on mine—so I roll us until I'm beneath him. We're not even kissing yet, just moving together, working our way up the bed.

Nathan settles over me, suspended on his forearms like

he's worried about crushing me, and God, that's exactly what I want. I *want* him to crush me. I want to feel him everywhere. But he's so cautious. And even though I think he's worried about hurting me, I think he's just as scared about getting hurt.

His ex-wife sure fucked him up.

"Kiss me." I curl my hand around his neck. "Please, Nathan. Please kiss me."

I'm just shy of all out begging when he finally settles onto me, and if I ever had any doubt if the attraction was reciprocal, it's completely gone now. Even with our clothes between us, I feel the hard length of him. The strain in his brow buckles when I hike a leg around his waist to lock him in. I want him lined up right where he needs to be. Right where *I* need him to be.

He lets out a hiss, his eyes roll back a little, and then his mouth crashes onto mine. I'm rocking against him, kissing him long and slow and then tugging his bottom lip between my teeth. My hands are everywhere: in his hair, on his chest, scratching up his back to grab onto his shoulders. There's a growl working its way out from deep within his throat, every nip and bite and kiss making him rumble with need.

I lick my way into his mouth and we're a tangle of tongues that creates a rhythm matching our hips. It's back and forth, fast and slow. I've never been more grateful for the sweatpants he's currently wearing. I think they are God's gift to sexually frustrated women.

Nathan breaks from the kiss and, for an instant, I think he's going to stop. But he just looks at me in a way no one else ever has. Like he's trying to memorize me. Not just memorize how I look but memorize this moment. Memorize the way this feels. He scans up and down, giving a little smile that I have the sudden urge to nibble on.

I pull him close and let my mouth move over his full lips before I kiss my way down to his throat and back up again. He smells incredible, and I can tell it's not just cologne. It's this heady combination of pine and bergamot, a little bit of sweat and a lot of lust. I want to devour him. I think I might be, actually, since I have to keep my teeth from sinking into his bottom lip when his hand suddenly moves beneath my shirt.

Nathan splays his large palm over my stomach.

I'm not wearing a bra because honestly, I thought I was heading to bed earlier, and when he discovers this, it's practically his undoing.

His thumb brushes against the underside of my breast and a moan trembles across my lips. That leg curled around his hips begs him closer. In answer, he grinds against me and I'm fully aware that I'm writhing beneath him as he rocks into me and his thumb strokes my skin. I want more. I want his hands fully on me. I want our clothes off and I want him inside me.

But he had insisted on just a kiss, and although this is admittedly much more than that, I don't want to push him.

Still, there's a need within me searching for a release, and it's going to find a way to get there.

I thread my hands into his hair and guide his mouth to the base of my neck as I continue to buck my hips against him. Yep, this will do it. He sucks just above my collarbone at the same time his hand finally palms my entire breast.

"Nathan," I groan into his ear. It sets him off just the way

I need it to, and his hips pick up speed, hitting me in the exact spot that I had only teased earlier.

I'm about to come undone. My gasps quicken into cries I can no longer control. His name is on my lips when his thumb strokes over my nipple, and when he rolls it between his fingers, I cry out, climbing, climbing, climbing until I'm splintering into a million pieces. My body trembles with shudder after satisfied shudder, and Nathan's rhythm slows until I'm left boneless and breathless beneath him.

I open my eyes to see him staring at me. A smile hooks up just one corner of his swollen mouth.

He leans forward and kisses the tip of my nose, then draws back to give me the guiltiest grin ever when he says, "Found it."

"I can't believe that just happened." It takes a moment for my mortification to fully form, but when it does, it hits me hard. "I'm not usually so responsive."

Nathan rolls to his side and props onto his elbow. "Why do you say that like it's a bad thing?"

"Because it's a little humiliating that I'm completely clothed and just orgasmed."

"You could not be more wrong." He's trying to be discreet, but his hand moves to his sweatpants to adjust himself. It's then I realize that while I just had the absolute time of my life dry humping the guy, poor Nathan didn't quite get where I am. "Quinn, that was sexy as hell."

"But you didn't..." I can't keep my eyes from moving down his body.

"It's fine."

"I could help take care of things."

He brings his head close so we're sharing the same pillow,

then gives me the sweetest, slowest kiss. "I said it's fine. That wasn't about me just now. That was all for you."

Whoa.

I can't compute what he's saying because I've never heard words even remotely close to them before.

"This isn't like a tit for tat sort of situation?" I ask.

He laughs outright. "No, definitely not. Although I am a big fan of your tits."

I might be blushing, but my face was already hot, so it's hard to pinpoint the reason for it.

"Sorry," he backpedals. "Too crude?"

"Definitely not. I'm a girl that likes to have her tits appreciated."

"I'd be happy to appreciate them any time you want."

I'm about to grab his hand and shove it directly onto the tits in question, but he turns onto his back and lets out a sigh. "I should let you get some sleep."

He's right. It's late, but sleep is the last thing on my mind. Still, I know he has a full day of construction on the docket, and I don't want to be to blame for any workplace related injuries or renovation miscalculations. But the thought of leaving this bed has me inwardly weeping a little.

I don't know how I've suddenly become so attached to this man that I almost crave him like air. The pull to be with him is stronger than anything I've ever felt, like a magnet drawing me toward him despite the things popping up in the way.

Our age difference.

The fact that we're still practically strangers.

And the reality that once he finishes the remodel and I'm done with house-sitting, we'll go our separate ways for good.

Still, I want whatever I can have of him, for however long I can have him.

That truth is lingering on the tip of my tongue, waiting for my head and heart to summon the courage necessary to speak it.

I've gathered almost enough when I turn to him and realize I'll have to wait for another time.

Nathan's asleep, his chest rising and falling peacefully, his handsome face filled with contentment. Contentment I think I might have a little something to do with.

As I slip out of the room and softly shut the door behind me, I feel like I've left a small piece of myself there with him. Given over a portion of my heart to a man I barely know.

And even though it probably should, that doesn't scare me at all.

15 /
nathan

WATCHING Quinn unravel before me last night was an absolute vision. But I knew the instant her regret swept through her. It came in the form of embarrassment, but she had nothing to be embarrassed about. She honestly acted like being that sensitive was a bad thing. She couldn't be more wrong. The thought that I was able to bring her to that place with our clothes *on* only gives me motivation for what things might be like once they're gone altogether.

I can't wait for her to moan from my mouth, my fingers, my cock. I want to set her off in every way possible.

Like me, she's up early. I hear her clanging around in the kitchen a little after seven.

I shower quickly, using the lavender scented shampoo and conditioner I find on the ledge of the tub, and then pull on my shirt and sweats from the day before. It's all I've got because I'm still not sure if I actually plan to move in, even if temporarily.

The offer was nice, but the last thing I want to do is play

house. After all, that's essentially what I was doing with Sarah all those years.

I keep my steps quiet as I descend the stairs, but three cats trail me clumsily, clomping and scratching on the hardwood as they barrel past.

Quinn's bending over, shaking some dry cat food into three separate metal dishes.

It's totally that Pavlov's dog thing, and I find myself part of it, too, since I start to salivate when a bell chimes on the oven. Whatever she's baking in there smells like heaven.

"Good morning, sleepyhead." Her face is full of light, all warmth and sunshine. "I hope I didn't wake you."

She stretches onto her tiptoes to pull down a mug from the highest shelf, exposing that delicious curve of her waist. The urge I feel to wrap my hands around her hips is hard to ignore, but she moves to the coffee maker and pours me a cup before I can act on it.

"I can't offer a coffee that might kill you, but this should have sufficient caffeine to wake you up a bit. How do you take it?"

"Black is good," I say as I reach out for the mug. Our fingers graze when I take it from her.

You would think after all the ways we touched the night before that something as simple as brushing fingertips wouldn't be enough to make me feel like my nerve endings are live wires, but apparently, it doesn't make a difference. Every interaction with Quinn is electric.

Her chest hitches when our eyes meet.

She's honestly one of the most gorgeous women I've ever seen. Big brown eyes. Honey-colored hair. A mouth that not only tempts me with its perfect heart shape, but with the things she says.

I'm falling. Hard.

It's not lost on me that I've barely known the woman a week. It has to be too soon for these feelings to be anything more than infatuation, but I'm okay with that for now. Infatuation is fun. Falling in love is the complicated part. I'm not in any hurry to venture into that territory again.

"Is Jace coming over today?"

She tugs on the handle of the fridge and finds the coffee creamer located inside the door. I'm not surprised that she's the type to fill over half of her cup with the stuff. She really is sweet all the way around.

"He has to work at the amusement park today and tomorrow, but he'll be back after that."

She brings her mug to her lips, and, for a moment, I'm jealous of a piece of ceramic. "So, you don't have any plans?"

"I mean, I've got stuff I can do, I guess. But if you're asking if I'm available for you, that answer is hell yes."

Even behind her mug, I can see the smile spreading on her face. She licks a little bit of creamer from her lips.

"What scene are you writing today?" I ask with too much hope in my voice. I cough roughly and down a big gulp of coffee.

"I'm not writing, but I do need your help," she says. "Not here, though. At my place on the coast."

"Road trip?" There's that damn hope infiltrating my words again. I can't help being anything but eager around this woman.

"A short one, if you're up for it. I've got a deck railing that I broke that needs to be fixed, otherwise my landlord is going to hire out for it, and that always ends up being so much more expensive."

"I think I can handle that. What kind of damage are we talking?"

"Well, the banister is shot, along with a half dozen rails. I'm happy to pay you whatever your going rate is."

Considering this house demo is my first real foray into construction, I don't have a going rate. But it's not like I would charge her even if I did. Just the thought of spending more time with Quinn and possibly getting to know her on a deeper level is payment enough.

"When are you hoping to leave?"

"The sooner the better. But there's one problem."

"And that is?"

"We'll have to bring the cats since I'm guessing we'll need to stay overnight."

I haven't suddenly transformed into a cat lover, but I can put up with them if it means being with Quinn. Hell, I'd put up with a rabid pack of dogs. Possibly worse than that. "I'll get their food and the carriers."

She snickers at how earnest I appear, but I'm fine with that. Her hip cocks against the counter, mug cradled between her palms as she lifts it to draw in another leisurely sip. "I'm glad the thought of sleeping under the same roof again doesn't scare you. I wasn't sure if I came on too strong last night."

"Is it possible to come too strong? That *is* the whole objective, right?"

Quinn practically chokes. "Oh. I see what you did there. That's good." She gives an approving nod. "That might find its way into a book."

"I hope so."

"Don't worry, I'll give you credit."

"Don't need any." I step a little closer. "You can use any of my material as your own."

I want to drop to my knees right there in the kitchen and give her some really explicit stuff to plagiarize, but the oven timer dings again, and it snaps her eyes from mine.

"Cinnamon rolls." She slips two oven mitts on. "I hope you like them."

"Is that even a real question? Who doesn't love a good cinnamon roll?"

"I never said they were good." I help her with the hot pad so she can situate the glass dish onto the tile to cool.

"They look amazing, Quinn."

"You're going to be less impressed once I tell you they came out of a tube. I literally just rolled them out and squished them into the dish." She reaches for a sealed plastic bag of icing. "Totally store bought."

"My taste buds don't know the difference. Seriously, thanks for making breakfast. Can't recall the last time anyone did that for me."

Her fingers are squeezing the white frosting from the packet, and when a dollop sticks to her thumb, she sucks it into her mouth. I swear to God, my dick just twitched. A harsh breath slips between my lips.

"Your ex didn't make you breakfast?" Quinn's narrowed eyes flick up at me and she looks almost offended to hear the news.

"Not in years. Sarah doesn't eat breakfast, so I guess she never thought of it. Plus, I'm not one of those guys that expects his wife to be in the kitchen cooking for him. I can get my own food. It wasn't a big deal."

"Sure, but making breakfast every once in a while is an easy way to take care of your man."

She doesn't mean it the way it comes out, but my heart can't help but snag on her words. I'm not her man. She's not taking care of me. But damn, what I wouldn't give to be hers. To wake up to her in my house, my kitchen. My bed.

"Some say it's the most important meal of the day," she justifies with a shrug.

Her hands are a mess of sugary icing and when she looks down at them and then back up at me, I can't stop myself. I close the distance between us and take her wrist in my grip. Lifting her hand, I bring my lips to her index finger. Our eyes lock. She's not breathing, just staring at me, and when I drag my tongue along the pad of her finger, she inhales, but it's shaky and open-mouthed, all nerves and expectation.

I draw her finger into my mouth and suck the icing from it, swirling my tongue around slowly. One by one, I repeat until all five fingers are licked clean. She still hasn't blinked.

"Are you just going to write my whole damn book?" she whispers in a rush. "Because that's some good stuff, too."

"I really don't want you to run out of subject matter."

"I have a feeling that's not possible with you around."

I glance toward the counter and see the discarded icing packet with a little frosting still left inside. It's not a fully formed thought, just instinct, when I squeeze the rest of it onto my thumb. I lift my hand toward her mouth, but she catches my wrist halfway. This time, she's in control when she thrusts my thumb between her full lips and sucks hard. That act alone has my eyes rolling back, but when she sort of

117

pumps my thumb between her lips—in and out several times —as she licks off the frosting, I lose it.

"Fuck," I hiss.

"I know," she says after releasing my thumb and wiping the excess frosting from her mouth with the back of her hand. "That would be fun, too. But we've got to get on the road. And we don't want these cinnamon rolls to get cold."

———

I offer to drive, and Quinn readily accepts. I like that. Not that I'd have any problem with her chauffeuring me around, but there's a stroke to my ego that can't be helped when she lets me take the lead. I want her to be able to relax in the passenger's seat, maybe even pen a few chapters if she chooses.

Her place on the coast isn't far; just a little over two hours. Though I've never been to the exact beach where she lives, I've explored the Northern California coastline many times in my youth. I remember catching starfish when the tide was out and getting stung by a small jellyfish hiding in the craggy pools along the shore when I wasn't watching where I was going.

The beaches up here are nothing like Southern California's, and that's what everyone imagines when they think of Cali. It's all sheer cliffs and large, jutting rocks dotted white from the seagulls that congregate on them. And it's freaking cold. You wouldn't dare go into the water without a wetsuit.

As we curve our way up Highway 1, I look out my window to see a group of surfers lying flat out on their boards, hoping to capture the next big wave to roll through. It's not something I've ever done, and at thirty-four, the thought of taking up a new death-defying hobby isn't one that sits well with me. What does that say?

My eyes travel across the windshield and over to Quinn. I wonder if she's ever surfed. I hate that I think it, but I also wonder if she's ever been with any of these surfers. Maybe not these exact ones, but a young guy with a carefree spirit seeking a brand-new adventure at every turn.

Honestly, I was never really that guy to begin with, even when I was her age.

Risk-taking has just never been my thing.

But now, this risk I'm taking with my heart feels like one of the most dangerous things I've done.

It's all unknown, and it's terrifying. And I'm beginning to wonder if I'm in over my head, one of those giant waves of doubt about to crest right over me and drown me.

"This next turn." Quinn breaks the silence and juts into my wayward thoughts. I hadn't really second-guessed this trip yet, and now is definitely not the time. I'm angling into her driveway. A little too late for turning back now.

I can see a row of condos up on the hill. She instructs me to take the long path that curves to the right, hemmed in by a beautiful garden of succulents and coastal vegetation.

"This is me," she says, closing her laptop and reaching for her tote bag to stow it away. "The one on the far end."

It's quaint, with weathered gray siding and a small deck off the front that wraps around one side. Immediately, I see the repair she told me about. There's a large portion of railing missing, a huge hazard considering how high her condo sits above the ground.

"Let's get our things and the cats inside, and then I was

thinking we could grab a bite to eat. My best friend works at the local bar just up the road. They're open for lunch during the day. It's mostly seafood; fish and chips and things like that. Would that work for you?"

"Sounds amazing, Quinn."

I get out of the truck and take my duffle bag from the access cab, then stretch over to grab the straps to her luggage, too. I shove both bags onto my shoulder to free up my hands to collect the cat carriers next.

"I can help you with some of that," she says, but I wave her off with a shake of my head.

"Nope."

She just smiles at me, looking a little longer than necessary. I wonder what she's thinking and if it matches my internal musings. I can almost see us like this years from now, traveling together. Maybe we'd travel so she could gather inspiration for her books. Maybe we'd visit new towns and places so I could fix up a few more houses to flip.

I'm stepping too far into a future that isn't a guarantee. Not only is it not a guarantee, but it's also only a wish at this point. A flimsy dream I can't afford to put my hope in.

I follow her up the deck stairs, each one creaking beneath us as we ascend. If I had more time, I'd replace the deck in its entirety. It's rickety and unsafe. But that's on her landlord, not her.

She fishes in her bag for her keys and pulls out a long chain with a fluffy pink ball at the end. The lock turns over when she fits the key inside.

"This is my place." It's theatrical when Quinn steps into the condo and does a little twirl, arms out on either side.

"Feel free to toss our stuff on the couch and let the cats out of their carriers. I'm going to use the restroom really quick."

The place is adorable, a total mirror of her. It's all bright and airy, with large windows and white subway tile in a kitchen covered with stainless steel and quartz. She's got a navy-blue couch along one wall, and an abstract painting easily six-feet wide hangs over it. There are plants everywhere, but based on the amount of time I know she's been away, I figure they are artificial. They're way too green to have gone without a recent watering.

I lower our luggage to the couch, take the cat carriers to the other end of the room and open them, and then continue my perusal. I don't know the name for the style of furniture, but I like it. It's simple with clean lines and natural looking wood where you can see the rings and imperfections. Her kitchen table is just a round piece of glass balanced on a black blocky base, and the four chairs tucked around it have thin legs and white plastic backs.

It's a big step up from Ikea quality, and I could totally see myself living somewhere like this.

My chest constricts.

No. No, I wouldn't live in a place like this, because this place is *Quinn's*. I wonder if it is just second nature for me to play out my life with her, though. Because that's what I did with Sarah back when we were teens, and it became our reality.

Not every relationship leads to forever. I know that. Don't I?

"Sorry." Quinn steps out from behind a door I assume leads to her bedroom and bathroom within it. Her fingers comb through her hair, and she gives me a smile that has me melting. She's so genuine it almost hurts. "You ready to grab something?"

I know she's referring to food and not her, but I still move forward and plant my hands on her waist and my lips on her mouth. Her surprise registers as a little squeak in the back of her throat, but then she fully participates and dives in just as deep, her tongue slipping into my mouth as her eyes fall shut.

Kissing her is like being set on fire from the inside out. Everything's hot, raging. I curl my hand around the base of her neck, threading my fingers into her hair as I tilt to gain access to her neck.

"Nathan," she whispers when I suck lightly on her skin. "If we don't get going, we'll never leave this condo."

"Not a bad plan," I say between lingering kisses.

"I promised Kimmie she would get to meet you as soon as we got into town."

That has me drawing out of our kiss to stare into her eyes. "Your friend?"

"Yep. The one who will be at the bar, waiting for us."

"You want to introduce me to your friends?" I'm sure I sound as surprised as I feel.

"In fairness, it's just one friend. I don't have a lot of others. But yes, I'd like for her to meet you. And for you to meet her."

I want to ask why, but I don't, because I feel the same. If Logan and Archie were in town, I'd sure as hell be bringing Quinn around to introduce them all.

She places a palm on my chest. "Also, I don't want you to think I asked you to come here with me just so I could take advantage of you."

"Take advantage of me?" I almost burst out laughing. In

what way could she possibly take anything from me that I wouldn't willingly give a hundred times over?

"Like, for research purposes, you know?"

"As I said before, I'm a vault of potential material just waiting to be cracked."

Her hand claps on my chest in a playful shove. "Then let's get out of here so we can come back and work on cracking that open."

I moan a little and press into her just to give her an idea of the way my body is currently responding to her words. "Quinn, you cannot say things like that and expect me to be decent to meet your friend."

"It's a ten-minute drive." She winks at me, gaze flitting down between us and then back up, which doesn't help the situation at all. "You should be recovered by then."

16 /
quinn

GLIMPSING Kimmie from across the establishment is like getting an instant hit of dopamine. That girl is my ride or die. Just the sight of her has me charging through the bar, bumping stools and clipping the edges of tables as I rush toward her.

We slam into one another in a hug that rivals a football tackle. Somehow, we stay upright.

"Don't you ever leave me for that long again!" She shakes me by the shoulders like a rag doll. "Your mom needs to hire a real freaking house-sitter, you know that? She's taken advantage of you for far too long, and I need my girl back at the shores with me. Tell her I'm tired of sharing."

Kimmie doesn't love my mom and my mom doesn't love Kimmie. I get it. Their personalities are like oil and water, and as hard as I've tried over the years to get them to mix, it hasn't worked.

Shoving me aside, Kimmie gives Nathan a hug with the same amount of force behind it. I can tell it jars him a little, but he's a good sport and reciprocates.

"You must be Nathan," she says, finally releasing him. Kimmie's almost six-feet tall and she's eye level with Nathan, but not in an intimidating way. Not much about her is. Her mile-wide smile—bracketed by adorable, pierced dimples— and fire engine red hair help take the edge off her multiple earrings and plethora of tattoos. She's the best kind of dichotomy. "I gotta be honest. I haven't heard enough about you yet, but I'm hoping all that will change now that Quinn's back in town."

"You know we're only here for the night." I had made that implicitly clear because I know my friend's level of enthusiasm and I'm often the one to temper it.

"I know. But I'm manifesting a car breakdown or tidal wave or some other cosmic intervention that will force you to stay longer."

I snicker because I don't doubt she is. "Can you get us a table?" I ask, looking around the place. It's uncharacteristically crowded for a weekday afternoon.

"You're here to eat? Not just to see me?" Kimmie walks us over to a booth with high seat backs wrapped in burgundy leather and a dim Edison light bulb hanging right above the table.

"Can you join us? When's your lunch break?"

With two hands cupped around her mouth, Kimmie hollers across the crowded room toward someone drying pint glasses behind the bar. "Walter! I'm taking my break!" She swings her gaze back to us. "Right now." Kimmie juts her chin toward the front of the restaurant. "I'll go grab some menus. Sit tight."

Nathan slides into the seat across from me.

"I'm sorry," I say, taking my place. "She can be a lot."

"She's great." He seems to mean it.

"Yeah? Because I obviously think so, but I know she's not for everyone."

"I like her vibe."

I want Nathan's approval, but more than that, I want Kimmie's opinion on Nathan. Some people get nervous introducing their partners to their parents, but my best friend's endorsement is all I care about. Not that Nathan and I are together. Still, before things go any further between us, I need Kimmie's input.

"Here you go." She reappears with the menus, and divvies them out before plopping down next to me, bumping her hip to mine to push me down the length of the booth. "But I don't really think the menu is even necessary. Our fish and chips platter is the best thing on it, hands down. Let's get three of those."

"What if Nathan wants something else?"

He lowers his menu and pushes it to the middle of the table. "If Kimmie stands by them, I'm game."

"I like this one." A coil of red hair bounces across her forehead as she nods toward him.

The praise settles onto Nathan's face as a small grin.

Damn, he's sexy, even when he isn't trying to be.

"So, Nathan, tell me what makes you good enough to date my girl Quinn?"

"Kimmie—"

She flaps a silencing hand at me. "Shhh. Let the man speak. I'd like to know why he thinks he's worthy of you."

"We're not dating," I get in, but Nathan's already answering.

"From what I can tell, I'm *not* worthy of her. She's incredible. Kind. Genuine. Doesn't take herself too seriously. I'll be honest; we don't know each other all that well yet. But what I'm getting to know, I really love."

It's suddenly a thousand degrees in here. Something must have caught fire in the kitchen because my cheeks singe so hard, I swear they're radiating. I flutter my menu to manufacture some kind of cooling breeze, but I still feel like I'm melting.

"I'll accept that answer," Kimmie says. "And you're right. She *is* incredible. Unfortunately, she has an *incredibly* difficult time choosing guys that will treat her like the queen she is. I want to make sure you're not like the other douchenozzles she's settled for in the past."

"This is all premature." I'm stuttering. My eyes look everywhere but at Nathan's. "We're not even together."

"Then it's the perfect time for me to issue this warning. Nathan, you appear to be a good guy, but if you fuck around with Quinn's heart, I will hunt you down, rip yours out, and feed it to the sea lions on Portuguese Beach. Are we clear?"

"Crystal."

"Alright, then." She smacks the table. "Let's get our grub on."

We share a pitcher of beer, three baskets of fish and chips, and an hour's worth of conversation. It's so easy. The three of us carry on like we've all known each other our whole lives.

I love that Nathan is so adaptable in a situation like this. As a bartender, Kimmie is really good at conversation. She can chat it up with anyone, no matter their background, interests, or personality. But I get the impression she really likes Nathan, and that makes my chest constrict right in the center for so many reasons. I'm happy, of course, but there's a twinge of trepidation here. This feeling that I'm getting a glimpse into a life I'm not sure I'll ever have.

When we've finished eating, Nathan moves for the check with stealth-like accuracy, discreetly snatching it from the server's hand before anyone else commandeers it.

Kimmie gives me a *'he's a keeper'* look. I know he is. That's the hardest part of it all. Nathan is boyfriend material; there's no denying that. If we had met under any other circumstances at any other time in our lives, I think I'd be all in. I'm just not sure I'm ready for that. And I don't think he's ready to jump back into a committed relationship yet, either.

I plan to just have fun while it lasts. The only moment that's a guarantee is the one you're currently living, right? So, I'm going to live it up.

"I should get back to work." Kimmie stands from the booth first. "It was great to meet you, Nathan." She goes in for another hug when he gets to his feet, too. "Don't be a stranger." She turns to me. "And seriously, tell your mom her house will be fine without someone physically sitting in it."

"It's more the cats that need watching than the house."

"Those fucking cats."

"Amen," Nathan mutters, and visions of Geronimo clawing his crotch flood my brain.

"I thought you liked the cats."

"I think he likes *you*," Kimmie says, eyes bouncing between us. "And he tolerates the cats because you're currently a package deal."

Nathan flicks out an index finger. "Bingo."

"Come by the bar tonight if you two are bored and I'll give you free alcohol." Kimmie kisses my cheek and keeps me close when she whispers in my ear, "But I don't see how you could get bored with a body like his to play with. Have fun, my friend."

I don't let my face register her words and instead follow Nathan as he makes his way toward the exit. When he reaches back to take my hand in his, it feels like the most natural thing in the world.

"Are you in a rush to get back to the condo?" He shoulders the door open and steps aside to allow me through first.

"Depends on how long you think it will take to repair the deck. I want to be sure you don't run out of daylight."

"Shouldn't take more than a couple hours." He rolls his wrist over to look at his watch. "It's still early. I was thinking we could go to one of the beaches for a bit."

"I like that idea. But we should still swing by the condo first to get a blanket. It'll be cold."

"Good call."

I do want the blanket to help combat the temperature, but I want it for other reasons, too. Rolling around in the gritty sand is not my idea of a good time, but cozying up with Nathan while the waves crash in our periphery, their unyielding back and forth creating a rhythm that we can replicate in a hot and heavy make-out session? Sign me up. *Yes, please.*

He keeps the truck idling once we arrive at the condo. I jog up the steps and into the house. I give myself a once-over in the bathroom mirror, deciding to scrub a toothbrush over my teeth and tongue for good measure. I've got a thick, quilted blanket over my shoulder and a smile on my face as I bound down the steps two at a time. Obviously, not the smartest thing to do with the deck's current level of disrepair, because when I land on the bottom rung, it completely snaps beneath my feet.

Nathan flings open the driver's side door.

"Shit, Quinn!" He races over. "Are you okay?"

I'm on the ground. Blinding pain shoots up my leg. It's like the time I tripped during a soccer game in junior high and rolled my ankle while the rest of my teammates trampled me like I was just a speed bump in the middle of the field. I was out for the rest of the season with that stupid injury.

"Dammit," I hiss, clutching my foot. The surging pain wanes, but my ears ring.

"This deck is falling down around you, Quinn. Your landlord needs to step up and replace the whole thing. Can you stand?"

"I think so." I take hold of his hand and wobble onto my feet. Both legs support me, and as I apply more weight to the injury, I realize it's not as bad as I originally suspected. "I don't think it's a sprain. Just twisted it a little."

"We can skip the beach."

"No." I shake my head. "I want to go to the beach with you. I just might need some help getting down to the water."

"Okay, but only if you think you're up for it. I'll carry you if I have to."

I don't expect to cash in on that offer, but when we arrive five minutes later and I hobble out of the truck and over to the cliffy staircase made from carved-out hillside and railroad ties, Nathan immediately scoops me into his arms.

Air whooshes from my lungs.

"Hang on," he instructs as he slowly descends, peering over me to make sure he has a proper footing on each precarious step. "Almost there."

The steep route isn't ideal in this situation, but I've always loved the seclusion it provides. Even though Highway 1 is just above us, there's a natural shelter created by the bluffs. Our own private beach.

We make it to where the dirt transitions into sand, but he doesn't put me down like I expect him to. I've walked through the sand before and know the resistance it creates. It's hard enough on your own, let alone bogged down with the cumbersome weight of another person. And yet, for Nathan, it seems effortless. He's stronger than I realized, and gentler than I suspected when he flaps out the blanket onto the sand with one hand and keeps me in his arm with the other. Gingerly, he lowers me to the beach below.

"You good?"

I give him a nod. "I am. Thank you, Nathan. You're quite the gentleman."

"I try." He bends to sit beside me.

My ankle feels almost entirely back to normal, but I hug my knees to my chest and keep pressure off it all the same.

"God, this is beautiful." His eyes are on the water. "I used to visit the ocean with my dad when I was a kid. I haven't been back in years."

It's the first he's mentioned of his family, other than his ex-wife. "Yeah?"

He nods, eyes forward. "Before he left, we used to do all sorts of shit together. Fishing. Hiking. Camping. You know, the obligatory father-son stuff."

I don't know if he's going to say more, but I'm thankful for the little glimpse into this part of his life. He's opening up, and I want whatever he'll give.

"But then, when I was sixteen, he fucked around with

his secretary and Mom made him move out. I remember being so mad at her at the time. I just couldn't understand why she wouldn't forgive him and let things go back to normal. At least until I left for college. Couldn't they just fake it a little longer? What harm would that do?" He gathers a handful of sand in his palm and lets it sift slowly through his fingers. He does this three more times without saying anything.

"I imagine that must have been hard on everyone."

"It was. I see things differently now. Faking it does nothing other than prolong the pain. In the end, it just makes the inevitable that much harder."

He's referring to his marriage, and if I hadn't already been certain, the way he rubs his ring finger with his thumb is a silent tell.

"I'm sorry about what happened to your mom, Nathan. And what happened to you."

He tosses another handful of sand out in front of us and then looks at me. "It happened to you, too. It sucks when people don't honor their commitments."

In fairness, Kyle and I weren't bound by anything as strong as vows, but I appreciate Nathan's sensitivity all the same.

"Does it make you at all gun-shy about the thought of opening yourself up again?" I reach down to tug the corner of the blanket over my shoulder. Nathan helps me gather a large swath of fabric to tuck around us, cocooning us beneath its heavy weight.

"I thought it would. But it's not stopping me from wanting to share everything about myself with you."

I shiver. It's not from the cold, but he interprets it that

way. Along with the blanket, he slides an arm over my shoulder to curl my body into his muscled side.

"I really like you, Quinn. I know we've only just met, so I don't understand it, but I also don't want to question it. I haven't felt this good in years. You make me feel something I didn't know was still there."

I get it. It's that way for me, too.

"But I also don't want to start something we can't continue," he adds. "I don't want to hurt you."

I lift my head from his shoulder, those green eyes stalling my breath. There's so much depth to his gaze, a pool of vulnerability I find myself sinking into. "I think at this point, it would hurt more if we don't explore where this could go. It would for me, at least."

His chest rises with a big breath. I don't resist when his finger hooks my chin, directing my face toward his. He waits a second, just staring at me, but then his lips press so softly to mine I almost whimper. It's gentle and reserved, chaste in a way that makes my eyes prickle with tears and pressure build in my throat. I'm overcome with an emotion I can hardly keep bound within myself.

This beautiful man with his beautiful heart is the most unexpected gift.

I don't know how we got here, but like Nathan said, I'm not going to question it.

I also don't let myself question my next move, the one where I'm leaning back onto the blanket, pulling Nathan by the shirt collar to come with me. I'm so grateful the blanket I chose is from my queen-sized bed, because even though we're the only ones on the secluded beach, I still want to be covered up for what I'm about to do.

He moves onto his side facing me and tosses the edge of the quilt over us, so we're sheltered beneath it completely. I don't let our lips lose contact. The initial innocence transitions into something else entirely when I slip my tongue past his lips, searching for a deeper connection. He meets me move for move, stroke for stroke. Kissing Nathan is a high and the only way I want to come down is if I'm shattering beneath him.

But right now, it's his turn.

My hands find his belt. He knows what I'm about to do. There's a hesitation made known in his staggered breathing, in the pinch of his brow drawn tight over his closed eyes.

But I'm not planning to stop unless he asks me to.

He doesn't. Instead, his fingers reach down and move with mine, loosening the leather strap until it's freed from the buckle. He brings his hand back to my face while our mouths mesh together, tongues tangle, and breaths mingle.

I work the button open, then slowly drag the zipper down.

Nathan groans loudly, but it's muted by the waves crashing along the shoreline in the distance, swallowed up in the chaos of the sea.

My own sounds of surprise rumble from my throat when my hand dips lower and I finally feel the full length of him. It's one thing to have our clothes on and envision what he's keeping in there. But holy mother of Moses, the man is packing something I've never come close to seeing—let alone touching—in real life.

"Wow, Nathan," I mutter against his lips.

"Yeah?" There's an edge of pride in his tone. "You think?"

"You did not tell me *this* was what you were working with." I slide my hand into the waistband of his boxer briefs and boldly curl it around his rock-hard erection. "I've only written about guys like you. I didn't know you actually existed. Thought maybe it was all a myth."

He nips at my bottom lip when I tighten my grip. "I'm glad I can serve as proof that we do, in fact, exist. Like your own personal Bigfoot sighting or something."

"I think you mean Big*dick* sighting." He snickers at the joke, but his laughter cuts off with a harsh breath when I start to stroke him.

"God, Quinn," he hisses. His forehead touches mine.

That encouragement keeps me going. I work him slowly up and down, root to tip, over and over, feeling his massive cock grow even more rigid within my hand.

"*Fuck.*"

Boy, do I ever want to, and I'm thankful for this small glimpse into his very big package, because now I feel just a little more prepared for when we finally do. This man is gifted beyond belief. I'm screaming internally at the thought that I might get to take this magnificent dick for a ride at some point in the future. I am a lucky, lucky girl.

But right now, the focus is on him.

Nathan has been such a giver; it's finally his turn to be on the receiving end.

"What do you like?" I whisper against his lips as my hand continues pumping him. "Faster? Slower?"

"What you're doing is perfect." His eyelids flutter. "Damn, Quinn. You're really good at this."

It's literally just a hand job, but I'm guessing he hasn't had many of those lately. And he's right. This *is* good, especially the moans and grunts of approval he's giving me. I swear, those sexy sounds alone make me wet. I'm suddenly a little fireball of hormones, and it takes all my sexual willpower not to jump the man right here, right now. Forget the fact that it's daylight and we're technically on a public beach. In this moment, it's just us and nothing else.

I don't stop stroking him. My hand moves faster, matching the quickness of our gasping breaths.

And even though I want to do this for him—want Nathan to finally have his moment to be appreciated in this way—I'm realizing it's not in his character to take without giving.

So I'm not at all surprised when his hand slips lower and squeezes my thigh, fingers curling into my flesh. They inch higher at the same time I rub upward on his cock, and all the blood in my body pools to the sensitive spot between my legs when he pushes the hem of my cutoffs and slides the cottony fabric of my panties aside.

Thank God for short shorts, is all I can say. This easy access is an absolute blessing.

A single finger swipes into me. He moans into my open mouth. "You're so wet."

No shit. My body has her hopes up and is doing her best to prepare for that colossal cock, but Nathan quickly proves he's just as talented with other things when he eases a finger all the way inside me.

My breath hitches. I make some sort of garbled noise.

"You okay?"

"Mm, hmm." I nod quickly, but I've lost track of everything up to this point. He thrusts his finger in and out several times, reminding me I was in the middle of doing something to him, too. But my synapses are misfiring all over the place. I don't know up from down. Like he senses my sudden disorientation, his free hand comes over mine still wrapped around him, guiding me back into a rhythm as we work his straining shaft together.

Holy hell, this is hot.

When he fits a second finger inside me, I swear I hear angels. It's too much, but somehow, still not enough. He pumps our hands over his length while continuously driving his fingers into me. When he curls them slightly, hitting a spot deep within, stars light up behind my eyelids. I'm in another universe.

Unlike Nathan's, my sounds aren't sexy. They're groans and squeaks and winded breaths that make my ears ring.

Apparently, I've sufficiently found my groove again because he removes the hand on mine to slip it under my shirt. I continue grasping his erection, working him up and down, harder, faster, wishing I could give him more than just this, even though he seems perfectly happy with what I'm offering.

Nathan tugs down one side of my lacy bra and covers my breast with his palm. I'm not incredibly busty, but I'm a handful, and apparently that's all he needs. I swear, his cock strains even more, grows even larger, when he squeezes my bare breast and then brushes back and forth over my nipple with his thumb, bringing it to a peak.

"You're fucking perfect," he grits out in a throaty moan. His fingers are drilling into me, his hand grasping me. I suddenly realize he's one of those guys that could probably walk and chew gum at the same time. He's mastered the art of worshiping a woman with his hands alone, and I'm thrilled to be the one currently benefiting from his touch.

"Your body is a goddamn marvel." He's not even able to really see me. We've got a blanket wrapped over us, keeping everything hidden beneath. But he's exploring me beneath his fingertips, and he obviously likes what he feels.

Things aren't any different on my end. I was overwhelmed with his dick at the start of this, but right now I'm completely awestruck. It's the eighth wonder of the world, in my humble opinion. I pick up speed, gliding my hand along his impressive cock, my hold tighter, my pace quicker.

"Quinn." His shaky breath hits my mouth. "Fuck. Yes. Keep doing that."

He matches my tempo, adding his thumb to rub my clit while his two fingers thrust so far inside me, I let out a yelp. It's so good, so deep. My nerves are in overdrive, his thumb making expert circles that have my toes curling, my nipples pebbling, my body clenching.

"Yes, Nathan. Right there. God, that's it," I cry out. "Don't stop. Please, don't stop."

"I'm not going to, baby." His hips thrust into my hand currently jacking him off. I can tell he's as close as I am.

He suddenly withdraws his fingers, and, for a moment, I feel like crying a little. But he moves them to my clit, rubbing their wetness over it before sliding them back to continue plunging in and out. His thumb takes over again. The slick sensation is even more incredible than before.

I moan and gasp, the only way I'm currently able to communicate. My hips rock into him as everything within me coils, wanting this—wanting Nathan—more than anything I've ever desired in my whole life. I writhe against him, completely shameless and utterly gone.

His mouth slams into mine, but it's hardly a kiss. It's all

teeth and lips and hot, erratic breaths accompanied by indecipherable words of need.

"Ah, that is so good. Yes, just like that," I somehow get out. "Nathan, I'm so close...I can't...I'm going to come."

"Me, too," he growls against my neck. "So... fucking...close."

We're a frenzy of hands and mouths and white-hot heat in pursuit of a release we're both working so frantically to achieve.

"I'm right there." His gravelly voice rasps in my ear, dripping with sex when he pulls back to look me in the eye and say, "I want to watch when I make you come like this. Ride my hand, Quinn. Show me how much you like it."

It's the final push that sends me careening over the edge. Everything once wound so tight within me explodes into fragments, my orgasm ripping through me, tense and tingling. Even as it racks my body, my muscles clamping around his fingers, my mouth on his and my heart hammering within my chest, I continue pumping him harder, faster, and he finally climaxes with a low, guttural growl.

Nathan's neck arches, body stilling. He shoves a hand between us, bringing his shirt down to cover himself as his release empties with each trembling pulse.

"Fu-*uck*." Somehow, he stretches the word into two syllables.

Our arms and legs wrap together in a need to be as close as possible, but Nathan jerks back. "Shit. I forgot. How's your ankle?"

I hadn't given it a second thought since we'd started this whole sexy seaside shenanigan. "Totally fine." A smirk lifts my lips and my eyes flit down. "How's your dick?"

"Never better."

He kisses me long and slow and sweet in a way that feels even more meaningful than what we just did to one another.

And suddenly, I understand why.

It's the first kiss we've shared since I've realized one important thing: I could absolutely fall for this man.

Maybe I already have a little.

17 /
nathan

"WHAT ON EARTH CAUSED THIS?"

Quinn's expression is all innocence, but I can read the guilt behind her eyes. "You don't want to know the answer."

Maybe I don't. "Wild night?"

"Wild morning." She smirks. "Doing yoga."

"Yoga?" I investigate the section of the deck missing the railing. "See? I *told* you yoga sucks."

"I lost my balance and just went over. In fairness, I think those boards were rotted out to begin with. And the pose was a really hard one."

Funny, because *yoga* and *hard* are definitely two words I associate with one another, but I know Quinn is referring to a different meaning.

She doesn't have to elaborate. If I were doing yoga on that ramshackle deck, I would have totally wiped out and taken the whole thing down with me.

"I'm going to need to pick up some wood posts for the balusters and a two by six for the handrail. Is there a lumber store nearby we can head to?"

She nods. "It's about fifteen-minutes from here."

We hop in the truck and drive north, the ocean on our left, rolling hills dotted with grazing cows on our right.

It's gorgeous here. I can easily see why Quinn chose this place to call home. It has everything. Sand. Surf. Even the fog settling over the coastline is oddly comforting, like a blanket pulled over the beach and tucking it in.

My ex-wife hated the ocean. Said it made her hair frizzy or something like that. I don't know, maybe the salty air does do something to women's hair, because I notice how Quinn's got these little wispy curls around her face that weren't there before. But she doesn't seem to mind. She looks beautiful, all windswept and carefree.

Her arm is out the open window, palm turned to meet the breeze that glides over the truck as I maneuver the twisty highway. Her head rests on her shoulder; her shoes are kicked off at her feet.

It's hard to keep my focus on the road. Everything in me wants to stare at her. I don't know what that's all about. I'm in awe. Not just about the way she looks, but who she is. I don't think I've ever met a person who draws me in like she does. Even the first time we met when she was all feisty and I was frustrated, there was something there.

But I'm definitely not frustrated anymore—not even sexually, and that's saying a lot.

We arrive at the do-it-yourself store, and she jumps down from the truck cab with gusto. In the back of my head, I'm still worried about her ankle, even though she's assured me it's fine. Without even mentioning my need for one, she grabs one of the flatbed carts from the lot and pushes it into the store. When I try to take it, she bumps me out of the way with her hip.

"I'll push it while it's empty. But once it's loaded down with lumber, that's all you."

"Fair enough."

The store is big like a warehouse, so I scan the aisles and the signs that hang overhead. "This way."

There's a wobbly wheel in the font that makes the cart swivel and fishtail. Quinn is using every bit of her strength to keep the cart going straight, but it clips the corner of an end cap of stain remover products, just about knocking an entire row of spray bottles from the shelf.

Quinn skids to a stop, eyes wide. "Whoa. That was a close one."

I come alongside her to grip the cart's handle. "Teamwork," I say, and with both of us at the helm, we make it to the lumber aisle with no additional run-ins.

"When I was a kid, my dad would always push me on these things when he'd make a trip to the hardware store." Her eyes are bright with the memory. "I used to pretend I was sailing on some big pirate ship. I'd even shout stuff like 'land-ho!' and 'ahoy, matey!', but I'm not sure I even really knew what that meant."

"You've always had a big imagination, huh?" I pull out my sheet of scrap paper from my back pocket to scan the shelves for the lumber I need.

Quinn's shoulders raise in a small shrug. "I got it from him. Dad encouraged my creativity. He never made me feel silly for playing make believe, even when I was too old to do so."

"Are you ever really too old for make believe?" I load the

cart with unfinished rails, tossing a couple more on than I'll need for good measure.

"I guess not. I mean, after all, that's sort of what we're doing right?"

I chuck that last board harder than I mean to, her words throwing me. "What?"

"This thing we're doing. It's all for the sake of fiction, and that's a lot like make believe."

That's when it hits me harder than a two by four to the head.

That whole episode back at the beach; that was all material for her book. A run-through. Of course, it was. After all, that's exactly what I told her to do: use me for inspiration.

While I'm over here falling for this woman, she's probably just mentally penning her next chapter. I can't even be mad about it. I don't have that right. But there's a pit in my stomach that grows like a sinkhole when I think about how real things felt for me. How impossibly good and perfect and even a little hope-filled that moment was.

Shit. I need to take a step back.

I scratch the back of my neck and suck in a deep breath.

"Did you get everything you need?" Quinn reads my hesitation as something else.

Snapping back into focus, I pull down the remaining board from a shelf higher up and slide it onto the cart. "Now I have. That's it."

She's still smiling, totally unaware that I'm experiencing a bit of a breakdown inside. I think that's just how I deal, though. Keep it all in. I can take it out later on the deck at her condo or on the tile entryway that still needs to come out back at the house. I have ways to sort through my emotions. I don't think any therapist would sign off on them, but it's how I've learned to cope.

"While we're here, want to show me the type of finish work you're thinking of for the remodel?" she asks.

"I haven't really thought that far ahead." I take the cart from her, not giving her the option to steer this time. I need to have control over something, and right now, a cart is about all I can manage.

"Let's look." Her hand meets my forearm, stilling me. "Since we're here."

I just nod. It's unfair to be angry with her, and I'm not. I'm just angry at myself for not working harder to protect my damn heart. It's still so raw and every time I let myself get carried away with Quinn, I'm splitting those wounds back open and pouring salt directly into them. It seriously stings.

We spend the next twenty minutes looking at light fixtures. Well, I'm just staring at them, but she's talking about things like pendants and chandeliers and wattage. It's all Greek to me. I'm not processing any of it, but there's an excitement in her tone and it's the same way she gets when she talks about her writing. This is clearly another passion of hers.

"Did you go to school for interior design?"

Her gaze snaps from the lighting overhead. "Me? No. I just like to decorate. Honestly, I thought I wanted to be an interior designer for a while there, but then Dad got sick, and I felt like I owed it to him to be a writer."

That statement takes me aback. "Why would you owe him?"

"I don't know." There's uncertainty in her eyes. "To continue his legacy, I suppose."

"Do you enjoy writing?" Now's my chance to get out of the lighting department and quite honestly, all the bright white is giving me a headache, so I take it. I push the cart toward the registers. "I mean, you're obviously good at it, but is it your calling?"

"I'm a creative person. Anything that lets me exercise that part of my brain is good," Quinn says. "For now, writing satisfies that for me. But I'd love the opportunity to decorate and design sometime. It's something I'd like to get better at."

"Well, I'm about to have an entire house for you to work with."

"You're going to want to hire a professional for that."

"No. I'd like to hire you."

She frowns. "But you haven't even seen what I can do."

"Yes, I have. Your condo. It's incredible." I push the cart up to the checkout counter and a young kid comes around with the scanner to tally up my boards. I move several around so he can locate the barcodes. "And that painting hanging above the sofa? You've got an eye for art, too, because that is phenomenal."

A pink blush comes over Quinn's face and neck. "I actually painted that."

"I should have known. Is there anything you're not good at?" I pull my wallet from my pocket and swipe my card into the reader.

"I'd say I'm mediocre at a lot of things, and not all that great at much. What's the saying? Jack of all trades, master of none?"

The cashier hands me the receipt and Quinn joins me to push the cart out the wide double doors that automatically stretch open as we approach.

"I wouldn't say you're mediocre at all. You're unbelievably talented, Quinn."

While we were in the store, the fog swept in, a hazy gray that lowered the temperature several degrees. Quinn runs her palms over her arms for warmth, then drops the tailgate on the truck when we get to it and stands close while I load the lumber into the bed.

"The entire problem with being a creative is that it inherently involves a lot of criticism. Everything from writing to designing to painting invites critique. It's hard to believe you're good at any of it when there will always be someone who doesn't like what you do," she says. She climbs into the passenger side of the truck when I get into the driver's seat. "But that's also what I like about it, I guess. There are no hard and fast rules."

It strikes me that there don't seem to be any actual rules when it comes to us, either. Anything goes, and I don't know where to draw the line.

"I'm a formulas guy," I say as I start up the truck to head back to the condo. "I like numbers. I like predictable outcomes." Hell, I got married because it was the next part of the equation.

"I'm going to draw the creative side out of you, Nathan. I'm going to get you to think outside the box."

She already has.

Here I am, falling for a much younger woman when I have no business getting into any sort of relationship. The rules I've played by my entire life have gone out the window.

It's too much. I need to switch gears. "What are you going to do while I'm working on the deck?"

147

"I'm hoping to get a little writing in." Her fingernail trails up my arm, making a lazy pattern. "I'm feeling motivated."

I shudder from the contact, but she reads that as shaking her off.

Recoiling, she drops her hands to her lap. "Maybe I'll just do some reading. I don't know."

This is where I should make some sort of innuendo, but it doesn't feel genuine, and I can't get the words out.

Even when we're back at the condo and I'm knee deep in repairs, there's a sick, hollow feeling in my gut again.

What happens when all the pages are written? When the house is rebuilt?

Quinn and I are temporary, at best. And even though I know that, I worry there will be permanent damage to my heart when all is said and done.

18 /
quinn

"SEX ON THE BEACH?"

I choke. "What?"

Kimmie holds a cocktail shaker over her head and jostles it wildly, making her bouncing boobs almost pop out of the neckline of her skimpy tank top. "Your drink of choice tonight. Sex on the beach?"

I blink. "Oh."

"Why? What did you think I was talking about?"

"Nothing."

Certainly not the fact that Nathan and I shared an incredibly sexy moment this afternoon on an actual beach, only to barely speak to each other the rest of the day.

I get it. He had the deck rebuild to tend to, but I can't help but feel like what we did suddenly switched something off for him. I don't know what happened at the hardware store, but there was an obvious shift between us. And I don't know how to get back to where we were.

It's the reason I suggested heading to Kimmie's bar for a drink. My sober brain wasn't doing any good sorting through things. Maybe an intoxicated state of mind might have better luck.

Or seeing my best friend could help. Kimmie's always been a pro at deciphering relationship woes.

"What's going on with you?" She pours the liquid mixture all the way to the sugared rim of a martini glass and slides it down the bar toward a brunette in a group of women about our age.

"Nothing's going on with me."

"Um. Yes." She plucks three maraschino cherries from a little dish and gives two to me, keeping one back for herself.

I pop one into my mouth. It's sweet and makes my taste buds perk up. "Nathan and I messed around this afternoon—"

"Hell, yes! I want the details. All of them." Her palms clap the sticky counter. "Or should I just wait and read about it in your next book?"

That's the thing. I don't want to use any of it in my book. It feels too personal, too private.

"I think I upset him," I say, ignoring her request for specifics. "It's like we had this really incredible, super-hot moment, and then he just shut down."

"Typical guy for you. Gets what he wants and then it's adios." She mimics a wave and whips her head, red curls bobbing all over. "But it honestly surprises me a little to hear that about Nathan. I don't know. He seemed more mature than the other guys you've dated."

"He's old, I get it."

"No, no." Her tongue is working on something behind her lips, and when she spits out a perfectly knotted cherry stem into her palm, I give her the appreciative grin I know she's going for. "It's not that he's older. He just seems more in tune with his emotions."

"Well, he's not cluing me in on them now, that's for sure."

The barstool swivels when I turn to look over my shoulder toward the door. Nathan's truck was having engine trouble on the way over, lights flashing all over the dash. He'd told me to go on inside while he stayed in the parking lot to check things out. It's been ten minutes, and he still hasn't made an appearance.

For a split second, I wonder if it's his plan to ditch me completely. But it's not like he could have orchestrated the light up dashboard. I need to stop with this whole self-doubt thing. It's not a good look on me.

"Maybe he's insecure about his...*you know*." Kimmie's eyes flit downward, then pop back up.

I pluck off another cherry. "Oh, trust me. He has nothing to worry about there."

Suddenly, there's a large body looming next to me, but it's not Nathan. This is some gym rat, and his idea of personal space must be measured in inches, not feet. He leans an elbow onto the bar, pressing in so close I can smell his hot breath.

"I'll have a Manhattan," he interrupts.

Kimmie full on rolls her eyes, even though it's her job to wait on him. "Up? Dirty?"

"Up *and* dirty," he says in a low voice that makes my skin crawl. Yuck. "What're you drinking?"

"Oh, I'm fine." I wave him off.

"Come on, sugar. Let me buy you a drink."

Kimmie's mouth is in a pout as she's mixing his martini.

She's not looking at me, but I know she doesn't approve of this creeper and the way he won't take no for an answer.

"I'm good with water," I say.

"The pretty lady will have a Cosmo."

A Cosmopolitan is the last drink I would order, no offense to the girls who like them. Cranberry juice just reminds me that my mom once read that it's good for post-menopausal health, and then proceeded to tell every restaurant we frequented they should carry it to support their older customer's dietary needs. I don't want to be thinking about my mom when I'm out drinking.

"I'm not a big fan of Cosmos," I interject.

"Then a Long Island."

"God, no." How much alcohol does this guy think I need?

"Two house chardonnays." There's a hand on my shoulder, and a smile already forming when I glance up to see Nathan. His lips land on my cheek before I can register what's happening. "Sorry that took so long."

A knowing grin spreads ear to ear on Kimmie's face even as she keeps up with drink orders behind the bar. She totally eats up this type of low-key drama.

The beefed-up jock slides down, but won't make eye contact with Nathan, or me, for that matter.

"Who's the dude?" Nathan whispers into my hair as he settles onto the barstool next to me.

"Just a Neanderthal that can't take a hint," Kimmie bellows, her loud voice clearly meant for the guy to hear. "And Nathan, I gotta say, I'm impressed with your order. Not too many guys are secure enough to drink a glass of white wine in a bar like this."

"Really?" He looks panicked for a moment. "Are there some kinds of drinking gender roles I'm not aware of?"

"Only if you don't want your man card revoked," Mr. Obnoxious cuts in.

"I can assure you, he has *nothing* to worry about when it comes to proving his manhood," I reply, snaking my arm into the crook of Nathan's elbow.

Kimmie's about to piss herself with excitement. She just lets out this little snort-giggle and pops the cork on a bottle of chardonnay that I know for a fact isn't their house white.

"The good stuff for you two."

She slides two healthy pours toward us, winking in a way only she can pull off. I tug my arm out of Nathan's so I can lift the glass to my lips.

"So, Nathan," Kimmie continues. "Quinn says you two had a good afternoon."

"It was productive."

I bristle. Was that all it was?

"I got the deck repaired," he elaborates. "Unfortunately, the truck is another story."

"Cosmic intervention!" Kimmie shouts, hands raised like she might as well be shouting hallelujah. "See? I *told* you I was manifesting. So, what does this mean, Nathan? That you and Quinn have to spend the night together? What a predicament."

I wish for a moment that we were at a proper table and not the bar, because I would be kicking the hell out of Kimmie's shins right now.

"I called a tow truck and they're going to haul it to an auto shop. The guy I spoke with on the phone said it shouldn't take more than a day. But until he looks at it, he can't give me a definitive timeline."

"Are you okay with that?" I turn to look at him. "I know you want to get back to work on the house."

"I've got time. It can wait."

I should be excited about the continued close quarters, but there's still something off between us. And even as we quietly sip our drinks and converse, it's all surface.

We've both polished off two glasses when we decide to call it a night. It's after eleven and the bar has shifted from locals grabbing a nightcap to college girls and bachelorettes looking to hook up with surfers. Little do they know, the locals have all gone to bed hours ago, their desire to chase an early wave a bigger priority than chasing tail.

Our Uber shows up within ten minutes, and I'm not at all surprised when it's Danny, Kimmie's brother and my landlord. The guy wears many, many hats in this quaint coastal town.

"If it isn't my favorite tenant," he says when we slide into the backseat.

"This guy's your landlord?" Nathan clicks his seatbelt and gives it a tug across his chest.

"Yep, the best one around," I answer.

Nathan's skeptical, and rightfully so. "That deck is a huge safety hazard, man. I repaired the damaged section today, but the whole thing needs to be replaced sooner than later."

"Yeah? And what are you? A building inspector?"

"I'm someone who obviously cares about Quinn a hell of a lot more than you do, and I don't want to see her get hurt."

My breath catches.

Danny leans forward over his steering wheel and squints through the bug-splattered windshield as he flicks on the turn signal to drive us toward the condo. "I get it. It could use some work. But I'm going to have to up the rent in order to pay for the renovation, and I doubt that's something Quinn would want."

"We can talk about this another time," I cut in.

There's tension in the car, a rubber band pulled taut, about to snap. I don't need Nathan and Danny getting into it right now.

"I'm sure you're aware there are renter's rights, and that involves the right to live in a safe environment. Just want to make sure you're keeping up your end of the deal in that area."

"Alright," I whisper to Nathan, hoping to put an end to it. I place a hand on his knee. He picks up what I put out there and the rest of the ride is quiet. Uncomfortably so.

My keys make the loudest jingling noise when I jostle them in the lock on the front door, but it's probably just the dramatic contrast to the stark silence stretching between us.

I flick on the kitchen light and place my purse on the counter, then grip the ledge, sighing out the big breath I've been holding.

"I'm sorry," Nathan says before I'm even done exhaling.

"What was that about?"

He looks up at the ceiling blankly. "I don't know."

"I mean, I appreciate what you did back at the bar with that guy. He was a threat. But Danny's a friend. *And* my landlord, may I remind you. One that has the right to evict me."

"You actually have more rights than he does."

155

"That's beside the point."

"I don't know why I got so possessive, Quinn. I'm sorry. I didn't mean to make things weird."

"Well, I guess they couldn't really be any weirder than they already were."

His face falls forward, eyes colliding with mine. "What's that supposed to mean?"

"It means we got each other off this afternoon and then something obviously changed."

"You're right. It did."

I didn't expect that answer. I hate that my throat scratches. I don't want the threat of tears muddling my emotions right now. "Why?"

"Because it meant something to me, Quinn. And I know it shouldn't have because it was just a trial run for your book."

"Are you serious?" I'm insulted, and a little inebriated, so my volume rises defensively. "I didn't realize that's what you thought of me. That I would just use you in that way."

"It's essentially what we're doing, right? Using one another?" He's not angry. He's just matter of fact and somehow, that feels worse. "You're going to help me; I'm helping you."

I absolutely cannot with this whole thing right now. "I'm tired. I'll get you a pillow and a blanket for the couch."

"Quinn." He steps closer, but I'm already beelining toward the linen closet.

"I'll put a call in to Ralphie at the auto shop tomorrow and ask him to speed things up with your car. I bet he can have the work completed by the afternoon," I say. "He owes me a favor, anyway."

"How small is this town?"

"He's Danny's and Kimmie's dad. And he's a good guy. Just like his son."

"Quinn, I said I was sorry—"

"It's fine, Nathan. It's been a big day. We can talk in the morning."

What I want to say is that I can't talk right now. That if I continue, more than just words will come out and I don't want to cry in front of him over this.

Because it's too soon to have the feelings I have for Nathan. And it's crazy that I'm so defensive over my actions because when it all boils down, we did sort of agree to use one another.

I just hate that it feels like this.

Like I'm losing something I never even fully had.

19 /
nathan

SOMETHING IS MASSAGING MY BUTT.

No. Not something. Some*one*.

"Get the hell off me, Geri," I hiss into my pillow. Reaching my hand back, I swat around but miss the mark. He keeps fondling my ass, alternating paws as a purr vibrates from his fuzzy chest like he has no shame. "You have absolutely no boundaries, cat. You know that?"

I've always been a stomach sleeper, but I contemplate flipping around just to get the guy's little mitts off of me. But then I run the risk of him pawing at my junk instead and let's face it, I've already had that happen once. I sit fully upright with a deep groan of frustration.

"Nathan?"

My bleary eyes squint at the digital clock on the microwave across the condo.

Two AM.

Quinn's voice cracks again. "Nathan? Are you up?"

I scrub my hand down my face. Shit. I didn't mean to wake her. I knew it had taken her a while to fall asleep. It was after midnight when the lamp on her nightstand clicked off and the warm funnel of light from her bedroom disappeared. I'd stared up at the ceiling with my eyes adjusting to the dark long enough to hear her soft breathing shift into a deeper, not-quite snore.

"I'm up," I finally answer.

"What's going on?"

"Nothing. Just trying to get Geronimo to respect my space."

Something that sounds just shy of a laugh echoes from her room. "I wish I had another place where we could put them."

My fists are in my eyes, but when I stop scrubbing and open them, she's standing in the doorway between her bedroom and the living space I'm currently in, her soft shadow a comforting presence.

Even without any light focused on her other than the moon filtering in from her large windows, she's breathtaking.

Hair piled in a messy knot on her head. She's in an over-sized navy t-shirt that hits her upper thigh, making me think it belonged to someone else because it's obviously too big for her. And she's got these adorable tube socks on with a thick stripe right at the top. I could never sleep in socks. I run way too hot for that, which is why I'm currently just in my boxer briefs. When that realization hits me, I grab my sweatpants from the armrest of the couch and shimmy into them while trying to remain seated.

"Do you want to sleep in here?" Her head nudges over her shoulder toward the room at her back.

"And make you take the couch? No, I'm fine."

"No, I mean sleep in here with me."

I clear my throat. "Quinn—"

"I don't have any other space to lock up the cats and their litter box is out here, so they kind of need to stay in this room. But we can close the door to my bedroom and keep them out so we can try to get a good night's sleep."

Sleep. Of course. Yes. That's what we would do in her bed. Sleep.

"I don't know."

"I'll keep my hands to myself." She lifts two palms up like she's surrendering. "Promise."

She's not the one I'm worried about.

"I don't want to make things weirder between us. You said they were weird earlier."

Quinn just shakes her head and paces the room to grab my pillow from the couch. Her hand takes mine.

"Come on. You're not getting groped by any more cats on my watch."

I follow her to the bedroom and damn, the entire space smells like her. It's lavender and mint and something kind of sweet like honey.

"I usually sleep on the left side of the bed, but if you have a side you prefer, let me know. I'm flexible."

"No, either is fine."

"Okay." She nods and places my pillow near the headboard but fluffs it up a few times before giving it a pat right in the middle. "Here you go."

I haven't shared a bed with a woman in a long time. Truth be told, the couch is not a foreign sleeping arrangement for me. Sarah said I moved around too much in my sleep and that it interfered with her REM cycle. She even wore a little monitor once to prove it. It was easier to tuck my pillow under my arm night after night and post up on the fold-out sofa than it was to put up any sort of fight. Pick your battles.

Quinn takes the corner of the comforter, peels it back, and slips in. I do the same.

"I've been told I toss and turn a lot," I suddenly feel the need to confess.

"I've been told I talk a lot," she says. "But I don't make biscuits, so at least I've got that going for me."

"I don't know what that means."

"Making biscuits?" She rolls over and props onto her elbow to face me.

"Yeah, why would you be baking in your sleep?"

"It's what Geronimo was doing."

"Your mom's cat knows how to cook? Who the hell is this guy?"

"Nathan, it's what they call that repetitive kneading thing that cats do with their paws. Making biscuits."

"Why would they give such a cute name to something so devious? He was feeling me up."

"They like squishy things."

"My ass is not squishy," I clarify. "It's rock solid."

"Oh, I know." She rolls back, snickering. "I think it's a sign he's comfortable around you. That he likes you."

I don't want to talk about cats. I don't think she does, either, but I'm not sure what else to say.

"Are you cold at all?" Her muted voice breaches the momentary stillness. "I have another blanket I can get."

"I'm good."

We're both on our backs now, eyes fixed on the shiplap pattern above us, hearts fixed on something else altogether.

"Nathan—," she says at the same time I utter, "Quinn—."

I take a breath. "You go first."

She doesn't speak for a few beats, but then she slides up the mattress, her back pressed against the upholstered headboard. I flip onto my side so I can see her.

"I don't think I'm ready to feel the way I feel about you," she says. I can see her hands wringing together.

I move up the bed, too. "How do you feel?"

"Like I'm falling for you." Her hands still. Her eyes drop to them. "I don't think when we came up with this whole helping each other thing that I accounted for that possibility."

"So, what do we do?"

"I don't know." She picks at a fraying string on the edge of the comforter, looping the loose thread around her finger. "I like having you read my book. Honestly, your input has been surprisingly valuable. And I'd love to help you design and decorate your place. I just think maybe we should take a step back from the physical stuff. Somewhere between my brain and my heart, the signals got mixed, and this is the only way I know how to uncross them."

Not what I want to hear, but what I expected.

"I think that's a good idea," I lie through my teeth. But it's one hundred percent truth when I say, "I'm having a hard time separating fact from fiction, too."

"Yeah?"

"Yeah."

"Okay. So, we just cut out that side of things."

"Cut it right out."

"And we're just friends, helping one another with work projects."

If you say so. "Yep. Just friends."

"I'm glad we see eye to eye on this."

She exhales long and slow as she slides back down. I tuck the covers up to her shoulders, not prepared for her to turn toward me, her eyes dark with something that makes my blood pump faster through my veins.

"Maybe..."

My throat catches on a shred of hope. "Yeah?"

"Maybe we need some finality."

"Finality?"

"Yeah. Closure." Her tongue wets her bottom lip. "Like one final kiss to put an end to things. A sort of period at the end of our sentence."

I'll take whatever I can get. "I'm on board with that."

"So just this one last time, and then we cut out everything physical. Agreed?"

I move closer. "Agreed."

"Okay."

My fingers graze her cheek, slipping a wayward curl behind her ear. If this is going to be the last time I get to touch her, I'm going to take my fucking time. Tracing my way down her jaw with my fingertips, I cradle her cheek in my palm and just hold her there, staring, because I don't want to rush this. I can't rush this.

Quinn scoots closer. I move to meet her halfway.

Her shallow breaths hit my lips and then the feel of her full mouth gently pressing to mine makes a desperate sound rumble within my chest.

Why does this woman make me feel like this? Like I'm not in control of my heart and who it's beating for?

She sighs as our lips move and she brings her body right up against me. Every curve, every inch of her is perfection. The way she kisses me is perfection. The only imperfect thing about this moment is that it's going to be our last.

I will time to stand still. I mean, that whole cosmic intervention stuff worked for Kimmie. Might as well try.

Time doesn't stop, but my heart does when she slips her arm around my waist, her nails scratching low on my back.

"Nathan." It sounds too close to a prayer on her lips.

I hold her in my arms and kiss her with all I have. Slowly, purposefully. I cherish her mouth as I coax my tongue past her lips and take the moment deeper between us. It's like we've been doing this forever. We read one another. We build a rhythm with our mouths, our bodies. It's pure bliss and absolute torture at the same time.

That torture takes on a new level when she pulls out of my embrace.

I'm not ready for this to be over so soon.

But this is what she wants, and I want Quinn to be happy. If cutting out the confusion does that, then so be it.

I'm collecting my breath and my thoughts when, suddenly, the sheets are shoved back and she's straddling me.

"Quinn?"

Her hands meet my chest, keeping me pinned to the mattress but not in a forceful way. I can hear her breath quiver shallowly in the stillness that surrounds us. See her chest rise and fall.

Leaning down, she takes my mouth again.

This kiss is something else. Something different. It's building, unlike the last kiss that trailed off toward a place I didn't want it to go.

Quinn pulls away and sits back on her heels. My wild eyes rove frantically over her, unfocused and unsure. My hands want to touch her, but I don't know if that's what she wants. I hold back.

What is she up to?

Her fingers grasp the hem of her shirt and lift upward in one quick move. I don't even have time to blink before her shirt is off and she's bare before me. Is this her idea of finality? Because I didn't envision this being a part of it, not that I mind at all.

Her hands move to her hair and untwist something that causes her caramel-colored curls to tumble down and spill across her shoulders. She shakes them out, making her tits bounce and making me rock hard all at the same time.

God, she's an angel. Maybe that's it—maybe I've died, and she really is one because I definitely don't feel tethered to Earth at all anymore.

Her hand reaches down and picks up mine, guiding it onto her breast.

The heaviest sigh I've ever exhaled parts my lips. I cup my hand to show her how perfectly she fits. "Do you have any idea what you're doing to me?"

She shimmies her hips slightly, but I know there's not a shred of naivety in the act. "A little."

"Tell me what's okay."

She takes my other hand and places it on her. "This is okay."

Instinctively, my thumbs brush back and forth.

This is not helping with the confusion, but there are parts of my body that aren't confused at all, so I zero in on those.

My head and heart? That's another story.

I choose to focus on the things speaking loudest in the moment, like my nerve endings that send a shockwave through me when she tosses her head back while she arches into my touch and lets out a needy moan. The vulnerable sounds she makes and the way her skin feels are doing things to my body that I'm absolutely positive she can read.

Even though she's on top of me, she feels too far away. I need to be closer.

I drop my hands to the curve of her hips and lift her off just enough so I can move to sit upright, too. She pushes up on her knees and then lowers back down onto my lap, bringing her breasts so close to my mouth that I can't resist the urge to flick my tongue out over a dusky pink nipple.

"Nathan." In an act of possession and permission, she threads her fingers behind my neck and pulls me in.

I look into her hooded eyes. "Is this okay?"

Her bottom lip is pinned between her teeth, so she doesn't say anything, just nods.

I spend the next moments lavishing all my attention on her, going back and forth between breasts, licking and sucking and swirling my tongue around each peak.

"Your tits are my newest favorite thing," I murmur against her skin as I leave kisses along the top of her cleavage, working my way up her neck because I need my mouth on hers again.

"Yeah?" She draws out of our kiss. "I've always thought they were kind of small."

"Not at all. They're a perfect handful." Both palms cover her chest and give a little squeeze, alternating between each breast. "Okay, maybe two handfuls."

I don't expect it when she starts giggling. Like full-on laughing.

"What?" Sudden insecurity draws me up short.

"Nathan, are you making biscuits?"

I'll be damned if she's going to compare copping a feel to being kneaded on by a cat.

In one swift move, I flip her onto her back. Air whooshes out of her lungs when she lands on the mattress. She's still laughing and it's flirty and playful and brings out a side of me I didn't know existed. At least not in the bedroom. I nip at her nose; she clicks her teeth like she's going to bite.

"I"—I kiss her jaw—"am"—I maneuver lower, trailing my tongue along her neck, licking my way down her breasts—"not"—my lips nudge across her nipple before taking it into my mouth to suck hard —"a fucking cat."

She holds me in place because it's clear she likes what I'm doing. She's right; she does enjoy having her tits appreciated.

"Oh, I don't know about that." Laughter vibrates through her chest. "You are kind of growly."

Playing along, I release a low grumble and give her my best roar, launching her into a fit of hysterics.

This woman has me doing things I've never done— feeling things I've never felt—and it scares the shit out of me.

We make out for a little while longer, but it's less sensual and borders on silly, which I'm actually okay with. Since this is it for us, I need things to end on a lighter note.

We're both winded from laughter when I roll toward my side of the bed. It's quiet for a few lingering minutes.

"Nathan Caldwell, you are a man of mystery, you know that?"

"Why's that?"

Quinn pops up. "It's a mystery to me that anyone lucky enough to be with you would ever let you go."

Nope. I *do not* want thoughts of my ex sharing the

bedroom with us. It's a place I can't have my head going right now. "I mean, you're kind of letting me go."

"I never had you."

"But you could." I don't sugarcoat it. "We could make this work, Quinn. There's obviously more between us than just offering up favors."

"I know," she says in a whisper. My heart thunders in my ears with each second where words go unsaid. "I can't rebound with you, Nathan. And I don't want to be your rebound, either. We both need time to heal on our own."

I've been trying to heal on my own for the last few months and it's been hell. The only time I've ever felt even remotely close to being healed is when I'm with Quinn. Can I tell her that? Will that scare her off completely?

"How about this?" Her hand moves right over my heart, and it isn't lost on me that she's already been holding it this entire time. "You finish the remodel. I'll finish my book. When all of that is done and enough time has gone by, then we can revisit things."

I'm a patient man, but what Quinn's asking feels like an impossible task.

Still, woven into that impossibility is a thread of hope, and I'm going to cling to it like it's a life preserver.

After all, it's all I really have right now.

20 /
quinn

I ROLL out my shoulders as I stir the cool water and the orange juice concentrate in the pitcher. The tart liquid swirls around the wooden spoon like a small whirlpool. It's not fresh-squeezed, but it's all I had in my freezer since I haven't made a grocery store run for the condo in weeks.

Thankfully, Nathan doesn't seem picky when it comes to food. I figure the toaster waffles I've already plated and the sausage links currently sizzling in the pan will do the job.

It's after nine but I don't have the heart to wake him.

He was wrong. He doesn't toss and turn in his sleep. The man is a freaking hibernating bear. Nothing would rouse him from his slumber. It wouldn't have been an issue, but we'd ended the night curled in one another's arms. His super heavy, super immovable arms.

I shake out my hands to bring some feeling back to them. When I woke up a half hour earlier, all of my limbs tingled from lack of circulation. Nathan's a big guy and while snuggling with him was all kinds of amazing, next time I'll need to be the one on top.

A shiver prickles the back of my neck.

There won't be a next time. At least not for a really long time.

Right. I know deep down this is for the best, but cutting things short—suspending them, whatever it is we're doing—will not be easy.

It's just that I know what's going to happen if we don't take an intentional step back. We'll both fall fast and hard, and then one day, one of us (my money's on him) will wake up and realize we jumped from one relationship straight into another.

I get that he's over his wife. She's done a pretty decent job ensuring that outcome. But he had a whole life with her and it's not like a few months' separation is enough to remove those memories, those feelings, and the hope I'm sure he had for their shared future.

I do not want all of that to just transfer over to me.

I think things will be easier on my end. I was never in love with Kyle. Sure, my pride was bruised because being cheated on never feels good, but when I envisioned my future, Kyle was never a part of it.

Certainly not in the way I've already fit Nathan into it.

Lifting the spoon out of the glass pitcher, I drop it into the sink with a clatter. I can see the waves crashing along the beach out the window hanging above the metal basin. Seagulls weave in and out of patches of fog, only to nosedive and break the surface of the tumultuous whitecaps, hoping to find a meal swimming below.

Mornings here do something to my soul.

That vast, almost endless expanse of blue water makes

me feel so small. Makes me realize I'm just a tiny piece of a bigger picture in the grand scheme of things.

It's almost unfathomable that we can be so minute—so insignificant—and yet feel things so deeply. Like we have an entire universe of potential emotion within us. We have these big, colossal moments that we feel like the crashing of stars or meteors exploding. But then, other times, our emotions are delicate and fragile, like the slow unfurling of a fresh petal.

That's what I have to focus on now. My heart has to be like that flower, waiting for the right time to fully bloom. I want things with Nathan to grow into something beautiful, not be plucked right out of the ground before we even have the chance to develop. Patience, grasshopper.

"Hey."

I turn to see Nathan leaning against the doorjamb, hair all mussed and more stubble than he had yesterday covering his jaw. He's gorgeous in an absolutely arresting way that makes me almost lightheaded, which isn't great since I'm currently working over an active burner.

I move the sausage around with a fork. Grease pops and splatters from the pan, spraying across the stainless-steel range.

"You didn't have to let me sleep so long." His sweatpants are slung low on his hips and he's barefoot as he pads toward me.

"You looked really peaceful."

"Yeah? I wasn't a wild kickboxer?" He untucks a chair from the kitchen table and sits in front of a plate I've already made up for him. "I felt like I should have wrapped you in bubble wrap just to keep you safe."

Meg Bradley

Giving the sausage one last turn, I grasp the handle to the pan and cross the space between us to roll a few links onto Nathan's plate.

"Thank you." He looks up at me with those mesmerizing green eyes and then takes the syrup bottle and squeezes it onto the waffles in a really meticulous zigzag pattern. "This is great, Quinn."

My smile is too big. I enjoy doing this for him too much. Taking care of him. For heaven's sake, even feeding him. Sure, all the physical stuff is emotional, but this is, too. Am I going to have to cut *everything* out?

I lower into the chair across from him. "I think your ex has painted you to be someone you're not, because I kid you not, Nathan, you did not move once. Didn't even budge."

He takes a big gulp of orange juice and dives right into the meal. "That's entirely possible. I do think one reason she wanted me out of our bed was because she often had another guy in it. I mean, obviously not while I was there. But subconsciously, I think she realized it shouldn't be shared. For as awful as Sarah was, she still had a conscience, I guess."

The mouthful of juice I swallow burns going down, but it's his words that taste like acid, not the drink. "I don't understand how someone could do that to you."

"Sarah's not totally to blame. I didn't give her the attention she wanted these last few years. I let things get too comfortable. Took things—took her—for granted." He chases a sausage link with the tines of his fork as it rolls across his plate. "She went looking elsewhere when I obviously wasn't meeting her needs."

"That's not how marriage works. You don't look elsewhere. You hunker down and figure out how to make things

172

work with the one you've committed to," I say with more aggression in my voice than I intend. I'm probably overstepping, but I don't care. "I realize I'm young and I've never been married, but those are just my two cents."

"Being young doesn't make you any less wise, and it doesn't make your convictions any less true." His broad shoulders rise as he sucks in a full breath. His eyes are fastened on mine when his brow draws tightly over them. "I don't want you to discount your beliefs just because you're younger. If I've learned anything, age isn't really a factor when it comes to maturity."

"Is it a factor when it comes to relationships?" This is the most personal conversation we've had, and even though I know I shouldn't press it, my curiosity has suddenly found a little courage.

Nathan holds his fork out in front of his mouth and pauses. "Until recently I was married, so I honestly never thought I'd be in the position to be in another relationship again. I haven't given a lot of thought to that piece of it." He pops the waffle into his mouth, chews, then swallows. "But I have given you a lot of thought."

"And what have those thoughts been?"

"Lots of things that aren't really breakfast discussion appropriate." There's that enticing quality in his voice and expression again. The man's words are like butter. "But I will say that your age hasn't stopped me from picturing a future with you. Eleven years is a pretty big gap, but it's not a lifetime."

There's something that's been brewing in my mind for some time now, but I've never offered it a voice. I'm not sure if now is the right time, but I decide to chance it. What do I really have to lose? "Did you want the baby to be yours?"

He places his fork on the table beside his plate. Straightens it. His eyes are on it for a while before he looks up.

"I actually thought it was mine for a minute there. I found the positive pregnancy test in the bathroom trash when I was taking it out. I mean, realistically, I knew it couldn't be mine. We hadn't been intimate in months, and to be totally candid, she always made me wear a condom because she said she hated the mess. But she was my wife. I was her husband. My first thought wasn't that it would be some other guy's, you know?"

I nod slowly.

"Did I want a child?" he goes on. "Yeah, I did. I wanted to be a dad. We had the house. The extra room for the nursery. I've said before that I've always viewed life in patterns and equations. Fall in love. Get married. Start a family. It was the next box to check." Nathan folds his arms over his chest and rocks onto the back legs of the chair. "I'm back to square one now. I need to heal. Then, hopefully, think about falling in love again. Marriage?" He shrugs. "I don't know. Maybe someday. And sure, I'd love kids. But if you're asking if that's something I want right now, the answer is no."

I don't know if he can see my palpable relief. I'm not ready for motherhood, not that it's something Nathan and I would ever explore any time soon. That's obviously crazy. But I do know that he's in a different stage of life, and if that was important to him, I would want him to be with someone who could give it to him sooner than later.

Even if our hearts feel the same thing but our timelines

don't sync up, it will never work between us. I would rather know that now.

"What about you?" His chin nudges forward.

"Do I want kids?"

He nods.

"I think so. Someday. But that someday is a long, long way off."

His head keeps bobbing, almost in an approving, processing way. "What else do you want out of life? If you could plan it, what would it look like?"

This requires some thought. I squint out a window toward the waves and watch as they encroach and retreat along the shore a few times, then bring my gaze back to him. He doesn't appear to mind waiting for my answer.

"I used to think I wanted to be a big, bestselling author. I saw it happen for my dad over and over and remember the joy it brought him. But I'm thinking that joy came from creating something he loved. And I'm not sure I love what I'm creating right now."

"Do you feel forced because you're on a deadline?"

"Not really. I haven't sold this book to a publisher yet. I was only in a contract for the first two, so my agent plans to shop it around. But there are these pesky things called rent and living expenses. I need to get paid, but sometimes it's really hard to put a price tag on art. And this current book doesn't feel like art to me."

"So, you're not sure if the whole author thing is long term?"

"I don't know." My eyebrows lift and so do my shoulders. "Starting over with something new seems like a challenge I'm not sure I'm up for right now."

"I get that, believe me."

"I know you do."

He gives me an intense look and there's probably more he wants to say, but he's restraining himself. "Thank you for the breakfast, Quinn. You really don't need to keep feeding me."

"Well, I'm not going to let you starve and there aren't many places to get a bite to eat around here. Man cannot live on fish and chips alone."

Nathan chuckles and it's low and deep and unintentionally sexy.

"Can I get you anything else?" I ask.

"No. This was perfect."

"Oh." I sit up straighter. "I forgot to tell you. I called Ralphie and he'll have the truck finished up by noon. Said it was the alternative or something."

"Alternator?"

"Yeah, that might have been it. Straightforward fix, apparently. We can head back to Brookhill by early afternoon if that works for you."

I don't want to go back yet. This is home for me. My place of refuge by the sea.

But I've got a house to sit, and he's got one to rebuild.

"I'll get showered and can be ready whenever you want to head out," Nathan says.

Apparently, the thought of Nathan showering does things to me because I feel a hot flush spread across my chest and a tingling in the depths of my stomach like a spasm. "Shower? Um, yeah. You should do that."

He lifts his arm and gives a little snort. "Do I stink?"

"No. Not at all. I actually really love the way you smell. It's earthy and a little spicy and super sexy," I blurt without censoring but then instantly realize friends don't talk about the intoxicating way the other smells, so I backpedal so hard I trip over my words. "Not that I really noticed, though. I mean...I, uh...I just caught a whiff once."

"I like the way you smell, too, Quinn."

Do I smell like anything other than drug store shampoo? I want to ask, but we're scaling back. Or trying to, at least. I jump to my feet to collect our dishes. Nathan's hand juts out and stills me, confiscating my plate to stack it on top of his.

"You made breakfast." He stands and nudges me out of the way. "I'll do the dishes."

"I don't mind cleaning up."

"Go take the first shower. I don't want to use up all the hot water anyway, and I don't mind taking a cold one."

Even if I were to challenge him, I wouldn't win. He's already at the sink with the faucet running, working up a lather of suds on the sponge and swiping it over a plate.

"I'll be quick," I assure.

"Take your time."

I do take my time because I know my hot water tank has approximately thirteen minutes of warm water in it and I figure Nathan won't need more than five. I let the streams rain down over my hair and face. I roll my neck side to side slowly, reveling in the way the hot beads pelt against my tense shoulders like a massage. With my purple loofah, I trace my body from head to toe and then grab the detachable showerhead to wave over me, rinsing the soapy bubbles from my skin.

I wish I had a bit more time because I'm instantly wound up and could use a good release.

But Nathan's in the kitchen and getting off in the shower

while he's busy cleaning up the mess I made from breakfast feels slightly insensitive.

Seriously though, I had no idea a household chore like washing dishes could be considered foreplay. I'm all hot and bothered just thinking about him with that damn sponge and that stupid plate. I run the sprayer between my legs and even though it's just to quickly clean myself, my hand moves of its own volition and locks in to keep it there.

The pulsating flow is toe curling. My teeth pin my bottom lip to trap in a breathy hiss and I press a hand to the cool tile for stability, spreading my legs wider.

It's not like I've just discovered this orgasmic tool. This showerhead has some mileage. But it's the first time I'm thinking of someone in particular as the warm, tantalizing spray rushes over me. It's the first time I'm picturing someone on their knees, their tongue lapping at me the same way the water caresses every inch of my core as I run the sprayer up and down, back and forth.

I shut my eyes and see Nathan before me, his dark hair drenched, his face buried between my legs, his strong hands curled around my thighs to hold me in place.

I'm going to use up all the hot water, but I don't even care.

I spread my legs wider.

And wider.

And wider some more, but not on purpose this time. The bottoms of my feet can't find purchase and begin to slip and slide over the wet tile. There's nothing to grab onto, and even though I claw at the wall with my nails, I feel myself quickly losing any sense of balance. The only thing to grip is the showerhead, so I wrap both hands around the long hose, pulling my way up it like a rope climber in gym class.

Momentarily, I find my equilibrium. My feet are planted.

Phew. That was close.

But just as I'm about to celebrate this small victory, things go from bad to worse.

Much, *much* worse.

21 /
nathan

I NOW UNDERSTAND the term blood-curdling, because when I hear Quinn screaming from the back of the condo, that's exactly what mine does.

Everything slows down. Coagulates. Even as I rush toward the wailing, my movements feel like they are in slow motion, like I'm wading through molasses, my feet and body lagging behind my brain.

Because my mind has already gotten there, has already made up a horrific scene in my head based on the sheer terror in her cry.

"Quinn!"

I kick open the bathroom door, expecting—but still not prepared for—the absolute worst.

"Shit, shit, shit!" she continues screaming, her voice raw and gurgled.

She's on the shower floor, but I can barely see her. Water is everywhere. It pours like a fire hydrant from above, from the place where a showerhead would be.

But there's no showerhead.

I fling open the glass door to see her struggling with what looks like one of those detachable sprayers, but it's coiled around her like a snake trying to constrict her naked body. Reaching back, I snag a towel from the hook and throw it over her, even though I know the fabric will be drenched in a matter of seconds.

"Quinn? What the hell happened?"

"I..." Water rains down her face and into her mouth as she tries to speak. She chokes and sputters. "I lost my balance and when I grabbed on, it pulled completely out of the wall."

The shower is filling faster than the drain can keep up.

She's still fighting against the water pummeling down on her, waving it off like it's a physical force. With both hands, I reach down and lift her into my arms. She's sopping wet, teeth chattering with shivers that make her entire body shudder against mine.

"Where's the shut-off valve?"

"Under the deck on the east side of the condo."

Settling her onto the foot of her bed, I crouch to eye level. Hair clumps around her face. I sweep several strands back with my fingertips gently before saying, "I'm going to go turn the water off. Wait right here."

It doesn't take long to find the valve. That thundering hum of water rushing through the pipes cuts off abruptly with a shrill, screeching sound, but my heart is still in overdrive when I come back into the house and hurry toward Quinn's room to check on her.

She has exchanged the soaked towel for a fresh one and is wringing her hair into a smaller hand towel.

"I think it's fair to say I've officially used up all the hot water." She blinks through her sodden lashes. "Sorry."

I can't help but chuckle.

I cross the distance between us.

"Are you okay?"

"Other than looking like a drowned rat?" She snickers. "Yeah, I'm fine."

"You're freezing." Damn, even her lips have a bluish tint.

I don't know my way around her room, but I figure it's a safe bet to assume she keeps her clothes in the tall dresser against the far wall. "Which drawer?"

"Top one on the right."

I'm not sure what I'm expecting to find, but apparently it isn't a drawer full of lacy things, because as soon as I slide it open and see her neatly folded collection of bras and panties, a cough catches in my throat.

"Oh." I drag in a breath. "Um, do you have a preference?"

There are thongs and boy shorts and these pink delicate panties I swear I've had actual dreams about her wearing.

"Do *you* have a preference?" Quinn bats her eyes at me.

I shouldn't. Still, I play it safe and pull out a pair of light blue cotton panties with a matching bra. I push them toward her. "Here you go."

The swell of her breasts peeks over the towel as she loosens it.

I flip around.

"You did just see me naked, Nathan."

My gaze travels to the ceiling and stays there. I grip my hands. "I wasn't really looking." A tiny white lie. "I was just worried about you."

"You can look now if you want to."

Who is this woman and why does she always say everything I want to hear? Still, I know I shouldn't look. We agreed to throttle back. But right now, the only thought I have of throttling anything involves a body part of mine that I'm trying desperately to ignore.

"I'll be in the kitchen if you need me." I move out the door without glancing back.

The dishes from breakfast are done and resting in the drying rack, but I run a towel over them vigorously, really swiping every last drop of water from their surface.

"I'm fully clothed." Quinn's voice carries over my shoulder. "You can safely turn around now."

I don't know how it's possible, but the sight of Quinn in sweatpants and a loose t-shirt is still enough to make me hard. Or harder, I should say. She's perfection in every form she takes.

"I'm sorry I just barged in on you in the shower like that." I flip the dishrag over my shoulder, lean back against the counter.

"You do have a habit of barging in on me," she mocks. "But in this instance, I'm glad you did. I was losing that battle with the showerhead."

"We can make another run to the hardware store and I'll pick up the plumbing I'll need to repair that."

Her arms slink over her upper half, head inclined. "How are you so handy, Nathan? I thought you got your degree in mathematics."

"My dad and grandpa were both contractors. When I was a kid, I helped them out a lot at their jobsites. I actually think they both thought—or at least hoped—that I would take over the business when Dad retired. But I discovered I had a gift for teaching when I started tutoring as a teenager." I shrug. "I don't know. I always felt like having a knack for something sort of made you obligated to use it. My mom used to say that. That if you had something someone else needed— whether that be something physical, a talent, or something you could just help them with—then it was your responsibility to make it happen."

"Your mom sounds like a wise lady."

"She is. She's been through hell and back and came out stronger for it."

"I'd love to meet her someday."

That confession hits me squarely in the chest where my heart is. And maybe that's because my mom has always owned such a big piece of my heart, and now Quinn's working her way into it, too. Of course, I'd love for them to meet, but I know how easily my mom would get attached to Quinn, and I feel the need to shelter her from that for now.

It's just too soon to tell what's going to happen between us.

———

Kimmie gives us a ride to the hardware store since her dad is still finishing up with my truck. That woman is something else with a mouth that runs nonstop. She has a story for everything, which I enjoy because many involve Quinn and give me a glimpse into her past.

Like the time they purchased kites at a local shop and took them down to the water, only to have the wind whisk them across the beach where they raced and tripped and faceplanted in the sand to keep hold of the rogue kites, ending up in some Youtuber's viral video. Evidently, there's even a remix song to go along with it. (I make a mental note to check that out later).

Or the time they first met when Quinn came into the bar with her mother who proceeded to get drunk on mimosas and tell Kimmie all the ways she was mixing her drinks wrong. Apparently, the two have had a strained relationship from the beginning.

But it's the story about Quinn's dad that has my lungs feeling tight, like I can't take a full breath.

I hadn't realized he'd only been gone a couple of years. He'd battled cancer for over a decade. They had thought he was in the clear, but it came back with a vengeance at Stage IV, with no real treatment options other than palliative care. Quinn's mom had been the primary caregiver, but Quinn came home every weekend from college to sit with her dad while he wrote. Sometimes—especially in the end, when he was too weak to type on his own—he'd dictate, and she would transcribe his words.

His last published piece had been typed entirely by Quinn, and he'd also dedicated it to her.

"I'm blaming it on the massive amounts of morphine in his system, but I still think that dedication was a touch manipulative," Kimmie says when we're back in the car on the way to the condo with the things needed for the bathroom repair. *To my dearest Quinn. Now that you've "written" a novel, it's your chance to do it all on your own. Make me proud.* " Kimmie snorts as she takes her hands from the steering wheel to make air quotes. "Seriously? Make me proud? Last time I checked, the dead don't have emotions."

"Kimmie." Quinn cuts her friend a look across the car.

"I know, I know. It's not socially acceptable to criticize

dead people since they can't defend themselves and all. But the other side of that coin is that it's not appropriate for dead people to dole out guilt trips beyond the grave, either."

"We've been over all of this before."

"Right, and I keep waiting for you to realize you need to be doing what makes *you* proud, not what you think your dad would want you to do with your life."

"I *am* doing what makes me proud."

I'm in the backseat of Kimmie's car so all I can see is the back of Quinn's head, but the rigid way she sits and the inflection in her voice clue me in that she's not being entirely truthful. Plus, she said before that her current novel doesn't feel right in the way she wants it to.

Shrugging, Kimmie pulls into the long gravel driveway leading up to Quinn's condo.

Something buzzes from the front seat. Quinn tugs out her phone from her purse.

"Oh, good. Looks like the truck is ready to be picked up. Should we go get it now? I just need to run in and feed the cats really quick first."

Kimmie throws her vehicle in *park*, leaving it idling. "We don't all need to go. Why don't I take Nathan and you can take care of those feisty felines?"

"You sure you don't need me to go with you?"

"Not necessary," Kimmie says before I can reiterate the same.

"Alright," Quinn agrees, but I can tell it's tentative.

Still, she steps out of the car, and Kimmie instructs me to move up front. "Unlike my brother, I'm not an Uber," she says, patting the passenger seat.

I give Quinn a quick squeeze on her arm before she heads

up to the condo, her head glancing over her shoulder several times until she finally steps inside. I shut the passenger door.

"There's something I want to talk to you about," Kimmie says as she maneuvers the sedan back onto the highway. "And I'd rather not do it through the rear-view mirror."

I buckle myself in both physically and mentally. "Yeah? Everything okay?"

"It better be."

I'm not following, but Kimmie doesn't give me time to ask for clarification. She's always one step ahead.

"My girl Quinn has some serious people pleasing tendencies," she dives right in, her eyes on me rather than looking forward through the windshield. "You've probably already noticed that. I mean, the girl is still trying to please her dad, and he's been in the ground for years. She does what's expected of her, or at least what she thinks others expect."

I don't know where this is going and I'm uncomfortable with the lack of attention Kimmie's paying to the road. Thank God we're currently the only ones on it.

"She wants everyone around her to be happy. It's why she didn't just say 'fuck off' to her mom when she asked her to house-sit for another two months. And it's why she keeps trying to write a bestselling book, because she thinks it's the goal her dad had for her. She's going to do it with you, too."

"How so?"

"She's going to choose your happiness over her own, whatever that looks like."

"Well, right now we're taking a step back from things. We talked about it last night. She thinks since we're both rebounding, it's best if we take some time off and explore the possibility of a relationship later down the line."

Kimmie's hands slap the steering wheel. I try not to panic when the car swerves over the yellow divide. She overcorrects and the vehicle swings the other way, bumping along the sandy shoulder.

"That's it! Dammit, she's doing it already." Her head shakes so forcefully it makes her entire body jostle along with her grip, so the car continues veering down the lane. It'll be a miracle if we arrive at the auto shop in one piece. "She wants to be with you, Nathan. I know that for a fact. But she's probably calling things off because she thinks that's what you want. Is it?"

"No, of course not."

"Then fight for her. Sure, it's fine if you both agree to take a step back. I get that. You both just came out of relationships. That's probably smart. But don't let her go, Nathan. And don't let her push you away because she eventually talks herself into thinking you'd be better off without her."

I can't think of a way to respond, and even when I pick up the truck from Ralphie's and it's just me and my thoughts within the confines of my vehicle, I'm speechless.

I picked up on Quinn's people pleasing vibe. She's easygoing and cares about other's emotions. And Kimmie's right; she does put everyone else first. She's obviously doing that with her mom, and from what I've learned about her relationship with her dad, it sounds like things weren't much different.

Kimmie's right about another thing. I *am* going to fight for Quinn. Whatever that looks like, however long it takes.

22 /
quinn

WE'RE in Brookhill by dinnertime.

Nathan made impressively quick work of the plumbing repair. I had offered the option to cash in on that hot shower, but he explained that since the glue he used to fix the pipes still needed some time to dry, we shouldn't use the water for a bit. So we packed up our things and the cats to head back to the valley, condo and truck repairs completed.

"Do you want to stay over again tonight?" I ask as he guides along the curb in front of his fixer upper. The driveway is still occupied with the massive dumpster, and boards and sheetrock litter the ground next to it, leaving no room for a car. "In the guest room, of course."

"I don't know—"

"How about this? You have a standing invitation to crash at my mom's place until your house has actual walls and bedrooms. I won't think anything of it. Nothing weird. Just a friendly offer to sleep over."

"I appreciate that, and I'll take you up on it. I'll help you get the cats situated and then I'll come back later tonight."

"I'm good with the cats," I say. "You do whatever you need to do around your place and let yourself in whenever."

We say our temporary goodbyes and I hate to admit it, but things are awkward between us. We both want more. That's apparent. But it's for that very reason that I feel we need to take a step back.

Nathan is someone I don't want to lose. Of course, I realize pushing him away like this might cause exactly that. But it also might give us the time to heal from our past hurts and be in a better emotional space, so when we do try this again, we're ready to give it our all.

Not going to lie, though. It's going to be brutal.

I mix up a box of mac and cheese on the stove, storing the leftovers in some Tupperware in case Nathan's hungry later. Is it okay to do that? I rationalize the gesture by noting the rampant food waste issue in America. I'm doing my part to combat that while simultaneously saving an entire meal for my next-door neighbor as I do my best to be a responsible citizen.

Who am I kidding? I don't know how to remove my desire to take care of Nathan from the equation. From any equation. It's practically innate.

It's dark once I've finished up with dinner. I've got my laptop open in my lap on the couch, the cursor mocking me as it blinks repetitively, the words blank from my mind and the screen.

Oh, come on Quinn. You don't need an actual muse. You've got this.

My inner voice isn't convincing. All I can think as I attempt to piece a rough chapter together is that I'm jealous that my characters get to pursue their feelings for one another. How pathetic is that? They're not even real.

Have I totally screwed myself over with this rash decision regarding Nathan? It felt like the right thing to do at the time, but now I'm not so sure.

I try to get lost in the story. It doesn't work. It's just a jumble of words, no emotion, no feeling.

I shut the laptop lid.

Sometime after eight I hear a light tapping at the front door.

I'd told Nathan to let himself in, but I guess he doesn't feel comfortable doing that. I get it. He's waltzed in on some pretty precarious situations before, so I understand the hesitation.

"Come in!" I holler as I stand from the couch. I do a quick adjustment of my outfit, smoothing my hands down my t-shirt and rolling the waistband over on my sweatpants so they're not so baggy in the butt. I'm going for coziness and not style, but Nathan never seems to care. I like that—that I'm totally comfortable in my own skin when I'm with him.

His feet click along the floorboards, pacing closer.

I meet him halfway.

Only it's not Nathan.

"Kyle?" My breath hitches in a gasp. "What the hell are you doing here?"

"I'm sorry, Quinnie." His eyes are so bloodshot I can hardly make out the blue irises within them. "I fucked up."

"You shouldn't be here."

That's when I get a putrid slap in the face of strong alcohol. "You're drunk." I glance toward his hand gripping a set of keys. "Did you drive?"

"I messed things up between us." He's got a thick trail of snot dripping onto his upper lip. The back of his hand comes up to swipe it away, and he sniffs loudly, all wet and bubbly. "I shouldn't have ever let you find out about Rachel."

"Really? That's what you got out of this? That you should have done a better job keeping your sidepiece a secret?"

He's so inebriated that he trips over his feet and stumbles forward, pitching his lanky body into my arms, so I have to catch him before he hits the floor.

"Kyle, you're wasted and we're over."

"And so are Rachel and me. Or Bambi. I think that's what I stored her name as in my phone. It was Bambi, right?"

"Why are you here, Kyle?"

He's swaying back and forth, a reed in unstable winds. I know if he hits the ground, I'll have an impossible time lifting his dead weight, so I loop my arm with his and walk him to the couch. Immediately, he faceplants onto the cushions.

"I did you dirty, Quinnie," he mumbles into a throw pillow. "You were so good to me, and I treated you like shit."

"Yep. You did." I move a stack of magazines from the coffee table and sit. "But it's okay, Kyle. I'm over it."

He lifts his head slightly, eyes unfocused. A string of drool drips from his mouth. "You're *over* me already? We just ended." He whimpers.

"Our relationship might have just ended, but the feelings have been gone for a long time now."

He looks ill. A sickly green hue coats his face and when his mouth pinches and he bolts upright, I know there's no time to move out of his way.

Getting projectile vomited on by my drunken ex was not on my agenda for the evening.

I'm frozen, just staring down at my soiled shirt when he retches again.

"Dammit, Kyle!" I leap to my feet.

"Quinn?" It's not Kyle's but Nathan's booming voice filtering into the room. He turns down the hall, freezing in the doorway.

"What the hell is going on?" He's at my side within seconds.

Kyle pukes a third time, and it's all the answer Nathan needs.

"Alright, buddy." Lifting Kyle to his feet, Nathan slinks an arm around the drunkard's thin waist for stability. "Let's get you to the bathroom before that happens again." Nathan makes eye contact with me. "I've got this. You go get cleaned up."

Something pinches in my chest and twists. "Nathan, you don't have to—"

Kyle sways, making Nathan skitter to the side with him as they fumble toward the downstairs bathroom, bouncing off the walls like a game of pinball.

"Whoa, buddy. Careful." He meets my eyes again over his shoulder. "No worries. Seriously. I've got this."

Guilt churns in my stomach, and it's more nauseating than the entire ordeal I just experienced.

In good conscience, I can't let Nathan take care of my inebriated ex-boyfriend. In what scenario is that okay?

Still, I head upstairs as instructed and peel my shirt over my head, immediately throwing it into the washing machine and setting the cycle to rinse. The sweatpants follow. Honestly, I'm better off showering, so I take a quick one, hurrying to get cleaned up so I can check on Nathan and the ex from hell.

Within ten minutes, I make my way back downstairs in fresh clothes, but not a better attitude. My frustration with Kyle simmers with each passing minute, bringing my blood and my patience to a boil.

I pad toward the bathroom. The door's cracked, a sliver of incandescent light shining through the small opening in a funnel of white. I lean against the closest wall but stay tucked out of view.

"She's the best," I can hear Kyle slur, his tongue tacky. "The fucking best, Nathan."

"I know. She is."

"Like, how could I have been so stupid to mess that up?" There's a hiccup after the mumbled words. "I had the best girl in the whole fucking world, and I had to go and ruin it."

"Quinn is one in a million."

"One in a *trillion*," Kyle corrects. "A gazillion, bajillion."

He hiccups again, followed by a long burp.

"Oh, shit," Kyle groans. The loud retching sound of Kyle puking again echoes against the porcelain toilet bowl.

"It's alright, buddy."

I step into the door gap. "Everything okay?"

Nathan's squatting next to Kyle, squeezing the guy's shoulders as my ex continues emptying his stomach forcefully, almost violently.

"We're good."

"Doesn't really look like it."

"I'm so sorry, Quinn," Kyle gets out between dry heaves. He spits into the toilet and falls back onto his haunches, tears and snot and sweat smeared across his pale face. I've never seen him look like this.

"You done for now?" Nathan takes Kyle by the shoulders again. "You think you can stand?"

"Mm, hmm." Kyle tries pushing onto his feet but it's unsteady, like a dizzy toddler wobbling back and forth after a ride on a carousel.

"Where can he sleep this off?"

"Oh." I don't know why I'm not prepared for that question. "I've only got the spare. Or we could throw him in Mom's room."

"No." Nathan's head cuts side to side. "The spare is good. Do you have an empty trashcan we can keep by the bed for him in case he gets sick again?"

"I do. I'll grab it."

There's a single Gatorade in the fridge, so I take that, along with the plastic wastebin from beneath the sink. Kyle's going to be dehydrated, and even though he's an absolute dick who put us in an unreasonable situation, I still don't want the guy to suffer. Hangovers are the absolute worst.

Nathan's saying something quietly when I enter the room. He glances up.

"Good call." He comments on the electrolyte drink in my hand. "He'll need that." He nudges Kyle with an elbow. "Can you sit up? Let's try to get some of this in you."

The lid comes off with a pop and twist. Nathan tilts the bottle toward Kyle's lazy mouth and it's like he's trying to feed a blind kitten. Kyle's eyes stay closed as he finally latches onto the Gatorade and takes a long swig.

"Alright. Maybe not so much to start with." Nathan pulls it back to set it on the nightstand. "There's a trashcan right here if you think you're going to be sick again. But I honestly don't think there's anything left in you. Try to get some sleep."

Kyle's hand wraps around Nathan's wrist, catching him. "I love you, man."

Seriously?

"Just try to get some rest," Nathan reiterates. He comes toward me and softly shuts the door behind him, leaving us alone in the hallway.

"Nathan, I'm so—"

"I'm going to stop you before you apologize for something you had absolutely no control over."

"You didn't have to do all of that."

"I've taken care of much worse," Nathan says. We walk down the stairs toward the family room to survey the damage. "My buddy, Logan, is a total lightweight."

"Sure, but I imagine it's different when it's a complete stranger."

"Kyle's not a complete stranger." Nathan gives a little shrug. "We have a few things in common. Most notably, the way we feel about you."

"I don't think he ever really cared about me."

"I think it's one of those situations where he realized what you meant to him too late."

Thankfully, the family room was spared from Kyle's *Exorcist* reenactment. It would appear my clothing got the brunt of it, and that's much easier to clean than rugs and upholstery. Small wins.

"Well." I rub the back of my neck, suddenly sore with tension. "I don't know why he thought showing up here two sheets to the wind was a good idea. The idiot drove under the influence. Does that clue you in on what an absolute piece of shit he is?"

"Driving while intoxicated is inexcusable. I'll give you that. I'm glad he made it here safely without hurting himself or anyone else." Nathan takes a seat on the couch, chucking the drool-coated pillow to the floor. I sit next to him. "But I understand the state he's in."

My face must communicate my confusion.

"It's awful to lose someone when all you want is to be with them."

"I imagine you probably had a few rough nights similar to this after you and Sarah called it quits."

"I'm not talking about Sarah."

My eyes whip up.

"Quinn, I respect that you want space. I completely get it. But denying these growing feelings I have for you is going to be a big emotional battle. I'm not sure I'm strong enough."

He's not alone in that. Is it crazy to admit that watching him care for Kyle was an odd turn-on? There's this nurturing side of Nathan that is so irresistibly sexy, and I can't shut off the way it makes me feel any more than I can convince myself chocolate tastes like broccoli or that there are eight days in a week and not seven.

"Getting a glimpse into the type of guy I typically go for isn't a huge red flag for you?" I ask. "I mean, I obviously don't know what I'm doing when it comes to relationships."

"If anything, it just makes me want to prove to you that you're worthy of so much more."

I really wish he hadn't said that. He's wearing down my resolve to keep things platonic. He's making me want to forget everything my brain says and only listen to my heart.

"It's been a long day," he finally says with a sigh. "I'm going to crash on the couch, but I want you to go upstairs and get some sleep. Don't worry about Kyle. I'll set an alarm on my phone and check on him every few hours. He'll be fine. Probably will hate life tomorrow, but that comes with the territory, and honestly, is a little deserved."

"Nathan, I can't thank you enough."

He pauses, his throat working on a labored swallow. Then his eyes are on mine and it's anguish and yearning and hope all wrapped into one pain-filled look.

"Hey." He shrugs, then lets out an almost silent laugh when he says, "What are friends for?"

23 /
nathan

I CAN'T BELIEVE I'm doing this.

I'm calling in the reinforcements.

There's a time in life when you must recognize you've bitten off more than you can chew, and with this stupid house, I devoured so much, so quickly, I'm choking.

At the rate I'm physically able to remodel it on my own, it'll be a year before it's ready to list. And Quinn and I have our agreement. She finishes her book. I finish the damn house.

It's not even nine in the morning, but I'm back at the fixer upper and I've got the bottles of beer chilling in the fridge. I'm going to need them. Archie is the king of *I-told-you-so's*, and I expect a whole slew of them spit-firing from his arrogant mouth. Logan's the quieter of the two, but he's dealing with his own marital strife, so I don't expect him to press me too hard.

I'm lucky, I realize that. Few men can say they have friends who would drop everything to bail out their buddy. At one point or another, we've all needed rescuing, so we don't even keep track of IOUs or favors. If one of the guys is in a quandary, you best believe we're going to rally around and help him out, whatever that looks like.

I just wish I wasn't the one needing rescuing time after time.

Like clockwork, Archie's sleek Ferrari Portofino M pulls up right at noon. The low hum of his luxury vehicle is like a purr that has this spellbinding effect on both men and women alike. I'm not all that into cars, but I appreciate the price tag and the hard work Archie has put in to own it. Or own several of them in varying colors, for that matter.

Still, I have to give him a hard time. It's what we do. "I'm surprised you even remember how to drive."

He steps out of the sports car, eyes shaded with designer sunglasses, both middle fingers thrust aggressively into the air. "Fuck you, too, Natty."

"He *doesn't* remember how to drive." Logan's clutching his stomach as he comes around the vehicle and then throws his arms over my shoulders in a massive, much needed hug. I make a mental note to ask him how things are going with Lauren later. If that embrace is any clue, not great. "Almost got us killed three times."

"*Two* times." Archie tucks his glasses into the inner pocket of his jacket. "That last time wouldn't have killed us, just severely maimed us. Plus, what was I going to do? Have Carlton drive and then just wait around while we rebuilt an entire fucking house?"

"Isn't that literally what you pay him to do? Drive you from one place to another and then wait until it's time to take you back home?"

They're arguing—always do—but it's the best damn sound in the world. I've missed these guys.

"Anyway." Archie's eyes slant toward Logan. "We're here and ready to work."

"In that?" My eyes give a long perusal of Archie's impractical attire. As an executive at a big San Francisco firm, the guy is always dressed to the nines. And even though he's not in a custom three-piece suit today, his loafers alone must cost more than I've spent on sheetrock and studs combined.

"No, of course not. I brought something to change into." Moving back to his car, he withdraws a duffle bag from the seat and swings it like a pendulum.

"You mean your assistant packed you some spare clothes," Logan corrects.

"What difference does it make? I'm ready to help our buddy, right?"

"And I'm grateful for it." I clamp a hand on his shoulder. "There's a lot to do."

"Lead the way."

I give them the tour, but there's not much to show. It's a lot of 'imagine this here' and 'that will go there,' but they nod and grin like they catch my vision. I had intended for this to be a solitary endeavor, but it's looking like not much in life is.

We work hard all the way through until lunchtime. For as much as I razz Archie about his posh lifestyle and delicate desk job hands, the guy is a machine. He alone tears out the entire cast iron tub from the upstairs bath, and the three of us maneuver the beast down the stairway and out into the garage where it'll wait for the guy who contacted me on Craigslist to pick it up.

I've taken Quinn's advice to use social media and not just

dump unwanted furniture and fixtures on the curb. I've even made a few extra bucks doing so, so that's a plus.

"You gonna feed us or what, Natty?" Archie runs a towel down his face when we pause for a break.

"I'll feed you. We can head into town. There's a diner that sort of reminds me of Jake's Place back home. You'll love it."

"Back home?" Logan pulls at the hem of his t-shirt to cool off, head cocked. "So, you're actually thinking of returning to Fairhaven?"

My mouth feels tacky from the slip up. "No. I'm not. I misspoke. Old habits die hard, I guess."

We pile into my truck—me and Logan in the front and a complaining Archie squished into the access cab—and take an open spot just outside the diner. A woman with an authentic hairstyle from the era the diner tries to emulate seats us, tossing menus toward us as she smacks her gum so emphatically, droplets of spit spray onto our table.

"Should we have asked to be seated somewhere other than the splash zone?" Archie bemoans loud enough for her to hear. She gives him one more dramatic chomp and saunters away. "Great place you've decided to plant some roots, Natty."

"I don't know that I'll be staying here, either."

Logan has the menu up to his face. "That's not like you, man. To have everything so up in the air."

"I know," is all I say as I read the specials posted on the board above the long counter. I decide on the French dip, fold my menu, and cross my arms, elbows on the table. "So, what's new with you guys?"

"I've got a fucking coworker from hell." Archie doesn't look up as he studies the lunch options.

"He means he wants to fuck the hell out of his coworker," Logan corrects.

"*That* is what you got out of our entire conversation on the drive over here?" Archie's menu falls away, and he pins our buddy with a death stare. "The woman is infuriating. I made the horrible, knee-jerk mistake of hiring her to take over our graphic design department and she's certifiably crazy."

"Don't you already have a head designer?" I ask. "That weird guy who only eats Slim Jims and Gogurts for lunch?"

"That guy's a dick," Archie sneers.

"I remember it being the other way around and that he seemed to think you were one," Logan chides around a haughty laugh. These two could go at it all day. "Didn't he literally present a bunch of cartoon dicks to the board for the company's new logo?"

"Are you really one to talk, bro?" Archie turns toward Logan. "Obviously, your wife thinks you're a big enough dick that she served you with divorce papers."

I jolt. "Lauren served you with papers? Shit, man. I had no idea."

"Things have been rough. What can I say?"

He shrugs like he doesn't care, but I know it must be ripping him apart inside. They've only been married three years, and I had heard things had been rocky lately, but I didn't see this coming.

"Tell Natty the best part." Archie gives Logan a goading nudge.

"The best part about my wife deciding she doesn't want to be married to me anymore?"

"No. The part about how you're still having to pretend to be in happily wedded bliss until the acquisition goes through."

"I didn't know your business was being acquired." Damn, I'm realizing my time away has severed more than just my relationship with Sarah. "That's great, Logan."

"The guy is under the impression it's a family-owned company. I mean, it technically was during our initial meetings, but not looking so much like one now." Logan rubs his neck. "I don't know. We're going on some team building retreat next month and Lauren has agreed to play nice while we're there. We'll see."

"Do you want her back?"

"Hell yes, I want her back. Is that even a real question?"

"Dude, read the room a little better than that," Archie says. "Not all men whose wives leave them want them back. Am I right, Natty?"

"Every relationship is different," I offer because it's all I've got and it's the honest to God truth. "If you want things to work out with Lauren, then I hope they do."

A different server comes around to take our order, which I'm certain is on purpose. Bubble Gum Betty is nowhere to be seen. We rattle off what we'd like and settle in with our drinks as we catch up on lost time.

I've known these men since we were twelve, starting out at a new middle school, acne on our faces, insecurities running through our blood. I love them like brothers and even though Archie can be a cocky ass and Logan can be combative, we're in it for the long haul. They've certainly put up with plenty of shit out of me over the years.

Halfway into our lunch, something in my periphery pulls

my attention out of the one-sided conversation Archie is having about the ridiculously slow speed of the new elevators installed in his high-rise building. The tip-top of first world problems.

Through the big glass window, I catch Quinn's long, twisting hair lifting in the breeze as she walks past. But there's someone on the other side of her, and it isn't until she steps into the diner that I'm able to make out who.

Fucking Kyle—all sobered up, looking more pathetic than ever.

"You good, buddy?" Logan swivels his head to track my gaze.

Archie hisses, clicking his teeth. "That is one fine piece of—"

"You will not finish that sentence." My voice is a warning and a threat.

"You know her?" Logan brings his eyes back to me.

"We've hung out a few times." I drag my napkin over my mouth, chuck it to the table.

"Isn't she a little young for you?" Archie's eyes bounce back and forth between me and Quinn. He's obviously doing the math.

"Isn't the new marketing exec a little too co-workery for you?" Logan comes to my defense.

Archie's mouth sets in a line, no retaliation forming.

"We're not like that," I say. I haven't withdrawn my gaze from Quinn, but she hasn't noticed me, not even when she's seated just a few tables away. "She's house-sitting the place next door to mine."

"Then why do you look like that?" Archie tips the rim of his water cup toward me.

"Like what?"

"Like you're ready to cut the nuts off the guy she's with and feed them to the family of squirrels outside."

I shake my head, trying to recover my expression. "He's her ex."

"What's he doing here with her?"

"My guess? Trying to get her back."

Our server returns with our plates, moving around orders until they settle in front of the right person. We all dig in. I chew more aggressively than normal, dunking my fries into my ketchup like I'm trying to drown them.

"You good there, buddy?" Logan and Archie exchange a look, but I almost miss it because my eyes haven't left Quinn and Kyle's table.

Kyle's hand reaches between them, dropping onto hers in a gesture that feels so fake, so rehearsed it makes my skin crawl.

She doesn't immediately pull away.

I throw my sandwich down.

"Excuse me for one second." I stand.

My buddies don't attempt to restrain me, but I know they've got my back if I need them.

"Quinn." I come up behind her table. She startles at the sound of my voice, then turns to look up at me with those doe eyes I can't help but get lost in.

"Nathan." Her face is all bright tenderness, like she's genuinely excited to see me. "I didn't know you were here."

"With a few of my buddies." I hook a thumb over my shoulder.

She jumps to her feet. "No way! Seriously? I want to meet them."

"Um, Quinnie." Kyle audibly clears his throat. "We're in the middle of lunch."

"I'll only be a minute, Kyle. Order me my usual. I'll be quick."

Hearing she has a usual that he knows makes my stomach turn over, but she's at my side, hand in mine, pulling me back to my booth before I have time to work myself up over it.

She drops into the open bench seat, sliding over to make room for me to join her.

Logan's eyes are silver dollars; Archie's are all coy and cunning.

"And who's this?" He says, popping a French fry into his mouth.

"Guys, this is Quinn. The neighbor I was telling you about."

She gives me a look. "Well, I'm a little more than just his neighbor." Sweat breaks out along my forehead, wondering where she's going with this, but she says, "I'll be helping him with the fixer upper once it comes time to make some design and decorating decisions."

"That house definitely needs a woman's touch," Logan agrees, nodding.

"And so does Nathan," Archie cough-speaks behind his napkin.

Logan's elbow meets his ribcage.

"Anyway." I talk over them. "This is Archie and Logan, my boys."

"Archer, actually." Archie extends a hand across the space to take Quinn's into his own. "Only Natty and Logan call me Archie."

"And I'm guessing you're the only ones who call him Natty?"

"Correct," I say. "The only ones who get away with it."

"I'm so glad to meet you both." She means it. Her entire being radiates with happiness. "Nathan's been a great neighbor."

I'm not prepared for her hand to squeeze my knee beneath the table. I stiffen in my seat.

"I've really enjoyed getting to know him," she adds.

My buddies are speechless, and so am I because her hand is traveling higher, her nails skimming along my upper thigh.

She tugs her hand back. "I should probably get back to my..." She pauses. "My lunch."

I slide out of the booth, letting her by.

She's about to leave but stops. "Are you guys going to be around for a while?"

"A couple of days," Archie answers for them.

"Why don't you come over tonight and we'll barbecue? I can pick up some steaks on my way home that we can throw on the grill."

I know she enjoys feeding me, but she doesn't have to go out of her way like this. Not for my buddies, too.

"Really?" Archie's amused eyes light up. "What time and what can we bring?"

"Six. And just yourselves and an appetite."

She gives another big grin, but before returning to her table, she throws me a wink that has both of my buddies' jaws dropping, and has my brain, my heart, and my dick more confused than ever.

24 /
quinn

KYLE IS STILL HERE.

I cannot get rid of this guy. He's like a freaking barnacle.

I had hoped my suggestion that we get a bite to eat before he set out on the road would serve as a large enough hint, but he's denser than I thought.

"What do you want to do now?" he asks, watching me put the credit card I used to pay for our lunch back into my coin purse. Of course, he not only ignored the check when it initially came but made up some sorry excuse about leaving his wallet in his other pair of jeans.

Whatever. I look at it as my last parting gift.

"Well, I'm going to head to the grocery store to pick up some food for tonight, and you're going to head back home."

"I could come with you."

Surprising me, he reaches around to pull on the diner's door handle first, letting me step out onto the pavement ahead of him like a human with honest-to-goodness manners.

"I'm fine on my own." I shoulder my purse and hug it close to my body. "Take care, Kyle."

"That's it?" His volume rises. "That's how we end this?"

"I *thought* we had already ended it when I stormed out of your apartment after finding out you were cheating on me."

"That wasn't the end for me, Quinnie. It still isn't. I love you."

"No, you don't." I walk toward my car parked in front of his. At least I was able to convince him to take his own vehicle to lunch. It would be all sorts of awkward to share a ride now. "When you love someone, you don't treat them the way you treated me."

"I was stupid. I've said that already. We all make mistakes, right?"

"We do. And it's a mistake for me to let this go on even longer than it already has."

I place a hand on his chest, but Kyle misconstrues the gesture. He cups his palm over it, grinning.

"Kyle, I'm going to stop you from groveling, from begging, and from humiliating yourself even more than you already have." I tug my hand back. "No hard feelings. Move on and find someone who makes you happy and then don't make the same mistakes with them you've made with me. Learn from this."

With that, I walk away.

It feels good to be done with him. *Again.* Like one more step in repairing the damage he did to my heart. One step closer to the end goal.

I spend over an hour at the supermarket, but a lot of that is because I watch a half dozen cooking videos on my phone as I roll through the aisles, trying to figure out how to put together a decent meal to feed three hungry men. It's this weird domestic side of myself that I didn't know even existed.

I get an odd thrill as I toss a few New York strips into the cart, followed by several stalks of broccolini and a bag of red potatoes.

To be honest, I'm not even sure my mom still owns a BBQ. I know my dad had one once upon a time, but I can't imagine the propane tank is full or guarantee that it even works. Thankfully, the store has several tanks available for purchase out front, so I add that to my tab and snag one on the way to my car.

I've got this. Totally.

And why am I doing this again?

I try to shake off my inner monologue, but she's questioning all my actions lately.

Because friends invite friends over for barbecues all the time. And it's totally appropriate to invite said friend's friends over, too. Right?

My subconscious isn't convinced. Still, I've already extended the invitation. The damage is done.

At six o'clock, there's a rowdy knock on the door.

"Are you wearing an apron?" Nathan mutters close to my ear when he steps inside and goes in for a hug. He passes off a bottle of wine.

"I am." I smooth a hand down my front and grip the neck of the bottle with the other. "It's weird, right?"

"It's freaking hot," he whispers against my cheek before pulling back.

Archer—Archie—goes in for a hug next and Logan just gives a cordial little head nod, followed by a flick of his hand. I glimpse the shiny silver ring on his fourth finger and assume he's married. Archer's not, I gather, based not only on the bachelor vibes he gives off like a single man pheromone, but also by the absence of any jewelry adorning his fingers.

"Where's the grill?" Nathan takes the plate of seasoned steaks from the kitchen island. I read they needed to rest and come to room temperature, and I'm suddenly worried I haven't given them enough time.

"Out on the back deck, but it hasn't been used in years. I'm not sure it'll even work."

"I think between the three of us, we can figure it out." Archer sidesteps around his buddy and commandeers the meat. "This way?" He points a finger toward the long hallway that leads to the backyard.

"Yep."

Logan follows on his heels.

All energy leaves the room with them. It's just Nathan and I, standing across from one another as silence settles over us like a heavy cloak. I almost feel trapped.

"So." He gives me a puzzled look.

"So."

"I thought we were taking a step back," he says, hushed even though his friends are already outside and out of earshot. I can hear them hooting and hollering, which leads me to believe they got the barbecue fired up and running. That's good, at least.

"We are."

"Yeah? Inviting me and my buddies over is taking a step back?"

"It's establishing a friendship. What we agreed on, right?"

"Sure." He nods, but it's not convincing. "But that thing under the table. That felt a little more than just friendly, no?"

"I'm sorry. I don't know why I did that."

"I'm not complaining, Quinn. I just want to make sure I'm reading things right."

Is he reading that I want to jump his bones at this very moment? That I want to kiss him senseless, devour him, and do things much too corrupt to take place in my mother's kitchen?

"I'll keep my hands to myself," I swear. I even go to the extra effort of making a little crisscross mark over my heart.

"You've said that before, and then you ended up straddling me. Topless, I might add."

"In fairness, I didn't say *you* had to keep your hands to yourself at that moment. But you're right. I need to back off."

His mouth pinches like he wishes he hadn't brought it up. "The last thing I want is for you to back off. But like you said, we need to get to know one another in ways that aren't just physical. Form a foundation that isn't only based on sexual energy."

Oh my God. *Yes.* That's exactly what this is between us. It's an undeniable sexual energy, an attraction. Lust; whatever you want to call it. Of course, there's more to the way I feel about him than that, but the driving force behind our connection is physical and has been from the beginning. No way around it.

Well, I suppose the way around it is to cut that out, which is exactly what we've agreed to do. At least we're kinda, sorta on the right track.

Another raucous shout echoes from the backyard, followed by a fit of hearty, booming laughter. Then there's an unidentifiable crash.

"Should we check on them?" I ask.

"Yes, but we probably don't want to see what we're about

to find," Nathan groans. "I have to warn you. When the three of us get together, we revert to our preteen days. There's no real way to avoid it, unfortunately."

"I think I can handle it."

I can, but apparently, I can't hide my laughter, because as soon as I see Logan and Archer flying through the air like a couple of oversized kangaroos, I lose it.

"I can't believe there's any bounce left in that thing," I say, gaping at the sight.

"This is amazing! I've always wanted one of these," Logan cheers. Archer bends at the knees the second Logan's big feet meet the trampoline, making his buddy's legs go ramrod straight. Logan jolts and collapses onto his back. "What the hell, dude?"

"Join us, Quinn." Archer's all out of breath. He flaps a hand at me while bent at the waist. "Show us how it's done."

"I don't think—"

"Come on," Archer pleads. "I promise not to steal your bounce like I did this asshole's."

I kick off my shoes and let him take my hand to pull me up onto the trampoline. It takes a moment to get my sea legs. I haven't been on this thing in at least a decade, but surprisingly, it all comes back. Like riding a bike, but even easier than that.

The three of us bounce around like idiots while Nathan tends to the grill, and he smiles each time I shriek with breathless laughter.

"Contest time!" Archer slows his jumping until the bounces peter out and he's standing still on the trampoline. Logan and I do the same. "Let's see who has the best bouncing skills."

"Why does everything have to be a competition with you, man?"

"Because life is more fun when it's a game."

"I'm in." I raise my hand, chest heaving since I'm still attempting to catch my breath and evidently, I'm in terrible shape.

"All-fucking-right. I like it." Archer gives me a high five and a grin that makes me believe he has no trouble in the dating department. This man oozes charm and the confidence to go along with it.

"Fine," Logan groans like he doesn't want to give in, but doesn't want to be left out, either. "I'm in, too."

"Natty!" Cupping his mouth to create a megaphone with his hands, Archer shouts across the yard. "You're going to be the judge."

"I'm cooking the steaks, bro."

"You can cook and critique at the same time," Archer counters. He's not about to take no for an answer. "Rate us on a scale of one to ten. You're looking for things like jump height, along with overall execution."

"In what world am I equipped to make those calls?" Nathan waves a set of tongs at Archer, clacking them once.

"You teach middle school. Don't tell me the kids don't have you doing shit like this all the time."

Nathan thinks on it, then shrugs like maybe Archer has a point.

Archer goes first. It's a standard, straight up in the air jump and I think he's mostly shooting for altitude.

"Six point five." Nathan moves his attention back to the barbecue. The steaks have perfect grill marks crosshatching them and the scent as they cook has my mouth watering.

"Six point fucking five? You've got to be shitting me."

Nathan shrugs halfheartedly. "I'm the judge. I have the final say."

"Fine, but you score me that low again and I'm going to challenge it." Archer steps to the edge of the trampoline and straddles the springs with his bare feet. "Logan, you're up."

Logan's feet are planted for a moment while he looks like he's gathering courage, but then he suddenly jumps up and does a forward flip, sticking his landing perfectly like a freaking gymnast. I like the guy; he's the opposite of Archer in that he's not as outwardly cocky, but there's obviously some fight in there that deserves to be noticed.

"Eight point nine."

"Eight point nine?" Archer is on the brink of a tantrum. "Where the fuck are you coming up with these decimals, Natty?"

"Do you want to take over the grill and do the judging?"

"Yes. Yes, I do." Jumping down from the trampoline, Archer makes ground-eating strides across the lawn and switches spots with Nathan. "Go show us how it's done, mister eight point six point five point two—"

"Alright, alright."

Nathan hikes a leg and climbs onto the mat. With his turn already over, Logan slinks off which leaves just Nathan and I on the bouncy surface.

"Hi," he says as he carefully ambles closer. The trampoline gives beneath him with every step.

"Hi."

"I'm sorry about them."

"They're great. Seriously."

"Archie's intense."

"Oh, and I know *nothing* about having an intense best friend."

That gets a chuckle out of him.

"You two just going to chat it up all day up there, or are you going to do some actual jumping?" Archer hollers.

"We should give him what he wants," I say.

"Do you trust me?"

I don't even have to think twice about that. "Of course."

"I'm going to double bounce you."

I remember doing that as a kid with my cousins when they would come over during the summer months and we would spend all our afternoons outdoors. I also remember soaring so high into the air, I swear I could see over the neighbor's roof. Am I still up for that?

"Take a few small warmup jumps, but on the third, I'm going to bounce you and you're going to fucking fly."

"I got this," I say, already thinking about the pose I'm going to strike once I'm sky high.

"Ready?"

I nod.

"One," he says as I get my legs set beneath me. "Two."

On the third he does as he says and jumps close to my feet, propelling me so high into the air, I panic. But just as I get to the apex of my jump, all my confidence returns, and I execute the best toe touch this trampoline—heck, even this zip code—has ever seen. My high school pep arts coach would be so proud.

I haven't even landed, and the guys are screaming like I just scored some big touchdown win.

"Ten!" Archer throws the tongs into the air.

"Ten!" Logan echoes. The guys legit chest bump one another.

But I'm lying on the trampoline mat, wishing I would have paid more attention to my descent because I land on my damn ankle and tweak it again.

"You good?" Nathan extends a hand to pull me up.

"Yeah." But I'm not and that's made known when I crumple into a heap after trying to put weight on it.

"Shit. Your ankle again?"

"I think so."

Nathan jumps down from the trampoline and scoops me into his arms, shouldering past his buddies who try to give me high fives on the way.

"Another cheerleader, huh Natty? Can't say you don't have a type."

Nathan spins around, and since I'm in his arms, my head whooshes with the disorienting movement.

"Don't you *ever* compare Quinn to Sarah again." He presses up close to Archer. I try to make myself as small as possible, but I'm obviously caught between them. "Understood?"

All playfulness leaves Archer's features. "Yeah." His voice is uncharacteristically void of teasing. "Absolutely. Understood."

Nathan shoulders the backdoor open and immediately goes into protective mode.

I'm lowered to the couch, a blanket tucked over me even though it's just my ankle and it's not like I'm sick or anything. Once he's satisfied I'm comfortable, he rushes into the kitchen. I can hear him digging around in the freezer. Ice clinks in the maker as he scoops some out to put in a plastic baggie. The freezer door swings shut.

"Put this on it for a while." Nathan returns and places the compress on my bum ankle, the look of anguish on his face matching mine when I wince at the cold contact.

He's agitated. I'm not sure if it's the fact that I keep re-injuring this stupid ankle, or if it's from his confrontation with Archer. There's a hard set to his jaw that hints at anger, and it's not a side of him I've seen before. I don't know what to make of it.

"You good here for a bit?" Even though the blanket is pulled all the way up to my chin already, he tugs it higher.

"Yeah, I'm good. But I really should check on the potatoes in the oven. I think they're close to being done and I don't want them to burn."

"I'll take care of the potatoes." His voice is curt, blunt with insistence. "And I've got to take care of something else, too. But I'll be back to check on you. Just don't move. Please."

I nod.

Nathan strides toward the backyard, evidently switching places with Logan because the friend comes sauntering into the house like he's not part of whatever is going down outside.

"Everything okay out there?" I struggle to get upright and balance the bag of ice on my ankle at the same time.

"Let me." Logan takes the icepack and waits until I'm situated before placing it on my ankle.

"Thank you."

He sinks into the loveseat with a warm smile on his face. "Of course."

He's handsome—both Logan and Archer are—with dark hair like Nathan's, but rather than green eyes, his are a striking blue that pops against his tan skin. I can only imagine that these three guys out on the town could really turn some heads and break some craning necks.

"To answer your question, yeah, everything is fine. Or will be once Nathan beats the shit out of Archer."

I jump to my feet but collapse when pain shoots through my hurt ankle.

"Whoa." Logan's hands come up. "I'm kidding. Take it easy there, tiger. They're just talking. It may not seem like it since we were literally just jumping on a trampoline, but we aren't kids anymore. Archer and Nathan have learned to resolve their differences in ways that don't involve fists and black eyes. They'll be fine."

The condensation forming on the plastic bag causes it to slip, so I readjust it. "That comment really pissed him off, huh?"

"Yeah, but I get it. I'm not one to talk about marriage because mine isn't going great—or going at all, really—but Sarah and Nathan..." Logan swings his gaze from mine. "They're complicated."

"I picked up on that."

"It's more than just the whole infidelity thing. I'm not going to beat around the bush. We all saw that coming. Even Nathan. Sarah would often talk about the men she would run into at the office or around town. Say things to make Nathan jealous, you know? Like if a guy at the store complimented her outfit, she'd make a point to wear it more often. Petty stuff like that."

"Just to get a rise out of him?"

"Yeah. I think so. I don't really know what motivated her. She wasn't always that way. As a kid, she was really sweet.

Popular, but not one of the mean girls. Popular because she was nice to everyone."

"What changed?"

"I wish I knew." Logan blows out a breath and drops his hands to his knees, back straightening. "I know money was tight in the beginning. She wanted a big wedding, but her parents didn't have the funds and Nathan's mom was already strapped working two jobs. They had a really small ceremony and even smaller reception because Nathan thought it would be the best way to cut costs and save for a down payment on a house. That was the other thing. Sarah was never satisfied with their place. Always wanted to gut it and remodel it. But she doesn't make a ton at her job, and Nathan's a teacher. He works hard, but he's not compensated appropriately for the time he commits to those kids. Teachers never are."

"Sarah wanted to renovate their house?"

Logan's head lifts in a nod. "A little ironic now since that's exactly what he's doing, only to a completely different place."

I wouldn't call it ironic. I would call it heartbreaking. Whether intentional or not, the motivation for this remodel stems from more than just a need to demolish something. I'm no psychiatrist, but the layers are peeling back and I'm not entirely comfortable with what I see.

"Anyway. I've given the boys long enough to work things out. I should probably go check on them, and on those steaks, too. Don't want the meat being neglected while Natty and Archie are duking it out."

"Of course. But Logan? One more thing?"

"Sure. What's that?"

I swallow and say in a small voice, "Am I like Sarah?"

Logan's features turn soft with understanding. "Not at all. I don't know you well, but other than that crazy impressive toe touch thing, I don't see any similarities."

Relief settles over me like the forecast of sunshine after a week of rain, warm and welcome. "Okay."

"And if it's any consolation, there aren't any similarities in the way Nathan interacts with you—or even looks at you—for that matter. Sarah might have had his last name, but you've got something else entirely."

25 /
nathan

"IT HAS BEEN A DAY."

Quinn passes me the last dinner plate. I run the dishrag over it and line it up next to the others in the drying rack beside a brittle fern that has no hope of ever coming back to life. Poor thing's a total goner.

"You could say that again," I agree. "Thanks for putting up with these dipwads all evening. They can be a lot."

"They're great. Best dipwads around." She turns so her backside presses against the counter's bullnose ledge. "Seriously, though. I really enjoyed getting to know your friends, Nathan. I feel like I got a glimpse into a side of you I hadn't seen before."

"You mean the irrational, hotheaded side?"

"No." Her big chestnut eyes catch mine. "The side that protects what he cares about. I mean, you were obviously super attentive to me when I got hurt again, but you also put in the work of straightening things out with Archer. I don't know what you guys talked about but based on your interactions during dinner and throughout the rest of the night, I'm assuming all is well with you two."

"We never stay mad at each other long," I say. "And I wasn't even mad at him. I just didn't want him saying stupid shit that isn't true."

Her bottom lip pins between her teeth like she's mulling something over. I guess her brain gives her the green light because she says, "Logan and I had the chance to talk a little."

"He's a good guy." I turn around so I'm up against the sink like she is and cross my arms over my chest. "I hope he works things out with Lauren because they're really great together. Unlike me and Sarah, I think they actually have a shot at forever."

"He told me Sarah had wanted to remodel your house."

I'm surprised that came up. What were they discussing exactly? "That's the thing about Sarah. She was never content."

"You're currently remodeling a house."

"I am." I don't know where Quinn is heading with this.

"Do you think that maybe there's a part of you that is doing this for her?"

My arms tighten. "Remodeling a house that isn't hers, in a town she doesn't even live in?"

"I mean, not *literally* for her. But is there a part of you, even a subconscious part, that's doing this because it's something she wanted, and you never gave it to her?"

"To make her jealous?" I thrum my fingers against my arm.

"Maybe not to make her jealous, but more of an 'F-you' kind of thing."

I heave out a long sigh. "I don't know. Like you said,

maybe it's in my subconscious, and in that case, I wouldn't really be aware of the motivation, would I?"

"That's fair."

"Would that bother you if that were the case?"

"I don't know." She pushes off from the counter and picks up a sponge to clean up the stray crumbs dotting the kitchen island.

"Hey." I cuff her bicep with my hand. "Would it bother you?" I need to know her answer.

"I think it would be unfair to you if it did. But truthfully? Yeah, it might bother me a little."

"And why is that?"

"Because it would mean that some part of you isn't over her."

"I'm over Sarah, Quinn. One hundred percent."

Her head lolls side to side. "But not really. Not if you're doing the very thing she always wanted you to do."

"But I'm not doing it for her. I'm doing it for me."

"I get that. I do. But it's like when you break up with someone and then go out and get a killer haircut and get your nails done and make yourself look fucking fantastic, all to make them realize what they could have had. There's still a small piece of you hoping they'll notice."

"Since this is literally my first breakup, I can't say I relate to that. Especially the manicure part." I chuckle half-heartedly to bring some lightness to the conversation, but everything remains just as dim. "Seriously, Quinn. There is no handbook on this stuff. I'm just doing what feels right."

"I know." She tosses the sponge into the sink. "I don't mean to question your motives."

"I don't mind you asking the tough questions. And it

means a lot that you're willing to bring these things to my attention. I just don't know if I'm able to give you the answers you want to hear."

"I'm not even sure what I want to hear."

"I don't understand."

She leans forward on her elbows over the island, head hanging. "If the baby had been yours, you would have stayed with Sarah, right?"

"I wouldn't have had a real reason to leave, I guess."

"But would you have been happy?"

"Happy? It's all relative. I know Sarah eventually wanted a child, so I wanted that for her. I'm not one of those guys that thinks having a kid is going to solve things or bring a couple closer. But you're right, I probably would have stayed and just kept doing what we were doing."

I take a long look at her, analyzing the display of emotion on her face. I can't make heads or tails of the deep line drawing her eyebrows together, don't understand the down-turned corners of her mouth that pinch with worry.

"Would you have stayed with Kyle if he hadn't cheated?" I volley.

"No. I mean, I probably wouldn't have ended it so soon, but eventually, I would have called things off. Because at the end of the day, I want a relationship where I feel loved and secure. Kyle couldn't give me that."

"I think that's what we all want."

"Probably." Her hands clap the counter, and she shoves off. "Anyway. Forget I said all that. Sometimes my thoughts wander into places they shouldn't." I recognize Quinn's forced smile immediately when her mouth curves into a placating grin. "I'm tired. I'm going to head to bed, and you should probably get back to the guys."

They went back to the fixer upper about a half an hour ago, and if I know them, they're already passed out in their sleeping bags, snoring so loudly they'd give a hibernating grizzly bear competition in the noise department.

"Thank you for being honest with me, Quinn. I hope you know you can always do that."

"I do. And thank you." Her lips press together. "Oh. One more thing. I sent over my latest chapters of my manuscript. Nothing super exciting, but if you want to read them, you can."

"Of course. Thank you again for trusting me with that. I'll look at them tonight."

I move to hug her, to pull her into my arms, but she's hesitant at first, feet locked in place. Then, something washes over her and she melts against me, her cheek to my chest, her arms snug around my waist. Her body almost trembles as she grips onto me like she would crawl inside if she could.

"Hey?" I pull back to look at her. My fingers sweep back a fallen lock of hair that she blinks out of her eyes. "You good?"

"I'm good."

Even with that verbal reassurance, I know something is off.

It's all I think about as I go back to my place and get ready for bed.

There's a melancholy between us that wasn't there before. We've always been so playful, so flirty. The emotions are deeper now, like we've opened up another part of ourselves and settled in, exploring our feelings in a brand new and scary territory.

That's what we wanted, though. To dive deeper emotionally. To connect with our hearts and not just our hormones.

But I hate that there seems to be a piece of Quinn that is hurting. And I hate that my response to my divorce and the way I'm processing it seems to be at the root of that. Maybe she's right. Maybe this whole fixer upper thing did subconsciously originate from Sarah's constant insistence that we do it to our own place. But I'm not doing this for Sarah now, and I'm not sure how to reiterate that. She's not a part of this picture. Not a part of my future.

I find the guys in the upstairs master bedroom, but they're not asleep. Several empty bottles rest on their sides, others have rolled to the corners of the room like runaway marbles. Both Logan and Archie are working on another round.

"Found your stash in your fridge and helped ourselves." Archie tips the neck of an amber bottle toward me. "Nice little collection."

"Shit, guys. You've only been alone for like thirty minutes."

"Logan's drinking away his sorrows."

"And what are you doing?" I cock a brow at Archie.

"Trying to keep up. Friends don't let friends wallow alone. Bro code number one."

"I'm not wallowing." Logan shoves Archie's shoulder. "I'm hydrating."

I tally up the bottles of craft beer. There are only eight discarded ones. Not terrible. Four each. But Logan can't hold his liquor and I'm not about to have a repeat of last night. I've witnessed enough grown-man vomit to last a lifetime. I remove the beer from Logan's hand and replace it with the bottle of water I had snagged for myself from the fridge.

"Quinn's a keeper," he says. Immediately, he downs half the bottle before coming up for air. "I really like her."

"I do, too." More than like. I'm falling for her, but I don't need to tell my boys that for them to know. It's painfully obvious.

"What's the hesitation?" Archie's sitting on the floor. He brings his knees up and loops his arms around them coolly, hands clasped and ankles crossed.

I can't let a good IPA go to waste, so I start in on Logan's. "She's hesitant because we just came out of relationships."

"I wouldn't call what you and Sarah had just a relationship."

Archie's not wrong. I've known the woman for over half my life and spent most of that time loving her. Or trying to, at least.

"Does she think it's too soon?" he prods.

"I mean, it is, right?" I throw back another swallow but keep the drink in my mouth before gulping it down with a hiss. "These feelings I have for her—can I even trust them?"

"Is it just the excitement of someone new?" Logan polishes off the water and crumples the bottle before rolling it over the floorboards to join the others.

"It's the excitement of *her*. Everything about Quinn sets me off. Her wit. Her talent. Her body. She's everything I'm looking for."

"She's a lot younger than you, Natty," Archie states.

"Yeah. I know that."

"Are you sure that's a good idea?"

"I'm not sure *any* of this is a good idea."

Logan shakes his head. "I don't think the whole age thing is that big of a deal."

"It's not, unless she picks up on the obvious." Archie's eyes bounce between us.

"And what's that?"

"That you're hitting the rewind button."

I don't follow. My brow lifts.

"Things didn't work out with Sarah, so you're starting over with someone the exact age you were when you got married. You don't think that's a little coincidental?"

"It's certainly coincidental, because I assure you, it's not intentional," I rally.

"We don't get do-overs, and I'm worried that's what this is trying to be." Archie's broad shoulders hike to his ears, and he brings his beer up to meet his lips. "That's all."

"Maybe it's not a do-over, but a fresh start," Logan interjects. It's nice that he's coming to my defense, but Archie might have a point, as hard as that pill is to swallow.

"Do you think Quinn thinks that's what I'm doing?"

Archie's hands go up, one encircling the neck on a bottle so it dangles loosely from his fingers. "Hey, I do not profess to know anything about the way the opposite sex's brain works. I'm just telling you how it looks from the outside."

"No. I appreciate that. You have a valid point."

"Let's talk about something else." That's Archie for you. Can only discuss the deep stuff for a limited amount of time before he emotionally short-circuits. "How's the sex?"

Of course, his mind would go there. "We haven't had any."

"You're shitting me. I don't believe that for one fucking second."

"Yeah." Even Logan gives me the side eye. "Sorry, Nathan. I don't believe that, either. Not the way you two look at each other."

"Okay. We've fooled around, but we haven't made love or anything."

"Made love." Archie harrumphs under a breath.

"Shut the hell up, man." Logan isn't having any of it, and I'm not sure if it's the alcohol or the tenuous state of his own marriage that makes his hackles rise. "It's a thing. Not all sexual encounters are one-night stands. But I wouldn't expect you to understand that."

"I don't doubt some sex is better and maybe even more emotional than others, but I don't know where this whole making love term came from. It's nauseating."

"Says the man whose idea of foreplay is sabotaging his employee's lunch order. How'd that go over for you?"

"Will you shut the hell up? I'm not interested in Zoey."

Logan just gives Archie a look that silences him right away. Whoever this new coworker of his is, she's obviously got him by the balls.

I pivot back to our earlier conversation. "We've decided to take a step back from the physical side of things until we get to know one another better."

"That's respectable," Logan acknowledges.

"And fucking unachievable."

"Stop being such an insensitive prick." Logan smacks Archie's shoulder.

"I'm just being a realist."

"No. I agree with Archie. It's going to be hell, but I want

a shot with Quinn, and I don't want to rush into things only to have it all implode. I think we could really have something good if we take our time and do things right."

"That's where I think you're getting hung up, Natty. There's no one right way to fall in love. It either happens, or it doesn't. And if it's happening for you both and you ignore it and put it off, it might just pass you by."

"Spoken like a man who actually has a heart." Logan stabs a finger right in the center of Archie's chest.

"Of course, I have a heart." Archie shoves Logan's hand away. "But I've also got a dick. And most of the time, it's more fun to listen to that."

26 /
quinn

NATHAN'S HOUSE is fully decorated.

Not in real life, of course. But based on the Pinterest board I spent all morning creating, there's not much left to design.

I let my creative juices loose, and the result is a modern farmhouse vision board with clean, contemporary lines, white oak woods, and pops of gold and black hardware that elevate things from rustic to present-day.

It's a place I could see myself living. I don't bother scolding myself for entertaining that brief thought. I've already beaten myself up enough over the conversation that definitely didn't need to occur last night. A girl can only take so much self-deprecation in a twenty-four-hour period. I'm going to extend myself some grace and press the pause button on that inner chastising dialogue for now.

But seriously, why did I feel the need to question Nathan's intentions with the rebuild? It isn't my place to insert my opinion into the life of a man I have no real ties to.

Plus, it's not like he's questioning my motivations for writing this silly book, even though I am each and every day.

Kimmie's right. I do feel the need to prove myself to my dad, which I realize is completely asinine because he's not even around to dole out his approval. Is it even my responsibility to carry out my father's legacy? Isn't it time I start creating my own?

I got an email from my agent this morning, asking me to send her my first draft within three weeks since she was heading out of the country at the end of the month and internet service would be spotty from then on. Twenty-one days. That's the number it takes to form a habit, I think. The routine of writing daily is one I've already established, but I commit to upping my wordcount and barreling toward the finish line, no looking back.

I spend the morning plunking the keyboard on my laptop and getting my characters closer to their happy-ever-after. It reads fine, but it's not the love story I'm currently interested in. Goodness, do I want things to move forward with Nathan. This pause—intermission—whatever it is, can't be good for my health because I feel like I'm about to explode, an over-inflated balloon ready to pop.

Around lunchtime, I decide to head to the sandwich shop in town that serves artisan subs with rare, rich cheeses and local jams and sauces. It's relatively new with an adorable young couple making everything fresh to order. Is it too presumptuous to grab a handful of extra sandwiches for the road? I figure the guys must be hungry and feeding them brings me this weird sense of joy.

Isn't the way to a man's heart through his stomach or something like that? I'm not going to overthink things here. I order four more sandwiches in case Jace is helping, too, and toss the brown paper bag into my passenger seat before pulling away from the curb.

It's beautiful outside today. Big, blue sky dotted with cotton candy clouds. I drive past the local community park and see some mommy-and-me playgroup gathered to take advantage of the sunshine. Toddlers waddle in the sandbox while their older siblings whip back and forth on swings and race down twisting slides. My light turns red, giving me some extra time to take in the sweet scene. Most parents look to be around Nathan's age. Established. Confident. Maybe even a little tired as they keep track of their brood, but happy all the same.

He says he doesn't want this, but Nathan is a nurturer. He can't help himself. And the thought of him with his own little family makes something scratch in my throat. It's not hard to visualize Nathan in this very moment, dusting off sandy knees or giving the merry-go-round a hearty push. He deserves this.

A car honks once behind me.

Lost in my reverie, I missed the light transitioning to green, so I press down on the pedal to get my car—and my thoughts—in gear.

I don't know when I'll be ready for a family. It might be ten years from now, and for me, that would be fine. I'm young. I have plenty of time. I know he said he could wait, but Nathan likely isn't thinking in decades.

When I show up with the sandwiches, you would have thought I had arrived with a four-course meal. The guys are beyond appreciative as they tear into the subs, talking around mouthfuls as they go on and on about my perfect timing.

"Nathan's one of those drill sergeants," Archer says, his elbow meeting my ribcage. "Said we couldn't eat until the house is completely done."

"That isn't even remotely close to what I said. I said once we finished hanging the drywall in the kitchen, we should think about grabbing some food." Nathan peels back the wrapper on his turkey sandwich. "You sure like to twist my words."

"Only because it gets you all twisted, and it's fucking fun to watch you get riled up."

I lift my hand to my mouth as I chew and speak behind it. "I can't believe the progress you guys have made."

"We'll be mudding and taping tomorrow," Jace chimes in. It's nice to see him working with Nathan again. He's always been a generous guy with a heart of gold, and I sometimes think that gets overlooked because his size often intimidates people, and they assume he's something he's not.

"From there, things should go pretty quickly," Nathan says. "I've got the county coming out soon to sign off on some stuff, and then I'll be ready for your creative help, Quinn."

"I might have already made an entire Pinterest board—complete with purchase links—full of my ideas." I make a face.

"Is that what you do for a living?" Logan asks. His sandwich is nearly gone.

"No. I'm actually an author."

"Anything I might have read?" Archer chucks his wrapper into a nearby trash bin filled with scrap boards and sheetrock, then lets out a silent roar of excitement when he makes the basket.

"I doubt it. I write mostly romance."

"And what makes you think I don't read romance?" His brows wiggle on his forehead. "My genre of choice, actually."

"I can't tell if you're kidding or not."

"He's not kidding," Logan confirms. "The smuttier, the better."

Nathan bends to pick up a hammer and loop it into his tool belt, but before he does, he waves it in my direction like he's pointing at me with it. "Maybe he's the one who should read your current work in progress."

Archer? Is Nathan seriously suggesting Archer read my book instead? Because I know what it led to when Nathan skimmed through my rough draft, and I can't imagine he'd insinuate I should do those things with Archer.

"I'd love to." Archer's face lights up, like this is an actual option.

"It's not really ready for anyone to read." I give Nathan a pointed look that he hangs onto for so long, it makes my eyes go dry. "But thanks for the offer."

"Absolutely."

The guys carry on discussing their current to-be-read piles, which I have to smile at because I did not know I was in the presence of such voracious bookworms. Nathan's right, of the four of them, he has the least interest in picking up a book. Despite that, he's the only one I want reading any part of mine, and I know the reason for that stems so much deeper than just wanting an extra eye on my draft.

"I should get going," I say once we've all finished eating. It's clear Nathan's ready to get back to work, though the rest of his crew doesn't seem as enthusiastic.

"I'll walk you out."

He follows silently on my heels but touches my elbow when we get to the edge of the driveway.

"I'm sorry." Those emotive green eyes collide with mine.

"For what?"

"For that whole thing I did back there, suggesting Archie read your stuff. That's obviously not what I want. I don't know why I said that."

"What *do* you want, Nathan?"

His gaze lifts skyward when his head falls back, shoulders sagging. "Sarah's in labor."

"What?"

"I just got a text from her mom that she's on her way to the hospital."

"Like, as we speak?"

His head drops, and he nods once. "Yeah."

"Wow." I honestly don't know what to say. "How does that make you feel?"

"I don't know." He cuffs the back of his neck. "I guess she's all by herself."

"Where's the father?"

"Not sure," he says. "Because apparently, she's not sure who the father even is."

My heart had been thumping at a disorienting rate, but now it's in my throat, clogging it completely. My eyes widen as understanding suddenly dawns. "Oh my God. It's yours."

"What?" Nathan looks like I've slapped him across his face. "Jesus Christ. No, it's still not mine. That's not even a possibility."

"So, she was cheating on you with multiple guys?" As soon as the words pass my lips, I recognize the unintended insensitivity in the statement.

"It would appear that way."

I touch his hand with my fingertips, needing some sort of connection. What I want to do is gather him into my arms. Hold him. Let him release whatever emotion he has stored up in whatever way he needs to.

But I pull back. "I'm so sorry, Nathan."

"Nothing for you to be sorry about."

"I can't apologize for something Sarah has done, but I can feel regret over the fact that it's hurt you. I care about you and don't want to see you like this." This time, I let myself take his hand fully into mine. "Is there anything I can do?"

"I just really need to get my mind off it. This whole thing is messing with my head."

"How can I help with that? Tell me what I can do."

He doesn't use the opportunity to flirt. I left him wide open for it, but he's hurting so much, there's not even room for the suggestive humor that has become second nature to us. This terrible woman just keeps breaking him.

"Can we hang out later this evening?" he finally asks. "We'll finish up here for the day in a few hours, and even though I know the boys mean well and will do their best to cheer me up, I'd rather have your company."

"Absolutely." I squeeze his hand. "Do you want me to plan something?"

"If you'd like to."

"Yes. I can do that. It's a date." The words are no sooner out of my mouth than I realize going on a date while his ex-wife is giving birth feels ill-fitting. "I mean, not a date-date, of course."

"I think I would actually like that, Quinn." There's a

spark back in his eye that was missing moments ago. "Let's go on a date."

"You sure you're up for that?"

"Honestly, I don't know what I'm up for. There's a chance that I'll be shit company and you'll never want to go out with me again, but who knows?" He shrugs one shoulder. "Maybe I'll surprise you."

I don't doubt that. Surprising me is one thing Nathan Caldwell keeps doing.

27 /
nathan

I'VE NEVER BEEN on a date that involved running shoes, but I've got to give it to Quinn, this is *exactly* what I needed.

I roll my wrist over to look at my smartwatch.

Mile three, and I feel like we're just getting started.

"Let's make a right up here." Quinn gestures toward the turn coming up ahead, where the road splits into two tree-lined directions. "There's a trail with benches where we can take a breather."

My shoes clap the pavement. My heart roars in my ears. And my head finally feels clear, a certified miracle considering all the junk that populated it just hours earlier.

Slowing up as we come to the first bench with one of those little dedication placards for someone named Mitchell Weatherby, Quinn paces in place to get her heart rate down, hands on hips, face upturned. A sheen of sweat coats her skin. Her breasts strain against her top as her lungs heave and I know I'm gawking, but it can't be helped.

I drop to the bench, out of breath for reasons other than just running.

"You good?"

"I am. Haven't raced like that since high school."

"I used to run a lot more than I do now. But every time I lace up my shoes, I never regret it. Even when I don't feel like running, I usually find that's when I need to." She leans back against the wooden slats. "And you know what else I never regret?"

"What's that?"

"Ice cream for dinner." The corners of her mouth tilt into a playful smirk. "And that is exactly what's next on our agenda."

"Ice cream?"

"Yep. Just a block down from the trailhead, there's a little lot where food trucks gather on Thursdays and Fridays. Nathan, we're going to drown our sorrows in sugar, chocolate syrup, and sprinkles."

But that's the bizarre thing. I'm not sad, even though I know my expression read that way earlier. Shocked. Confused. If I feel sad about anything, it's for Sarah's baby, because it's the only truly innocent one in all of this.

"Ice cream sounds perfect."

"I get that this isn't your conventional first date, but I don't know." Quinn's slender shoulders touch her ears. "I thought of all the things I would do if I were in your situation —the things that might make me happy and take my mind off everything—and since we're trying to get to know one another, I thought this might be a good way to show you that side of myself. But now that I'm saying all this out loud, I'm realizing it sounds somewhat selfish. It's your heartbreak we're trying to heal. Not mine."

"Not selfish at all. I want to get to know you better, Quinn. This is a great way." My hand comes down on her thigh in a gesture of reassurance that almost crosses the line into something else. "And I know this is going to sound unbelievable, but I'm not heartbroken."

"You just found out Sarah has been unfaithful to you with more than one guy. That must make you feel something."

"I feel a whole fucking lot. But oddly, heartbreak isn't one of the emotions." My hand is way too comfortable on her leg and if I let it stay there, I'll never want to remove it. I pull it back and fold it with my other in my lap. "Honestly—and I realize this is going to sound insane—but the main thing I feel right now is relief."

Doubt draws up Quinn's eyebrows in an arch over her questioning eyes. I get it. It doesn't make any sense.

"It's a relief to know I'm not the only man that couldn't satisfy whatever Sarah was looking for. All this time, I thought Donovan was filling some need in her I couldn't. But knowing she was with other men, even when she was with him? I don't know. That just shows the problem lies within herself, not with me."

"The problem was never with you, Nathan. When people cheat, it's for so many different reasons, but most often, it has little to do with the actual person they're cheating on."

"I'm seeing that now." I lean forward on the bench, elbows perched on my knees. "Hey, do you know much about basketball?"

"What?" My comment is out of left field, I know, and Quinn's not ready for it. "No. Not really."

"So, in basketball, there's this thing when a player shoots and misses, but it either hits the backboard or bounces off the rim. Basically, it doesn't make it into the net because it wasn't on the right path toward the basket."

Quinn's head slants in concentration.

"When that happens, there's the chance to score again. It's called a rebound." I angle my head to look over my shoulder at her. "In basketball, a rebound is a really good thing. It's another opportunity to make the basket. To come at it from a different angle. To recover from the previously missed shot, take a step back, and get things right the second time around," I explain. "We've been saying it this whole time like it's a bad thing, but I *want* you to be my rebound, Quinn, because it means something different to me. It's not that I'm rebounding with you because I'm not over my ex, or because I can't be alone, or because I'm looking for you to heal something broken within me. I want to rebound with you because my life wasn't on the right path before, and now I have a shot to get things right with you. I've learned what didn't work, I'm in a different place, and I'm ready to give love another chance."

I can see the confession settling in, see the process it takes for the things I've said to move from my mouth to Quinn's head, and finally settle somewhere deeper in her being.

"Damn, you have all the words, Nathan." Her lips bow into a smirk, then a full-fledged grin. "Maybe I should just give you my laptop and have you write the book."

"The only romance I'm interested in writing is my own, and the only other person I want to share it with is you."

Then, wordlessly, Quinn reaches for my hand, her fingers gently closing over mine, and we sit silently until all that exists in this space and this moment is us.

"You have a little something." She runs her thumb along my bottom lip. "There. Got it."

For good measure, I sweep my tongue out to wipe away any leftover chocolate syrup.

Ice cream for dinner should be normalized. Every other time I've had ice cream, it's been as a treat or a dessert, not an entire meal. Tonight, I don't hold back. I get the triple scoop, complete with banana split, whipped cream, and extra cherries, which Quinn quickly seizes for herself.

"Three scoops of vanilla?" Quinn wrinkles her nose. "Not feeling super adventurous, are we?"

"Do you not see all these sprinkles?" I wave the loaded bowl beneath her face. "It's like a unicorn exploded on it."

"Is that what unicorns are made of?" She plucks another cherry from its stem, making a delicious popping sound with her mouth. "I always thought they were made of rainbows."

"These are *rainbow* sprinkles," I add, sticking by my earlier assertion. "And it's fucking magical." Digging in, I shovel another spoonful of the cool treat into my mouth.

Quinn runs her tongue along her single scoop of coffee ice cream as she twirls the cone in her grip. Honest to God, my dick jolts, wishing it could trade places just for a second, because that's all it would take.

We walk back with our ice creams in hand rather than eat them quickly and run because 1.) the side-ache situation is real and 2.) it's getting dark out and we don't have long until the sun slips completely from the sky. We need to walk and talk, eat and move.

We've got one mile left to go when my phone buzzes. Must be Archie or Logan, letting me know they've made it home safely. Before I left this evening, they told me they would clear the next three weekends to come back and help with the rebuild. It's not something I would have ever asked of them on my own, but I'm damn grateful for their continued generosity.

I balance the ginormous sundae in one hand and fish my cell phone out of my pocket with the other.

Not Archie.

Not Logan.

Sarah.

I feel like I've just been punched in the balls.

"Everything okay?" Quinn laps at her ice cream as it melts down the side of the cone in a sticky trail.

"False labor."

"Sarah?" There's a hitch in Quinn's step, a falter she tries hard to recover. "I hear that's pretty common with first time pregnancies."

I jam the phone into my pocket, wishing I could stuff away my frustration, too, but it's so big there's no place for it to go. "I don't know why she feels like that's information I need to know."

I wish she hadn't texted me. Of course, she had been in the back of my mind all evening. It's a little impossible not to think about something that life-altering. Birth is a big deal.

"Probably because she knew her mother had messaged you and that you'd be curious about how things went."

"I'm not curious."

Quinn's feet plant. "Nathan, of course you are. I'm curious, for goodness' sake, and I don't even know the woman."

"It would be so much easier if she just kept it all to herself. Moved on with her life and left me completely out of it."

"Sure, but isn't a small part of you glad to be in the loop? You're a caretaker by nature, Nathan. And before you go worrying that I'm threatened by that or think that maybe you still have feelings for Sarah because of it, don't. I saw the way you came to Kyle's aid, and I know for a fact that you can't stand the guy. You just can't help yourself. It's who you are."

"So, I'm the consummate caretaker, huh? What does that make you?"

"Well, if you ask Kimmie, I'm a people pleaser. And I can't say she's wrong there. I have this inherent need to make the people around me happy."

"I wouldn't say you have to work too hard at that. I, for one, can't help but be anything but happy around you."

"I appreciate that, and with us, it doesn't feel toxic because it's reciprocal. But in other relationships—especially with my parents—I would say it tiptoes into the unhealthy realm."

I flip my spoon over to pull off the ice cream packed into it with my bottom teeth. "How so?"

"House-sitting, for starters. I don't want to upset my mom by telling her what a monkey wrench it has thrown into my life. She's happy in Italy, possibly even finding love. It's easier to just go along with it."

"But what about you? Don't you want to please yourself?"

Quinn registers the innuendo before I do, her eyes turning into silver dollars.

"I don't mean like pleasure yourself." Laughter brackets my words. "What I mean is, isn't your happiness important, too?"

"It is. But it can wait."

"I'm not sure if you recognize it, but that's what we've been doing, too. Delaying happiness."

Quinn's eyes swing over to mine. "You think?"

"I do. But I get it. And I don't want to rush it. I will not ask you to change who you are, Quinn. And when it comes down to it, I want to please you, too."

I let those words sink in, landing somewhere between vulnerability and insinuation, right where I intend for them to.

I want to make her happy. Emotionally. Physically. I want every part of Quinn to be satisfied. And right now, based on the sweet look on her face as she licks her ice cream cone and walks side by side next to me, I'd say I'm doing a pretty decent job.

28 /
quinn

TWO WEEKS GO BY, and Nathan and I have shared at least a half dozen dates in that time. We've done the traditional things like gone to the movies, out for coffee, or stayed in to curl up on the couch as we binged home design shows that provided so much inspiration, I pulled out my notepad to jot down ideas while the episode aired.

As always, I've enjoyed being with him, but each time he leaves, something in me deflates when he doesn't go in for a kiss. I figured we would have worked back up to that by now, but Nathan's not only taking things slow, he's seemingly moving in reverse.

I understand. He's tired. He's at the stage with the remodel where he's up with the sun and finishing well past dark. It's physically exhausting work. On the weekends, his buddies join him, and they work triple time, knocking out the really labor-intensive things like flooring and baseboards. Anything that requires more than two hands.

Last night, Nathan even mentioned listing the place soon. I don't know why, but when he said it, the fine hairs on the back of my neck prickled, a shiver moving along my spine.

Logically, I know this is the next step in the process. But I'm not ready for someone else to live in the space I've gotten so used to Nathan inhabiting. When I ask him where he plans to go, his answers are always vague.

"Wherever my next project takes me."

Things are up in the air. With the house. With us.

But we'll need to make some decisions soon, and it's a discussion I can't keep putting off if I want to maintain any semblance of sanity.

Today, I spent the morning writing a few chapters that I sent off to Nathan before lunchtime. He has been keeping up as I write, offering sound advice that truly elevates the story. I'm still not in love with where it's going, but as my agent says, you can't edit a blank page, so I'm grateful just to have some words—any words—to work with.

As I'm returning my laptop to the coffee table, I glance over at Geronimo curled up next to me on the couch cushion in a swirl that makes him look like a furry cinnamon roll. Silly cat. I give him a gentle nudge.

Normally, that would be met with a paw swiping at me, claws bared, but he hardly flinches as I push along his spine just a little more aggressively.

"Geri?" I jostle him. "Geri? You okay, buddy?"

The cat slowly rotates his face toward me, his chin covered in drool that I immediately register as a bad sign.

"Oh no, Geri. What did you get into?"

Curling my hand under his belly, I lift him off the couch, but he's a limp noodle, all dangling legs and hanging head.

He lets out a low moan that tries to sound like a meow but fails.

"Shit."

I scroll on my phone, tapping my foot as I wait for Nathan to pick up.

"Hey, Quinn. What's up?"

"Nathan, something's wrong with Geri."

"I'll be right over."

I'm not even sure he's had time to hang up the phone, Nathan arrives at my doorstep so fast.

"What's going on?" He's already moving toward the downstairs hall closet where Mom keeps the cat carriers. He rustles around and retrieves the largest one.

"I thought he was just sleeping, but he's acting really lethargic and sort of salivating in this weird way that isn't normal for him."

"Have you called the vet?" With two hands, Nathan withdraws Geri from my arms and gingerly places him inside the carrier, then latches it. The cat doesn't even try to hiss, sign number two that things are going from bad to worse, and quickly.

"Not yet."

"Okay. We can do that on the way."

We're in the car in a flash and seated in the waiting room at the veterinarian's office in no time flat. I try not to look at all the other sad pets surrounding us because I really don't feel like crying and an animal in distress triggers the waterworks for me. I blame *Marley & Me*.

"You okay?" Nathan's arm moves over the back of my chair, and he draws me into his side.

"My mom will never forgive me if I kill her cat."

"First off, you haven't killed her cat. And second, I'm sure your mother understands that things like this happen. Animals get sick. Geronimo's lucky you were there. And he's in the best hands possible. We got him here quickly. The vet even said that."

I know Nathan's right, but irrational guilt consumes me. I had one job—keep the cats safe—and I failed to do that. Well, two jobs: take care of the cats and water Mom's ferns. I've done a piss-poor job with both.

"Hey." His thumb moves to my chin and tilts up. "Don't cry."

I shove the sleeve of my shirt to my cheeks and sniff. "I don't know why I'm crying."

"He's going to be okay."

I don't think I'm crying over Geronimo. Not entirely, at least. It's this man next to me, the one who dropped everything to take his feline nemesis to the vet because he instantly recognized the distress in my voice.

I'm a big girl. I know I can do these things on my own, but at this moment, it hits me I *don't* want to do them alone anymore. I want Nathan to be the person I call when things go sideways. Today, tomorrow, and for as long as possible.

"Nathan, the thought of you no longer being right next door might have a little something to do with the tears."

He leans back so he can fully take me in. "I'm not going anywhere yet, Quinn."

"I know you're not. But this situation isn't permanent; me at my mom's and you at the fixer upper."

"I know."

"So, where will that leave us?"

I expect this to kick off a brainstorming session, but Nathan's face remains blank.

"Have you given any more thought to where you might end up once the house sells?" I ask as a prompt.

"Yeah, I have. I've been thinking about it more lately since that timeline is getting closer." His fingers mindlessly stroke my shoulder while he talks. "I still have my job at the middle school, and Archie owns an apartment complex in the city that he said I could rent a room out of. I think that's going to be my best route."

"You're thinking of going back home?" My eyes begin to water all over again.

"It's the only viable option I have right now."

"So, then..." I swallow forcefully. "This? Us? This is just a blip?"

"It's not a blip, Quinn. We can do the long-distance thing. It's not that far."

"I'll be back at my condo. That adds another two hours."

"We can make it work."

"Should we, though?"

He pins me with a staggered look. "Why wouldn't we?"

The door suddenly opens, and a vet tech dressed in turquoise scrubs with pink hearts steps into the waiting room, clipboard in hand. "Is the owner of Geronimo here?"

It takes a moment to locate my voice. "Yes. Right here."

I stand from the chair, swaying as my head goes light.

"Careful." Nathan's hand moves to the small of my back.

We are guided down the hallway and into a room where the doctor waits for us with a very drugged up Geronimo.

The vet delivers the good news, but it's just mumbled words that tinker around in my brain and never quite untangle. Something about a toxic houseplant, dehydration, and a prescription that should make Geri feel better in a few days.

Those fucking ferns.

"Well, that's the best-case scenario, right?" Nathan looks across the car toward me once we're back on the road. When I don't respond, he picks up my hand, pulling it closer to rest on the center console between us. "Hey. You okay?"

"I'm not sure. I don't know why I'm so emotional lately."

"Today was a big scare. I get it. That little furball even got my heart racing."

Sure, seeing Geronimo so sick was distressing, but the news that Nathan might go back to Fairvale is what prompted my current unraveling.

He'll be back in his hometown.

Working his old job.

Hanging out with the people he used to hang out with.

Falling into the same routine.

And he'll be close to Sarah again.

I'm not sure why, but when I thought she had started this new life with a new man and a little one on the way, that provided me with a level of certainty that she was out of Nathan's life for good.

But now she'll be a single mother, and even though I don't know her, I can only imagine she'll be tempted to lean on Nathan. I don't worry about him falling for her again—she's hurt him too badly for that—but I also have a feeling he won't be able to stand by and let her struggle all on her own. That's not who he is.

If she were to call him in the middle of the night with a

colicky baby she couldn't comfort, would he really be able to ignore that?

From what I know of him, no.

And maybe it's not my place to ask him to.

Nathan drops me off at Mom's with Geronimo, and I throw away every freaking plant within the house. Most are dead already, anyway. There's something strangely satisfying about chucking the brittle ferns into the trash, dirt clods tumbling out of the plastic containers as the roots separate and stems snap.

The cats sit at my feet throughout the entire ordeal, yellow eyes wide.

"No more fern munching on my watch, kitties."

After I fill their dinner bowls, deciding it's been a hell of a day and that they deserve wet food, I pour myself a glass of wine that threatens to spill over the rim when I walk upstairs to my bedroom to slip under the covers and review my latest chapters.

Not going to lie, the reality that Nathan has these words in his possession makes my armpits sweat.

My characters haven't had sex, but this is where she finally gives him a blowjob, and let me just say, the woman's got mad cock-sucking skills.

I should have given Nathan a warning, so he at least had the option to gloss over this part.

Hoping it's not too late to issue one, I pull out my phone.

> Me: Skip chapter fifteen if you haven't already.

I bite my lower lip when the dots pulse on the screen almost immediately.

> Nathan: Too late.

Shit.

> Me: I'm sorry. I hope you don't think differently about me. It's all fiction, remember?

> Nathan: I have some suggestions for edits.

Double shit.

> Nathan: You around if I come by and give them to you?

It's suddenly sweaty armpit central around here, and I practically break out in hives. I'm gnawing on my cheek at this point. Every inch of my skin crawls.

> Me: Yeah. I'm around.

That's all I can say.

You know that grimacing emoji? The one with two dots for eyes and that row of clenched teeth? My face is literally its doppelgänger right now. I can feel the tension in my jaw, the rounding of my shocked eyes.

Immobilized by fear, embarrassment, or maybe an equal combination of the two, I can't move from my bedroom when I hear his knock on the door downstairs.

Me: It's open. I'm in my room. You can come up.

I close my eyes. I'm not the praying type, but I start mumbling into the void, demanding to get swallowed up by the mattress whole so I don't have to sit through a lesson on how to write a sexy BJ. It might very well be the death of me.

I hear Nathan ascend the stairs and move down the hall. He raps on the open bedroom door with a single knuckle.

"Knock, knock."

"Oh." I down a mouthful of wine. Damn. That burns. "Hey. Come in."

"Sorry." He looks around the room. "I didn't realize you were already in bed."

"I'm not," I say. "I mean, I *am*, I guess. Like, I'm *literally* in bed. But I'm not asleep or anything. This isn't me sleep talking. I'm totally coherent. Wide awake."

And completely off my rocker.

Nathan chuckles. "Gotcha. Just winding down, huh?"

"It's wine-down time!" I thrust the glass into the air. Stupid thing to do, because purple liquid sloshes around, twisting out of the top like a whirlpool. My comforter is a Barbera bloodbath. "Crap."

"I'll get a towel to clean that up."

"Don't bother." I whip the quilt off the bed. Yep, totally forgot that I'm in just an oversized t-shirt and socks. No pants land in full effect.

Nathan's eyes travel toward my bare legs. "It feels like maybe I shouldn't be here."

"Why?" He's seen me in this exact outfit before, so I don't understand the sudden hesitation.

And that's when I see it in all its purple silicon glory.

"Oh my God." I scramble for the rogue vibrator and chuck it into my nightstand. The drawer slams so hard, the lamp teeters. "I wasn't using that."

"It's okay if you were."

"I *promise*, I wasn't. I didn't even know it was in there."

"It's kind of hot, Quinn."

I pinch the center of my shirt and tug on the fabric. "It is hot in here, right?"

"No. I mean, it's hot to see you with that."

Where are we going with this? Because he hasn't even so much as kissed me in the last few weeks, and here we are, talking about stray sex toys.

"You said you had some suggestions for the recent chapter I sent?" My voice fractures on a hiccup.

That I'm willingly pivoting the conversation toward blowjob talk just shows how utterly mortifying this entire encounter has become. I will not be betrayed by a forty-dollar G-spot vibrator. Not today.

"I do have some suggestions." He nods slowly and moves a step closer. "Not sure where I should start."

I'm not sure, either. How does one begin an oral copulation convo?

"Can I sit?" His gaze redirects toward the bed.

"Yeah." I guess this is going to be a lengthy lecture. Oh, joy. I shimmy over to make room. "Of course."

The mattress dips as he presses a knee down and then lowers so he's in front of me. "Before I dive in, I want to talk about something you brought up today."

I feared I was already experiencing tachycardia with my elevated heart rate, but now it thrums even harder for a completely different reason. At what rate does it self-combust, if that's a thing? Because I'm definitely testing the limits of normal heart function here. "What was that?"

"When you said maybe we shouldn't continue this"—he waves his hand in the gap between us—"once I've moved."

I hastily rake a hand through my hair, tempted to rip it out by its roots. "It's just that I sometimes wonder if this is only temporary for us. You know, like a summer fling."

Hurt edges into his eyes, and even though the lighting is dim, I can see the turmoil my words create.

"This is not a fling for me, Quinn. I hope over these last few weeks together, I've made it clear that I'm trying to build a solid foundation for a relationship with you."

My mind travels back to all the moments we've shared. The commonplace things we've done, like pushing carts around the grocery store side by side or combining our laundry in my mother's washer, sorting out and pairing off socks while we rocked out to 80s hair band music. We've made each other laugh, we've sat in comfortable silence, and we've talked late into the night about our upbringings, our most embarrassing adolescent moments, and even the fears we've never felt comfortable sharing with anyone else.

In every sense, we've become closer, both in our friendship and with our feelings.

"I'm ready to take things to the next level with you, Quinn. I'm tired of putting off what might be the best thing to ever happen to me." His voice is ragged, emotionally raw. "I'm certainly not entertaining the idea of ending what we've started simply because we won't share the same zip code anymore."

Nathan crawls over the bed, stalking toward me, heated determination in his eyes.

My breaths quicken when his face comes close, and a gasp releases between my lips mere seconds before his are on mine. I don't mean to moan into his mouth, but the relief that washes over me is uncontainable.

This has been a long time coming.

My hands are in his hair; he gathers me into his arms. We pause long enough to really look at one another, to recognize the matching desire reflected in our expressions and in something deeper. Something that feels a lot like the center of my soul.

Then our lips collide, tongues plunging into each other's eager mouths.

This kiss is more than just the beginning of a really great make-out session. It's the unspoken confirmation I need in order to trust things are going to be okay between us.

That we're finally all in.

Nathan's hands grip my backside to lift me onto his lap. I'm clumsy and uncoordinated, but I cross my ankles behind him, my head falling against the headboard as his mouth trails unhurriedly down the slope of my neck, alternating licks and kisses as he moves.

When he comes to the collar of my shirt, he draws back and looks up.

"This needs to go."

I couldn't agree more. I wrestle out of it and make the decision that he's also wearing too many clothes. With my help, he discards his t-shirt to the foot of the bed.

"Much better," he says when we come back together.

My nipples scrape against his bare chest, making them

instantly hard. Wow. That felt good. A shiver of delight spreads through me in a tremble that jiggles my breasts.

The grin on Nathan's face in reaction to the sight is downright adorable.

"Tit appreciation time?" I decode his expression, maybe a little too impatient for the answer.

"You fucking know it."

He presses his full lips to the swell of my breasts, and I lean back to give him better access. Unhurriedly, Nathan plays with my nipples, rolling his fingers gently over them, pinching before sweeping his thumbs back and forth over their peaks. Like he can read my mind, he lowers his head and lets his tongue take over, and he sucks one beaded nipple until I sift my hands into his hair and guide him to the other to continue his adoration.

I swear, just Nathan's tongue flicking over me is enough to make me come. There is a low flutter in my belly, a weightless sensation that rolls through my core.

"You like that, don't you?" His warm breath hits my skin, eyes locked with mine while his tongue resumes teasing.

"Yes." It's a hissy sound from my lips. "I love it."

He drags his mouth from one aching nipple to the other, then reaches between us to take my hand. He places it over my breast.

"Play with yourself," he directs. "I don't want to neglect any part of you while I'm busy over here."

There's just enough command in his tone that I don't feel shy about taking my nipple between my fingers and lightly twisting. God, it feels good.

My eyelids flutter. The sensation and the visual of his lips on me while I pluck my nipple is almost unbearable in the very best way. And it's then I understand why he wants me to feel myself up while he's also cupping my breast.

So he has a free hand to do other things.

His fingers slip low and tease the waistband of my underwear, swiping along my hip bone, back and forth. It's torture and delight mingled with each lazy stroke. Anticipation builds like a tempest churning inside me, and my stomach hollows out on an uneven breath.

"You good?"

"Yes." I'm fast to answer. I don't want him to stop for one second. "So good."

He works the heel of his hand over my panties. In no time, he's going to discover the evidence of my arousal. I worry I should be embarrassed, but when his finger moves along the soaked fabric and an approving groan rumbles from the depths of his chest, I let go of any shame or uncertainty. He's obviously pleased with his discovery.

"You're always so ready. So responsive." He hooks my panties to the side, and a single finger glides along my slit. "Fuck, Quinn. So wet for me."

Nathan's mouth returns to my breast as his finger curls up to my clit and then back down without ever slipping fully inside. I writhe beneath his touch, needing more. Even with my own fingers pinching my nipple, his mouth moving at my breast, and his hand rubbing against my most sensitive spot, it's not enough. There's an edge that I've reached and I'm hovering so close, but I can't get to where I need to be.

Nathan knows.

He stops what he's doing, and he yanks me forward quickly, then bends me back onto the mattress before taking my hands in his, pinning them up by my head while his mouth journeys down my body.

I can't keep from squirming.

"Nathan?" His name catches roughly in my throat. "What are you doing?"

"I told you I had some suggestions for that recent chapter you sent over." He lets go of my hands and follows the curves of my body until he gets to my thighs, gripping on. Those full, tempting lips plant a featherlight kiss just below my belly button. "I'm doing a little editing."

29 /
nathan

THE WHOLE TIME I was reading Quinn's latest chapter, I wondered what this guy did to deserve a blowjob without even thinking of going down on his girl first. In my opinion, Quinn got that part backward. Maybe a little of her people pleasing tendencies infiltrated their way into the novel, but I'm about to set that straight.

"Nathan." Her anxious fingers tangle through my hair, attempting to pull me back up. "You don't have to."

"I fucking *want* to." To make that crystal clear, I dip lower and swipe my tongue along the inside edge of her panties. "Are you okay with that?"

Quinn's teeth roll over her bottom lip as her hips involuntarily arch upward. She releases a shallow moan. "Yes."

"Good," I murmur against her skin.

I take her underwear and drag slowly. To help me, Quinn wiggles until they're far enough down her legs that she can kick them off. Whatever inhibition she initially harbored is gone now that she's draped across the bed completely and exquisitely bare before me. She's fucking breathtaking. I want to stare at her—take in every perfect inch of her delicate curves, her soft pale skin—but I have more pressing matters that involve her seeing stars and losing her goddamn mind.

I come back and gently run my nose along her inner thigh. I feel like I've waited a lifetime for this moment.

I sense her legs clench, her body ready but apprehensive all the same.

I get it. This moment is intimate. I'm just grateful she trusts me enough to do this with her. To satisfy her in this way.

"Spread your legs for me, Quinn."

Her chest rises with a big breath. "I'm trying." A hand flies up to her eyes, covering them. "I'm sorry. I feel sort of exposed."

"You are." I grip her ass firmly, my fingers pressing into her flesh to keep her in place. "But you're so damn beautiful. Every single part of you."

She whimpers. Has no one ever told her this before? I suddenly feel the need to make up for every idiot in her life that made her feel anything less than the goddess she is. I've used my tongue to speak it aloud, and now I'm going to use it to convey that truth in another way.

Holding her still, I press my lips to her pelvis, testing to see how willing she is to give up control and let me devour her in the way I want to. In the way I need to.

She bucks up to meet me.

Alright. We're doing this.

I push her knees out farther on either side, and in one long stroke, I run my tongue over her from her entrance to her clit, pausing when she quakes against my mouth.

"Nathan." Her head thrashes on the pillow. "Oh my God."

"How does that make you feel?" I rub my chin against her hip bone and prop myself up to look into her hooded eyes.

"Amazing."

I do it again, but this time, I don't wait for her reaction before I repeat, licking her arousal over and over. I've thought about tasting her for so long, it's hard to believe this is actually happening. I want to get lost in the moment, but I also want to remember every hitch in her breath, every tremble of her body, every gasp and moan and cry she makes as I bring her to that promised place of euphoria.

"Yes," she groans in the sultriest voice ever to meet my ears. "Oh God. Right there. Don't stop."

I suck on her clit, then let the tip of my tongue flick across it again and again before sucking some more.

"Nathan." Her hands shoot down to the back of my head, pushing me deeper. I spear my tongue inside her and Quinn's entire body tenses. She's close.

When I suddenly pull back and get to my feet at the edge of the bed, I think she's going to throw something at me. The look of sheer frustration sends a chuckle straight through my chest.

"What?" Her mouth pops open. "Wait. Where are you going?"

I don't answer. I move toward her nightstand, and that frustration instantly morphs into disappointment.

"Nathan. I don't have any condoms here."

I slide open the top drawer. "Not what I'm looking for."

She props herself up, her eyes going wide when I pull out her vibrator and then quietly shut the drawer back into place.

"I can't..." Her hair whips all around her gorgeous body, head shaking vigorously with doubt. "I won't last."

"You will." I walk back to the foot of the bed.

"I don't think I can."

"Quinn, you will. And you won't come until I tell you to."

She wets her bottom lip, nodding apprehensively but conveying her trust.

I flip the vibrator on. "What setting do you prefer?" It buzzes in my hand.

"I don't know." She can't form thoughts, but I understand. Her body is filled with so much need, she can't interpret anything other than her demand for a release.

"Let's find out."

She's so wet. I slip the toy inside without too much resistance. When it bottoms out, she flinches.

"You okay?"

"Yeah." Her neck arches. I move the vibrator around but stop when she lets out a yelp. "Oh, shit. That's it. Right there."

"And is this speed okay?" I keep it on the original setting for a moment before clicking into a higher gear. "Or this?"

"Holy fuck. Yep, that's the one."

"What about now?" I press the button again. "Too much?"

Quinn inhales sharply, all choppy and erratic. "I don't know." Her legs start to shake. "It might be."

Wanting her to last and be able to drag out every ounce of her pleasure, I lower it back down a level and hold the device inside before withdrawing slightly and pressing it in deeper than before.

"Nathan." She's grasping at the sheets, fisting the fabric in her hands, legs kicking out.

"Keep still," I instruct. "Do you want me to continue?"

"Yes." It's almost a shout. "God, yes. Please, don't stop," she begs. "Please."

I don't. I keep the vibrator in place while I maneuver Quinn on the mattress to bring her closer to the edge, so I have a better position for what I'm about to do. Then I get on my knees.

Her hands keep clawing at the bed, needing something to grip onto.

"Play with your tits again."

She doesn't hesitate. She grabs each one, squeezing and clutching her chest while she moans loudly.

Shit. I'm about to blow my load and my cock hasn't even been touched yet.

This is the most sensual thing I've ever witnessed, ever done. How is this real life?

Quinn rolls her nipples between her fingers, her mouth open as she gasps from everything we're putting her body through. I almost forget what I'm about to do, the uninhibited sight of her so disarming. Snapping my head, I refocus my attention and drive the toy in and out.

"That feels so good," she cries. "So good. I'm not going to last much longer."

"Not yet."

I have to angle the vibrator to make room, but once I position it just right, I lower my mouth and bring my lips to her clit.

"Oh!" Her entire body lurches.

My free hand moves inside my shorts and grasps my erection. It's not going to take long on my end, but when Quinn finally reaches her climax, I want to be right there with her. *Need* to be right there with her.

I let the vibrator work her from the inside while my tongue continues flicking over her sensitive bundle of nerves, back and forth, up and down. Her sounds, her taste. It's going to be my undoing.

Pumping my fist over my length in rhythm with the vibrator plunging in and out, I make quick circles with my tongue as she builds closer to her orgasm.

We're both breathing hard, moaning, grunting, and sighing our pleasure.

Almost there.

I pick up speed and slide my fist up and down my cock frantically while my tongue laps at her pussy.

"Nathan." My name is a request for permission. She's holding on by a fucking thread. "Please?"

I yank out the vibrator.

My mouth instantly covers her, licking and sucking and swirling my tongue while Quinn's hips thrust to meet me. I let her fuck my face and savor every goddamn minute of it. With a sharp cry, she falls over the edge, her body shaking and shuddering as she pulses against my tongue.

"God, Nathan. Yes!"

I grip my dick with both hands and come hard to the sound of her screaming my name.

My mouth stays on her until the very last tremor of her orgasm ripples through her body and she's limp, boneless with exhausted pleasure.

Barely able to breathe myself, I fall back onto my heels.

Once all of our sounds have quieted and our panting

levels out, I finally ask, "You alive up there?" I clean myself up with my discarded t-shirt and move to my feet.

Quinn is curled into a tiny, satiated ball, her voice all dreamy when she says, "Honestly? Not sure."

I'm certain I already know the answer, but I ask the question still. "Did you like my rewrite?"

She pulls the pillow out from beneath her head and smothers her face. I chuckle when she lets out a little muffled scream, then drops the pillow to her chest. "Are you kidding me? I've never experienced anything like that in my life."

"In a good way?" I find her underwear all tangled in the sheets and pass it to her.

"In a phenomenal way."

She makes room for me in bed. Are we doing the post-sex cuddling thing? Because if we are, I'm all for it. To invite me closer, her head lifts so I can slide my arm under it, and she curls against my side, hiking a leg over my thigh. Once we're both comfortably settled in, Quinn's finger draws lazy figure eights across my chest.

"Nathan?"

"Hmm?" I press a kiss to the crown of her hair.

"Did you ever imagine you'd be taking care of two pussies in one day?"

Oh my God, this woman. I can't get enough of her.

"I gotta say," she continues. Her fingernail skates lightly across my skin. "I think between myself and Geronimo, I'm the more appreciative of the two."

My hand smooths over her hair. She smells like mint and lavender and sex, and I inhale the intoxicating scent deeply, making my chest rise. "I don't know," I play along. "We did save Geronimo's life."

"That's true. And you just tried to kill me. Death by orgasm."

"There are worse ways to go, I suppose."

I kiss her forehead. I want my lips on Quinn all the time.

Her hand pauses its exploration. "I'm afraid to ask, but how did you learn to do all of that?"

Damn, I hope that's not a hint of insecurity I detect. She has absolutely nothing to be worried about. This was a first for me, too.

"I just listened to your body and what you needed. And I might have picked up a few pointers from all of those spicy books you made me read. I promise, that's not something I've ever done in that way, either. I wasn't sure if you would like it."

"Like it?" She goes a little rigid. "Nathan, that was hands down the world's best orgasm. You deserve a medal, or possibly even a monument named after you. At the very least, a gold star."

"High praise."

"What can I say? I call it like I see it. Or feel it, rather." She lifts her chin and kisses me on the mouth, sweet and slow. "I know I was the one who put the brakes on everything, but I'm kicking myself for that now. Imagine if we had been doing *that* these last few weeks. I feel like I should have taken advantage of the naughty neighbor situation we've got going on."

"I think we're doing everything just right." I move my hand to her breast. I've officially decided tit appreciation is a twenty-four-seven type of thing. "Plus, we've got time. I'm not going anywhere yet."

She just sighs, but I note the apprehension there.

"Hey." I need to cheer her up. "What do you say we make some final decisions about the house tomorrow? I'd love to get the fixtures and lighting ordered."

"Yeah? That would be fun. I have tons of ideas and I can't wait to see them come to life."

We spend the next hour scanning through inspiration pictures on her phone. I lean up against the headboard and she sits between my legs, her back to my chest in a way that lets me rest my chin on the top of her head. In every scenario, we just fit together.

If I'm honest, I think I'm falling in love with Quinn.

Yes, the whole intimacy side of everything is great, but her joy is infectious. Her excitement, catching. When she shows me each photo, her voice gets higher, and she talks fast in this endearing way that just makes me smile.

I knew demoing the house was what my head needed to process my new stage of life.

It just never occurred to me that rebuilding it with Quinn was what my soul might need.

30 /
quinn

I COULD NOT BE MORE excited.

Okay. That's a lie. I was pretty damn excited last night when Nathan brought me to the brink of death via orgasm.

The man has some serious tongue-action skills. Skills I want to explore all freaking day long, but we've got home décor on the docket and that's what currently has me riled up.

I have visions. Concepts. Honestly, at this point, they should just give me my own HGTV show. My mind is overflowing with shiplap possibilities and marble countertop makeovers.

And Nathan has given me free rein. As in, *here's-the-credit-card, purchase-what-you-think-we'll-need* freedom.

Last night, when I was showing him a handful of my ideas, he just kept nodding and smiling, nodding and smiling. Sure, it might have had something to do with his own handful of boob at the time, but the guy is easily agreeable. What can I say?

He slept in my room but was up early to give Geronimo his medicine and whip up a scrambled egg and bacon breakfast that he plated and brought upstairs for me to enjoy in bed. I could get used to this. Not the whole living in my mom's house part but settling into a routine with Nathan.

I dress quickly, pairing my favorite cutoffs with a Smashing Pumpkins 1997 concert shirt my mother had in a pile for Goodwill. Lip gloss and a little mascara are all I need because I swear my cheeks are still flushed from last night's orgasmic exploits. Sneakers laced, teeth brushed, and hair twisted into a loose bun, I shove my phone into my back pocket and my notebook under my arm to head next door, ready to get things underway.

Am I too old to skip? Because my feet are tempted to as I cross the distance between Nathan's house and mine. There's a float to my step, a lightness in my being that I attribute to good sex and the prospect of unconstrained creativity. My two favorite things.

I expect Nathan to be in the garage where he spent most of yesterday sorting through the last salvageable pieces of hardwood. He has the dumpster scheduled for pickup later this afternoon, and I know he's trying to cram any remaining pieces of debris and unwanted materials in before the hulking thing is gone from the driveway for good.

Even though the garage door is open, Nathan's nowhere to be found.

I open the door leading into the interior of the house. Instantly, I hear Nathan's voice, coupled with others. But it doesn't sound like Archer and Logan, or even Jace.

It's a man and a woman. The woman's pitch is too high, her inflection too excitable. And the man is equally eager.

Whoever they are, they're much too giddy for this early hour. I didn't realize I would need coffee for this.

"Hey!" I shout around the corner. It's one of those situations where I recognize they are already deep in conversation, and I feel the need to announce myself before butting in with my presence first.

"In the kitchen!" Nathan hollers back.

I follow the recently drywalled hallway toward their voices.

I have no clue who this couple is, but the way they look at me with huge eyes and cartoonishly large smiles leads me to believe I'm missing something.

"Quinn," Nathan says, moving toward me to take my hand. "Meet Becca and Ryan. They're currently renting a house up the street and popped in on their morning walk."

For pleasantry's sake, I shake their hands and reflect the goofy smiles still plastered to their faces.

Nathan's fingers thread tighter over mine. "They're interested in the house."

"Oh." I fumble back, visibly faltering. "Wow. That's great. Yeah?"

"It's wonderful." Becca's voice is so breathy, it reminds me of my manufactured cadence back when I was a fairytale princess. "I can't believe how lucky we were to find this house before the finishing touches were put in place. It gives us the opportunity to make it entirely our own. A totally blank canvas."

That's when I understand why Nathan still has a secure hold on my hand. So I won't drop right onto the floor in complete disillusionment.

"They're interested in purchasing the house as-is," he

says softly, like I needed any clarification. My face might be blank, but my emotions aren't. I'm experiencing too many to convey, so it must look like I've short-circuited.

"And with a cash offer well above market value and a quick two-week escrow," Ryan chimes in, clearly Mr. Money-bags in this equation. He's too proud as he presents this information.

"Two weeks?" I'm hoarse with shock.

"Maybe less," Ryan boasts.

I turn to Nathan. "Can you excuse me for a second?" I wriggle my hand out of his and head for the door.

I hear Nathan mumble, "I'll be right back. Feel free to take a look around," and then catch the sound of his shoes clapping against the hardwood and then concrete as he chases me out to the street.

"Quinn!" he calls after me. "Quinn, wait."

I pace along the curb, reminiscent of the first day we met in front of his gutter crib. "Is that what you want?"

"What?"

"A two-week escrow and a cash offer?" As soon as I say it, I realize that yes, this is exactly what every house flipper should want. It's a dream deal.

"I didn't think anything would come of it when they stopped by and asked to take a peek at the place," he reasons. "But they sound interested. And what they've proposed as an offer is so much more than I thought I could get for this place. It would be stupid for me to turn it down."

He says the words, but I'm the one who feels them.

Stupid for thinking we had more time. Stupid for letting all the time we *did* have pass us by because I worried about jumping into things too quickly. And stupid for implying for even one second he should pass up this opportunity.

"I'm so sorry, Quinn. I know how excited you were to pick out all the finishes for this place."

"I wasn't that excited," I lie.

His hands meet my hips. "I know you were. And I was, too. But I think the reason they're so pleased with this place is because they get to make all of those decisions. I understand that. It's the opportunity for them to take it from a house to a home."

Unmerited jealousy surges through me. I wanted to be the one to make a home with Nathan. Even though we wouldn't be living in it together, there was this fantasy in my head that I knew I could partially fulfill by doing this with him.

Now all of that is gone.

"Maybe they'd like to see some of the things you came up with?" His eyes travel to the notebook wedged under my arm.

"No. I'm sure they have their own ideas. It's fine."

"Quinn. I'm honestly so sorry. I don't know what to say."

I pause, taking in the obvious distress in his tensed brow and troubled green eyes. He truly is torn up about this.

"I'm going to head back to Mom's to check on Geronimo. He seemed a little funky when I left."

"I can go with you."

"No. It's fine. You go show Becca and Ryan around. Let them know the blood, sweat, and tears you put into this place. I'm sure they'll appreciate hearing all about it."

His smile is weak, but I recognize it's all he can give. I don't have much to offer, either.

"I'll sync up with you later," I say. Then, as confirmation that I'll be okay even if I don't totally feel it, I lift to my toes to give him a kiss on the cheek.

When he's back inside, I pitch the notebook straight into the dumpster.

———

The End.

I genuinely did not think my fingers would type these words again. For so long, the story felt aimless, the couple's happy ending existing somewhere in the hazy distance. But, like driving through a thick morning fog, as I inched my way closer to the finish line, things once far off filtered into clear view. Sure, I could only see my immediate surroundings, could only write scene by scene, word by word, but the pieces fell into place beautifully when I paid attention to the story on a more detailed level.

"I love it," Cora Scranton, my agent, croons into the phone line. "There are some things we'll want to button up and a few plot holes that need fixing, but I like this new direction for you, Quinn. It's noticeably different from your last books."

"You think?"

An espresso machine gurgles in the background. Baristas bark names and orders. Cora is always on the go. Always multitasking her life to the very last drop. It's for that reason I'm not surprised she's taken the opportunity to call me from the airport before her vacation is set to commence in just a few short hours.

"I can't pinpoint exactly what it is, but your voice is...I don't know. It's more believable for lack of a better word." There's a muffling clamor and I assume her hand has temporarily covered the mouthpiece when I hear a 'thank you' uttered to someone close by. "I can sell this. It hits all the right beats and gives readers that swoony feeling they're going for. I'll work on my suggestions on the plane and will try to squeeze in some time while in Bali, but don't go freaking out on me if you don't hear anything on my end for a bit. Internet is rumored to be shitty."

"Which is the entire reason you booked this resort," I cut in. "Go. Unplug. Have a great anniversary trip and don't you dare check your email or spend time working on my manuscript while you're in paradise. It can wait."

"You and I both know if I can't check my email at least once a day, I'll break out in a rash. But thank you, I will do my best to put things on the backburner. Maybe not the back-burner. Maybe still on a front-ish burner, but with the flame turned down to a low simmer. Not gonna lie, I'll be thinking about some very specific scenes while I'm sunbathing on the beach with the hubs. Thank you for that."

"I do what I can," I note with a chuckle, even though Nathan should get the credit. "Safe travels."

"Thanks, dear. Talk soon."

I click to hang up. While we were talking, I felt the buzz of a few incoming texts, but I sit a moment before pulling those up.

Relief is such an odd sensation. There's a portion of it that's incredible, this overwhelm of peace that soothes you from the inside out like a balm. But even in the midst of that, there's a shell of worry you've been so used to existing in, it takes a bit of time for that to crumble and break away.

I'd been tied up in knots over this manuscript. I can't fully sink into the praise Cora has just given me, even though it's everything I'd hoped for. She's pleased, and that's the first step in getting this thing out in the world. It might not end up a bestseller, but it's my best work, and there's a tremendous sense of accomplishment wrapped up in that.

Would my dad be proud? Truthfully, I don't know, but I don't think that's my focus anymore. As I wrote, I found myself doing it more and more for me, less and less for him. It was good practice in shedding some of those people pleasing tendencies and focusing on my own goals and dreams for once.

And, as Cora said, it's believable. I know the reason for that.

It's hard to convey the turmoil and elation of falling in love if you've never experienced it. That's why I'd missed the mark in my other novels. I was reaching for something I'd never touched on my own. Don't get me wrong. You don't have to experience something to be able to write it. I get that. I personally don't know any woman who has been ravished by a half-man, half-beast with a kingdom of fae but it has been written many times over. And quite well, I might add.

But a piece of yourself goes into every word, every sentence, every character and arc. And now I have more pieces to give.

I have love and hope. Even a little despair and uncertainty. But my human experience gave life to those characters through those words, and the result is something I will forever cherish, even if the story ultimately never sees the light of day.

With a refreshing sigh, I scoop up my phone.

> Kimmie: I hope you're not busy today because I'm currently in Fern Hollow filling up my tank and have a bagful of cronuts on my passenger seat with your name on them.

How is my best friend thirty minutes away and just now telling me this? A closer look at the timestamp on her text shows she's actually only five minutes out due to the discrepancy in the time the text was received versus read. Shoot.

> Me: Did we have plans I forgot to write down?

> Kimmie: No. I just got a rare day off and decided a visit was in order. This whole seeing you once every few weeks is not cutting it for me. I'm a needy bestie. We both know that.

> Me: Indeed, we do.

> Kimmie: Get your running gear on because we're going oh you shut the fuck up, you turkey! I have the right of way, jerkwad. Get the hell off my tail!

> Me: Everything okay?

> Kimmie: Sorry. Voice-to-text. Some asshole idiot thought it was a good idea to cut me off.

Me: I will leave you to road rage in peace. See you in a few and drive as safely as your blood pressure will allow.

Kimmie: See you soon.

31 /
nathan

KIMMIE'S at Quinn's place.

I don't know if that will be a good thing, or a colossally bad thing.

When I deliver the news to Quinn that escrow closed even earlier than expected and that Becca and Ryan are requesting their keys by tomorrow, it might be nice for her to have a friend around. Might make my sudden absence a little less noticeable. Cradle the bomb I've just tossed into her lap.

Am I disappointed I won't get one last night with Quinn? Of course, I am. We still haven't had sex, even though we've shared the same bed and countless intimate moments. I don't know if I've been saving it for right before I have to leave— some romantic sendoff—or if I've been putting it off so I don't connect with Quinn in a way I'll never be able to come back from.

I don't have plans to end things. That's not my angle. But there's going to be a shift in our relationship now that we won't be living next door. It's not something we won't be able to handle. Couples do it all the time. It'll take work, but I've got it in me, and I know she's committed, too.

Still, it sucks.

I've opened the bank account app on my phone at least a dozen times this morning, hoping to be seduced or at least comforted by the extra zeros. It doesn't do the trick. Sure, they're shocking, but they don't get my heart racing the way a simple, thoughtful look from Quinn does.

Damn, I'm really going to miss her.

I'm about to walk over to her house fueled by a new sense of courage paired with a strong cup of coffee when I get an email notification that everything with the key hand-off is good to go. I scroll down and bold text from unread messages catches my eye. There's a lot of spam. A few emails from my school listing important dates for conferences and prep days. One from the Brookhill library saying a book I've checked out is overdue.

And there's an email from Sarah.

I don't know how I had glossed over it before. It was sent from her work email, of all things, and I didn't have that address saved, so it reads as her first initial, our last name, followed by the at symbol and her company's info. Not one I would recognize off the top of my head.

I click on it.

There's no real way to prepare to see a picture of the woman you've been with since high school cradling her newborn child. A child that isn't yours. There's fluffy language announcing her little blessing, but I can immediately tell I'm just one recipient on a longer list of emails.

Sarah looks good. Tired, but that's to be expected. And her daughter—Mikayla Marie—is an absolute doll. Sweet ruddy face with a nose that can only be described as a pert little button. I see a bit of Sarah in her, and not an ounce of myself, though I'm not sure why I'm trying to find it.

She's not mine. I know that truth, head and heart.

Sarah and I have started our new stories, and as much as it scares me to do so, I need to begin this new chapter with Quinn. The one where I tell her I'm moving out of the fixer upper.

For now, sweeping the driveway seems like a good stalling tactic. Can't let the new owners move in with dirt all over the place. First things first. The broom scrapes against the concrete as I move, creating long symmetrical grooves in the layer of fine dust. It's like one of those thera-peutic desktop sandboxes with the little wooden rake. I sweep back and forth for so long, you could eat off the ground without so much as a stray bit of sand working its way into your food. It's freaking clean. All I'm doing at this point is wearing down the bristles on a perfectly good broom.

And wearing down my resolve to just get it over with and spill the news to Quinn.

I need to act fast before I waste so much time, the announcement ultimately comes as a plate of freshly baked cookies from her newest neighbors.

I have to be the one to tell her, and I've only got today to do so.

Working my phone out of my back pocket, I pull up Quinn's number. Her profile image melts my heart into a ball of warm mush. I'd snapped the photo that first day on the beach, when her hair whipped around her like the wayward tails of a kite, mingling with the fresh ocean air. Even through the unruly strands, you could piece together her smile, the one that makes it impossible not to mirror it.

God, what this woman does to me.

I punch a text asking if she's around, but rather than wait for the reply, I decide to walk over and see for myself. No more dilly-dallying on my end. If I only have until tomorrow before I'm on the road, then I want every single second spent with Quinn.

"Nathan." As always, her face reacts before her words. I've never seen someone's features morph so fully. She goes from blank to ecstatic in a finger snap. "I'm so glad you're here. Kimmie and I were just heading out for a run, and I was telling her we should ask you to join. If you're lucky, maybe we can even snag some of that unicorn ice cream. The truck should be there."

"Howdy Nathan!" Around a mouthful of what looks like a pickle, Kimmie shouts the greeting from the kitchen.

I peer past Quinn into the house. "Hey Kimmie!"

"Do you want to come with us?" Quinn's eyes widen.

"On a run? I don't know."

"Worried you can't keep up, old geezer?" Kimmie wedges by Quinn and smacks me straight in the gut with the back of her hand.

"I was actually coming by to talk with Quinn about some-thing. Privately."

That's all I need to say. Kimmie catches my drift and is instantly on it.

"Oh crap." Performance mode activated. She clutches just below her waist and doubles over. "I think I just started my period."

"You did not," Quinn insists. "I know for a fact you've

already finished it because you told me you cried over a basket of coconut shrimp last week at work, and you only cry over shrimp when you're menstruating. These are facts."

"Because it's so sad that they just decapitate them and serve up their bodies, but for some reason, leave the tails on. Like, they get to keep their tails, but not their heads? Who made that decision?"

She has a fair point.

"Either way, that dill pickle must've been bad, because I've got a rumbly tummy and I don't want to be on mile marker number three when I've got to go number two."

Yep, this woman is eccentric, but it's working in my favor. I think I just might get Quinn alone.

"You do understand that pickles last, like, *forever*," Quinn asserts. "That's the entire point of pickling."

"Oh no!" Kimmie makes a face. "Nature calls."

She jumps back into the house and shoves us both off the stoop before slamming the door.

"Not sure what that was about."

"I think she's just giving us some space." I take Quinn's hand in mine. "What do you think about a walk instead?"

"Sure. I'd like that."

I rarely get this nervous around Quinn, but today, my palms collect with sweat and my voice unintentionally cracks each time I open my mouth to speak. I try to urge my feet forward, but they lock up right in front of my house like they won't let me take another step until I've come clean.

Okay, okay. I can do this.

"On second thought, can we talk here?" The tailgate to my truck is dropped, an open invitation for us to sit while I get everything off my worry-constricted chest. "Would that be okay?"

"That works for me."

The answer isn't born from her usual easy-going nature, but out of a place of unease. Quinn is agreeable because she's hesitant, just waiting for me to finally say what's clinging so tightly to the tip of my tongue, it's a miracle it hasn't already freed itself and tumbled out.

My hands meet her waist to boost the little jump she takes to get onto the truck. Once she's comfortable, I remove my cell phone from my back pocket and hoist a leg to climb up, too.

"I have to be out of here by tomorrow."

Her eyes capture mine. "Seriously?"

"Yeah. Everything went through faster than we all thought. The money's pending in my account."

"Nathan, that's great." Fabricated joy accounts for the smile on her face. "I'm so happy for you."

"Thank you. I mean, it's great that I was able to sell this place, not so great that I have to leave you so soon."

"Soon is all relative. If you think about it, we've been neighbors for over a month at this point."

"Yes, but we've only been together for a portion of that. It feels like we're just getting started," I say. "Hey, hand me your phone."

A dart of confusion tugs her brows, but she takes her cell out and passes it my way all the same.

I pull up her calendar, specifically, each weekend, and add my name to the days.

"I'm going to visit you every weekend until your mom is back. After that, we'll figure out another plan."

She collects my phone from the truck bed, about to do the same, I figure, but pauses.

The picture of Sarah and Mikayla still graces the screen.

"Oh." Quinn's mouth settles into a line. "Goodness. She's beautiful."

"Aren't all babies? Or is it that they all look like aliens? I can't remember."

"Not the baby, although she is a perfect little cherub. But Sarah. She's stunning."

I incline my head to look at the photo over Quinn's shoulder. "Maybe on the outside. I'll give you that much. But she's proven to be pretty ugly on the inside, and that's what matters."

Quinn just takes in the picture for several quiet moments before finding my calendar and adding **FaceTime with Quinn** to every Tuesday and Thursday evening.

This is us making it work, I guess.

She passes the phone back and looks at me, then blinks away.

"Hey." I tip her chin.

"I'm sorry." A muffled sniff doesn't stop a tear from spilling down her cheek. She shoves a hand to her face to blot it away, but I glimpse it. "I don't know why I'm being so sensitive."

"I get it. I am, too. I think we spent so long fighting this, thinking it wasn't time, and we didn't realize time was actually running out. But it's not over for us. Things will just look different."

She sputters a frustrated sigh. "I just feel like I'm never ready for these abrupt goodbyes. With my dad. With the Ainsleys. Heck, even with Kyle because that timing wasn't my decision, either. They keep sneaking up on me, coming out of left field."

"This isn't goodbye, Quinn. It's a pause." I pull her into my chest and strum my fingers along her back.

"It seems like that's all we know how to do. Press the pause button. When do we finally get to go all in on our happiness?"

I don't have the answer she's looking for, and rather than fill in with half-believable words of assurance, I just fasten my arms around her. Hold her. Provide her with the steadiness she needs in this moment in the only way I know how.

"I've fallen in love with you, Quinn."

She stills in my arms. "What?"

"I have. I'm in love with you. You've given me every reason to be, and not a single one not to. I wasn't sure what this feeling was, the one where all I want is to be near you, protect you, care for you. I've never experienced it so intensely, so quickly before. But then it occurred to me I've never experienced love in the way it's intended to be felt, either." A smile returns to her face, forming ever so slowly on her sweet mouth. "I love you, Quinn. I think I have for some time, actually."

I don't even need her to say it back. This isn't one of those declarations that demands a reciprocal answer. It's just a truth I want her to hear from my lips while we're face to face. Still, when she angles her head to look up at me, a quiver of anticipation makes my body heat, makes my nerves buzz just beneath my skin. It would feel so good to hear those three words, but I'm fine waiting for them.

Turns out, I don't have to wait more than a few breaths.

"I love you, too, Nathan."

"Yeah?" I don't mean to sound surprised, but honestly, I am a little.

"I knew it the moment I wrote the very last words of my book. Something was different, and that something was you. You interjected more than just romance into my edits. You gave me a model for true and selfless love, something I've never experienced, either. And let's face it, you cleaned up my ex's vomit *and* came to the rescue of a cat that tried to castrate you. I mean, when am I ever going to find another guy that will live up to that?"

My mouth hooks into a smirk at that. She's got a point.

"You know," I say, "most people wouldn't call the dissolution of a ten-year marriage at the hands of infidelity lucky, but I don't know how else to describe it. Because all that led me to you, and I consider myself the luckiest man on the planet to be the one holding you in my arms right now."

"Lucky in love. I think that's the term for it."

I smile into her hair. "Sounds like a title to another romance novel you should write."

"I'm sure that one already exists. I'm more interested in writing the one where the handsome older man and his flighty next-door neighbor conquer all odds, time, and space to get their happy ever after."

"I think we're already writing it."

She runs her hand along my chest. "I think we are. And I can't wait to turn the page."

32 /
quinn

I WANT to tear up this page. Put it in the paper shredder. Set it on fire.

It's been two weeks and I haven't seen Nathan.

We had plans for a visit last weekend, but something popped up on his end with documents that needed signing ASAP and despite trying to juggle our calendars, we couldn't get them to sync up. I assume the papers are for the place in the city he's renting from Archer. Housing contracts are important, and I understand things like that can't always be moved around, but disappointment still shrouded me like one of those weighted blankets. I had really wanted to see him.

We've managed to FaceTime more than just Tuesdays and Thursdays. We've talked every night, gotten each other off via super-hot phone sex, and fallen asleep with our cell phones wedged between our ears and our pillows as our words and eyelids drifted off. It'll have to do for now. I'm trying not to be the needy girlfriend who wants to be around her significant other twenty-four-seven, but I'm tiptoeing into that crazy girl territory.

My schedule just isn't as busy as Nathan's. I realize he's gearing up for the school year, likely drafting lesson plans and creating seating charts. I don't want to interrupt that. But I'm still waiting to hear from Cora regarding the changes to my manuscript, so I'm not knee-deep in edits or deadlines at the moment. Or in anything, really.

I've started plotting my next book, a story that centers on a side character from book one. I enjoy this stage. There's so much prospect in a new book. The ideas are in their infancy, with many possibilities for their future. It's an exciting time, but I can't appreciate it for what it's worth because I still feel like I'm in limbo.

I'm waiting.

Waiting on my editor.

Waiting on my mom.

Waiting on Nathan.

I have to say, it's not my favorite place to be.

Hell, I'm even currently waiting for my Door Dasher to show up with the crab rangoons I ordered over an hour ago.

Patience is not a virtue I presently possess.

I fight a grumble of frustration when I drag up the app on my phone and see my food is nowhere in my vicinity. Not even in the same city.

Irritation swells in my stomach like a bout of bad food poisoning.

Something isn't right, but it's not the missing takeout order that has me in knots.

I've texted Nathan three times today and while I understand he has things going on and might not have his phone Velcroed to the palm of his hand like mine is, he's pretty prompt in his replies.

I don't want to bug him, but my concern is quickly transitioning to full on worry.

What's the harm in another check-in? I compose and send a quick text; nothing too heavy, just a note asking him to call when he has a chance.

That's reasonable, right?

If I were to ask Kimmie, I'm sure she'd give me some belabored speech about men and their inability to communicate through anything more complex than grunts and hand gestures. She would probably tell me to get in my car, drive my ass to the city, and talk to him in person. Maybe that's not such a crazy idea. Not to track him down, per se, but to surprise him.

Guys like that sort of thing, don't they? Spontaneity? When a woman takes initiative?

Problem is, I don't really know where Nathan is right now. I've yet to visit his new place, and each time I suggest it, he's either tied up on campus or not currently at home. I don't want to think he's being cryptic because he's hiding something, but the longer I go without communication, the easier it is for my suspicions to grow legs and walk themselves into that paranoid part of my brain.

You know what? I'm just going to do it.

I might not be able to track Nathan down easily, but Archer has a prominent online presence, and within four minutes, I have the address to the apartment building that he not only lives in but owns. Must be nice, huh?

This is vastly out of character for me, but I'm committed and decide to run with it. And if I'm going to surprise Nathan, I'm going all in, and that means taking it all off. Since it's not practical to show up totally naked—what with the risk I run of getting pulled over for indecent exposure—I slip into the black lace nighty I bought online last week and cinch the belt to a long jacket I had stored in a closet at Mom's from ages ago.

Even as I'm on the highway, I get a naughty thrill from the rush of it. That only I know what I'm wearing beneath the nondescript beige coat, paired with the thought of Nathan's face when I let him in on my little secret, has me pressing the gas pedal firmly, accelerating the car along with my heart rate.

But traffic is a bitch and what should only take me an hour stretches into two. And apparently two hours is a sufficient amount of time to second guess my life's choices in their entirety, and this most recent decision has my face flaming in humiliation.

Who am I kidding? I'm not the type of woman who can pull off this sort of shit. I don't do sexy surprises, and I don't know if this is something Nathan would even like.

Spontaneity is for the birds.

If I weren't so hungry, I'd point my car back toward Brookhill and scrap the whole thing. But I've got to eat and now this visit to Nathan's is more of a mission to feed my hungry tummy than it is to fly by the seat of my sex kitten pants. I really hope he has a stocked fridge, at the very least the fixings for a sandwich I can whip up before I set back out for home, tail between my legs.

GPS guides me into an underground parking garage and the piece of paper in my hand containing Archer's apartment number leads me up the elevator to the top floor.

Of course, it's a penthouse suite. What does this guy do for a living?

When the double doors yawn open, I'm met with a long marble hallway that I wobble and clip-clop down in my stilettos. Don't know why I thought five-inch-high heels were the way to go, considering I'm rarely in anything other than my Chuck Taylors. Apparently, I'm pulling out all the stops on being awkward tonight.

With zero confidence, I blow out a frazzled breath that lifts the hair framing my face.

This was a royally bad decision, and each step toward Archer's has me questioning my brain function. I'm not currently operating on all cylinders.

I get to a massive black door and pause. It's modern and opulent, and there's a little intercom button just to the left that I jam my finger into.

"Hello?" Instantly, I recognize Archer's voice and my shoulders sag from the warm familiarity of it.

"Hey Archer. It's Quinn."

I hear the lock turn over and then see the smiling face of Nathan's best friend giving me a thorough once over.

"Not the company I was expecting tonight." He has a half-consumed glass of wine in his grip, and based on the lazy drawl of his words, my guess is it isn't his first. "Come on in."

I step into the apartment. It's past being merely spacious and borders on colossal, with huge floor-to-ceiling windows that draw in the city and its sparkling lights from beyond the glass. It even smells like wealth, if that has a scent. Everything about the place oozes money, much like the man within it.

"Can I take your coat?"

"No!" In a panic, I slap away Archer's proffered hand. "I'm so sorry. I mean, no thank you. I'm a little chilly. I'll keep it on."

"Alright then. What about a glass of wine? Something to eat?"

"Something to eat would be amazing."

I really don't want to be known in their friend group as the half-naked girl who shows up unannounced requesting snacks, but I don't think it can be avoided.

"What're you hungry for?" Archer tugs on something I swear is a cabinet, but it opens into a refrigerator with a rainbow-colored assortment of foods stored within it. "I've got every fruit and vegetable you can think of, or I can call Carlton and ask him to pick up something else if you have a hankering for something specific."

I don't know who Carlton is, but I'm not about to put him out and based on the grocery store display of items already in Archer's fridge, I'm sure I'll be fine.

"Maybe some grapes?" I shrug. "Whatever's easy."

He gives me a brusque nod and then gets to work creating a whole ass charcuterie board because apparently a handful of grapes won't suffice. There are soft, crumbly cheeses and sliced salamis, and even a little dollop of something I think might be caviar, but I'm too embarrassed and unrefined to ask.

"I prefer my grapes in liquid form." Archer tops off his wineglass from a bottle that probably costs more than my monthly rent and then slides the butcher block charcuterie board across the counter. "Have a seat. Make yourself comfortable."

Keeping the opening to my jacket cinched tightly so I don't flash the guy, I shimmy onto a barstool and dig in.

"So, Quinn. What brings you to the city tonight? Though I'd be flattered if it were the case, I don't think it's to visit me."

I crunch down on a plump green grape. "I'm trying to track down Nathan."

Something streaks across Archer's features, but it's obvious his profession has given him practice in maintaining a stoic expression. It's a total poker face. "I see."

"He's not returning my texts, and the last few times we've tried to meet up in person, it hasn't worked out. So, I got this bee in my bonnet to just show up and surprise him, but your address is the only one I could find online."

"I wish I could help you out, but he's not here."

"I figured as much. Didn't think you two would be bunking or anything like that. But would you be able to give me his apartment number? It's in this building, yeah?"

"I don't have it, Quinn." Archer lowers his glass and splays his palms on the counter. I don't like the look of pity mixed with affection he levels at me. "And no, he doesn't live in the building."

"But I thought he was going to rent an apartment from you."

"That was the original plan, but..." Archer withdraws eye contact and softly coughs. "But things have changed."

"Things changed as in he's no longer living in the city?"

"Something like that."

I heave out a hot breath. "You've got to give me more than that to work with, Archer."

"I can't, Quinn. I'm sorry."

"Seriously?" My voice lifts by several octaves as my spine tightens. "Do you even know where he is?"

"I do."

"And you won't tell me?"

"I can't tell you."

The ambiguous texts from Nathan intersect with Archer's obvious evasion and leave me so far out of the loop, I'm nowhere in the general realm of understanding.

I'm also no longer hungry.

"I have to go." I scrape the barstool back from the massive island, not even self-conscious when my jacket flaps open and I feel a rush of cool air skate along my thighs.

I'm sure Archer just got a glimpse of my "surprise" for Nathan, but he doesn't acknowledge it, and somehow, that makes everything so much worse. He knows why I drove all the way here and yet he's not offering anything. He's as tightlipped as a vault sealed shut.

"Thank you for the food," I say. "I appreciate it."

Archer follows me to the door, shuffling slowly at my back since these damn shoes won't let me storm out at a sufficient speed. I rip the high heels from my feet.

"Quinn, I really wish I could tell you what's going on, but Nathan asked that I didn't."

I'm not mad at Archer. I'm not even mad at Nathan, just confused in a way that feels a lot like the hurtful sting of betrayal.

"I understand." Yet I don't. "I'll see you around." I probably won't.

"Please, drive safely."

I just give Archer a little nod as I head toward the gilded elevator.

As the penthouse door shuts softly at my back, my phone vibrates within my jacket pocket.

I don't mean to, but the hope that it might be Nathan lifts my spirit just high enough to have it come crashing down when I see it's not.

It's Mom.

> I'm home! (And you're not). The cats were acting like they hadn't eaten in days, so I fed them. When can I expect you?

I don't have the bandwidth for this right now. As the elevator sluggishly descends toward the parking garage level, I punch out my reply.

> Glad you made it back safely. I'm heading to the condo for a few days. Catch up with you later.

33 /
nathan

"THAT WAS FUCKING ROUGH, buddy. Don't make me do your dirty work like that again, okay?"

There's a sharpness to Archie's tone that lets me know he's not entirely kidding. I feel like a dick for making him cover for me, but it had to be done. I didn't really have any other options.

"I know," I groan my apology through the line. "And I'm sorry I put you in that situation. I didn't think she would show up out of the blue like that."

"She was trying to surprise you, Natty. I didn't get a good look, but I'm pretty sure she had something intended for your eyes only beneath that ugly ass coat she was wearing."

That comment wallops me right in the chest. "Shit. Seriously?"

"You should've seen the hope extinguish from her eyes when I told her you weren't renting a place from me. She's onto you, Natty, and I think she's suspecting the worst."

I figured that might be a problem. As much as I wanted to keep this from Quinn, I owe it to her to protect her heart, and that means being honest. She's proven her trust over and over, and I don't want my obscure behavior lately to jeopardize that.

As soon as I end the call with Archie, I text her.

> **What are you doing?**

I'm not owed an answer, I recognize that. She has reached out to me countless times today and I haven't even given her a simple reply. Still, I hope she's a bigger person than I am, and when I see the dots on the screen, something catches in my heart at her inherent goodness.

> **Quinn: Heading to my condo.**

> **Me: Meet you there?**

I don't hold my breath for a reply, which proves appropriate because I don't get one. A wordless hour drags on before my phone finally receives a text from her number.

> **Quinn: I'll be there in thirty minutes. You can come anytime.**

Thing is, I'm already there, just sitting on my dropped tailgate watching the waves batter the shoreline, letting the white noise of the ocean ratchet down my sky-high anxiety.

There are two ways this can go but I only focus on the possibility of it ending supremely well. What does Kimmie call that again? Manifesting? I'm manifesting the shit out of that hope.

It's how I spend each passing minute until I finally see the beam from two headlights pierce through the coastal fog as they swing into the driveway and cut a path toward the condo.

In the stillness, the engine hisses as Quinn kills it. She steps onto the gravel in her bare feet, her emotions worn on her sleeve as always. That's usually a comfort. Right now, it's a kick in the goddamn nuts.

"You beat me," she acknowledges flatly. I try to mask my frown when she tugs the sash on her jacket even tighter around her waist.

"I made good time." I take a tentative step to meet her. "Hey, can we talk?"

"I'd really like to get inside." Her arms mimic the belt around her middle when she weaves them over her chest. She's not letting me into that jacket or under her skin, apparently. "It's been a long day."

"It'll only be a minute." I don't want to push her, but I gently clasp her elbow to lead her to the back of my truck where most of our important conversations seem to take place.

Quinn's eyes are blank, her mouth tense. Still, despite the frustration she outwardly feels toward me, she joins me on the tailgate.

"Quinn, I'm sorry I've been MIA."

That gets a snort I'm aware I deserve. "You could say that."

"I've been doing a lot of thinking."

Those arms bind even more snugly. "It's never good when a conversation starts with those words, Nathan."

I want to do everything I can to reassure her that I don't intend to hurt her, but the damage is already done despite my wishes. I need to push on.

Without preamble, I dive in. "Quinn, you said yourself I was a caretaker. That it's in my nature and who I am. I've been giving that a lot of thought lately, and you're right. At my core, I want to take care of everyone. I can't help it."

"Oh God." Her arms unclasp and it's like they were the only things holding her together because her entire frame collapses and she has to use the side of the truck bed to hold her up. If she didn't seem so averse to it, I'd reach out and keep her steady myself. "You're going back to Sarah, aren't you?"

"I am not going back to Sarah." Shit. I probably should have prefaced our conversation with that, but to be honest, it never occurred to me that this could still be an assumption. While I know things with Sarah are completely over, Quinn needs a guarantee in that area, and I owe her one. "However, I do think I'm at a stage in my life where I'm ready to take on more. Take on something—or should I say someone—else."

Hope hasn't returned to her gaze, and that worries me. I'm not being clear enough.

"Nathan, if you're saying you've realized you're ready to be a father, I completely understand that. And I respect it. I'm just not in any place to become a parent yet, and as much as I'd like for things to work between us, I can't hold you back and keep you from pursuing that dream."

"That's not what I'm talking about. I'm not ready to be a dad. Not to a human, at least."

Quinn's brows squiggle. "I don't follow."

Jumping down from the truck bed, I reach the passenger side and tug on the door. It squeals so loudly it draws up the fine hairs on my neck.

"Nathan? What's going on?"

I don't want to leave Quinn waiting any longer than I already have, so I grab the handle to the carrier and meet her at the back of the truck as fast as my legs can get me there.

"Quinn, I'd like to introduce you to Peeve."

As if on cue, the tabby kitten squeaks out a meow the moment I say his name.

"You got a cat?" I momentarily fear Quinn's going to slip right off the tailgate from shock.

"I did. Rescued him from a shelter in the city. He's eight weeks old, likes to chase ladybugs, and canned albacore is his dinner of choice."

Immediately, she unlatches the wire door and withdraws the little guy, bringing him near her chest to nuzzle close. I can hear his loud motor going already.

"*This* is the reason you've been so evasive lately?"

"I wanted it to be a surprise and knew if we spoke, I'd let the cat out of the bag. Pun intended." I shrug, knowing it's still not a valid excuse but praying she'll forgive me because I need her to be tracking with me for what I have in store next. "Hey. It's getting cold out here. What do you say we take this little guy inside and get him settled in?"

She's too preoccupied with the fluffy kitten to do anything but follow my lead, so we tread up the steps to the condo in time with the heartbeat ringing in my ears like a fucking metronome. I'm glad she's distracted and doesn't realize how scared shitless I am.

We finally get to the top of the deck, but rather than walk toward her front door, I change direction at the last second.

An unreasonable amount of nerves push my heart into my throat, and I pulse with the fear that things could go completely sideways at any moment. This is a crapshoot. I know that.

Quinn's mouth slips open when my hand finally dips into my pocket to fish around for a key. Without looking right at her, I fit it into the lock on her next-door neighbor's place.

My newest fixer upper.

"Nathan? What are you doing?"

"Getting Peeve settled into his new home."

The door swings wide on its hinges with a soft moan but Quinn stays rooted in place, mouth still agape in absolute confusion.

"I bought the place from Danny." I nudge her into the entryway and shut the door behind us but keep my hand on the small of her back as a steadying point of connection.

"Are you going to renovate this place?"

"I am. I was hoping you might want to help me out with that. I know you've got a great eye for design." I give her a wink, but it goes unnoticed.

"And then you're going to sell it?"

She's pieced together that I bought the entire place and selling it might very well mean the end of her lease. That's a concern I never intended for her to have.

"Not going to sell. I'm going to live here, next door to you, my favorite place to be."

She almost drops Peeve; her entire body goes boneless. Readjusting her hold on the little kitten, she keeps the questions coming. "What about your job?"

"Believe it or not, they have middle schools out here, too," I say, inserting a little lightheartedness into my tone, hoping it's okay to do so. She's not quite there yet. "I've already got a long-term subbing position lined up for after the holidays.

And I put in my notice at my old job. They were sad to see me go, but it was time for a change."

Quinn's mouth works on a swallow. "I don't know what to say."

"Say you're happy?"

"Nathan, I'm more than happy." Yet the words don't match the sudden tears skating down her cheeks.

"You're crying." I thumb away the salty tears, and something about seeing them, touching them, has a scratchy lump forming in my throat. When did I become a sympathy crier? With Quinn, I can't help but take on every emotion.

"I'm overwhelmed."

"I know. I worried it might be too much."

"It's definitely not too much." Her lips meet mine and press deeply, like she's stamping those words on me.

Settling Peeve back into his travel carrier and moving it onto a couch I picked up secondhand from the consignment store down the road, she slips her arms around my waist, beckoning me to her.

"No one has ever made me feel the way you do," she utters with so much confidence I can't place any doubt in those words. They are a declaration. A testimony. "I can't believe I thought you were going to end things."

"Quinn, I just told you I loved you a couple of weeks ago. Do you think my feelings change that quickly?"

"I don't know. I mean, we were both able to move on from our exes pretty fast."

"Because they gave us more than enough reasons to. But you?" I tug her hips. "You've only given me reason after reason to fall even more in love with you."

"Is that so?" She's refined the coy look to a T. It crosses

her gaze before she releases me from our embrace. Then her hands move to the sash belted around her waist. Hell, yes. "I might have another reason."

"I think I'm really going to like this reason."

"I hope you do." With a jostle of her shoulders, her coat slips from place, falling to the floor in a puddle of fabric at her bare feet. She ups the seduction level when her tongue wets her bottom lip, eyes capturing mine. "And here I was, wanting to surprise you, when you're the one surprising me."

"I think it's fair to say we both surprised each other."

I take her in, my mind toggling between wanting to touch every inch of her and needing to appreciate the beautiful vision before me.

"I see you have a couch," she notes through the smile curving her mouth. A single brow arches like a hook drawing me in. "But what about a bed?"

Damn. I like where this is going. "Yep. Got one of those."

"Want to show it to me?"

"Oh sweetheart, I'm about to show you a lot more than just my bed."

Those words, combined with the act of scooping her into my arms to carry her into the bedroom, have Quinn launching into a fit of giggles. It's the best fucking sound ever.

I kick open the door and playfully fling her to the mattress.

"Oomf!" Air rushes out from her lungs as sweet laughter fills the room. She scrambles to sit up and pats the quilt. "Wow. I like it. Nice and firm."

"You think that's firm?" I'm feeling frisky, too, so I reach for her hand and bring it to the raging hard-on I've been sporting ever since Archie alluded to Quinn's little present for me.

She clutches me through the fabric of my jeans, bottom lip trapped between her teeth. "I think we should get naked."

"I couldn't agree more."

I like the little black number she's wearing, but I fucking love the sight of Quinn in nothing but a come-and-get-me grin.

For a moment, I'm speechless. Nearly breathless because it's almost too much. The way I feel about this woman has my ribcage tightening, has a warm ache pooling in my stomach. I love her, and I want to be with her in every sense and expression of the word.

I let her undress me first. She's methodical, unhurried in her quest to free me from the layers I'm presently wearing. Her hands wander up and down my stomach once she lifts my shirt over my head, and my muscles clench in response to her touch, a wake of chills chasing each gentle caress.

"Your body is beyond impressive, Nathan." She flattens her palm over my abs and thumbs each defined ridge.

"It's all yours."

"And I'm yours." As an invitation, her fingers move to the thin straps on her lingerie, but I beat her to it and untie the cute little bow right between her breasts. The gown flutters open.

I groan because she's goddamn gorgeous. "You're going to get tired of me telling you how perfect you are all the time."

"Nathan, that is not something a girl ever tires of hearing. I promise you cannot wear out that statement."

That's something I'm about to test. I move closer so my mouth can come down and meet the subtle slope of her neck.

"This is perfect," I murmur right beneath her ear. I work my way lower. Pressing a kiss to the curve of her breasts, I say it again. "And this spot right here? Perfect, too."

"See?" She shrugs, then shivers when my mouth continues its perusal. "Not even a little bit tired of it yet. Keep it coming."

I do as I praise every part of her, from the crown of her hair to the tips of her painted pink toes. If Quinn had any question about the way I feel about her body, that's nothing but a memory now. She's a temple and I've just spent the last few moments worshiping every fucking inch of her.

But I'm not done yet. I press my hand over her heart and my gaze stays solidly locked in with hers when I say, "And this? The most perfect part of you."

"Nathan." She covers my hand with hers, so I feel her heartbeat thumping beneath my skin, then lowers onto her back but doesn't break eye contact. "Make love to me?"

She does not have to ask twice.

I remove my jeans, followed by my boxer briefs, and make a beeline for the nightstand to get a condom. She captures my wrist mid-mission.

"I'm on birth control. And I'm clean. After everything with Kyle, I got myself tested."

You wouldn't think a statement including that fucker's name could be a turn on, but somehow, that's exactly what this information does. Because it means we can do this with absolutely nothing between us. Is it my birthday? Because I cannot possibly think of a greater gift.

"That's the best fucking news." I wear a grin from ear to ear. "I am, too."

Even though we always used condoms, I still didn't trust

Sarah, so I secured the first appointment possible to get tested after things imploded. At the time, I had no idea what a necessity that precaution would prove itself to be. Every once in a while, I get things right.

"Come here." Quinn's up on her knees, beckoning, hand outstretched.

Shit. Why am I suddenly nervous? I'm not a newbie to this sort of thing. But then it strikes me that yeah, that's exactly what I am.

I've had sex. I've fucked. But I've never been this intimately close with someone in this way before, and I'm so damn grateful Quinn is the one I'm about to experience this with. Never have I wanted to surrender every piece and part of me to another person, give up control by giving over all of myself.

Quinn has done this to me.

And I can't wait for what I'm about to do to her.

34 /
quinn

MY LEGS ARE DRAPED over Nathan's shoulders, my body still rolling from the freefall.

"Damn, Quinn," he groans between my thighs. "You're still coming."

I am. Not sure how it's even possible, but I keep pulsing around his fingers, trembling against his lips.

Usually, I'm only good for one orgasm. But rather than taper off as I come down from being fucked into oblivion by Nathan's magical tongue, it's like my body is gearing up for more. Jittering in anticipation from the promise of another round of orgasm-record-shattering sex.

"You good, sweetheart?" He moves over me, arms bracketed on either side of my quivering body.

"So good."

Lazily, his tongue drags across one breast, then the other. "Are you ready?"

"For more of that?" My eyebrows shoot up. "Yes, please."

He does a single push up to kiss me on the mouth. The wild hope that somehow his enormous dick will miraculously slip inside when his body comes flush with mine isn't granted. Dang it. I won't lie and say I'm not a little worried about it fitting. I understand anatomy and the way things work, and being worked from the inside out by Nathan's colossal cock defies all sense of reason and rationale.

"Breathe." His gaze narrows. "Just take a long, steady breath."

As a demonstration, he fills his lungs, waits for me to do the same, and then exhales with a shallow hiss. Is it sad that I need step-by-step instructions on something that should be completely innate? I'm sure Nathan didn't think we would be taking time out of our night for lessons in respiratory function.

"You're going to be fine," he assures. "I'll take it nice and slow."

"I think I owe you a blow job first."

He stills above me and grunts. "Uh, I'm probably going to be the first guy in the history of mankind to turn that down." His head hangs a little. "I need to be inside you."

Maybe the BJ offer was my way to delay my death by dick impalement, but I'm honestly glad Nathan opted out. Even though I'm still not convinced his massive erection will be readily welcomed, I'm not one to back away from a challenge. Especially when the reward is guaranteed to be so toe-curling and tingly.

Nathan repositions so he's supported on his forearm while his other hand comes down to grip the base of his shaft. When he notches himself right at my entrance, I must involuntarily gasp because he angles to look at me. "Keep breathing, baby."

Oh. Had I stopped? I blow out all the air from my rigid

body. "I'm sorry. I don't know why I'm so tense. Couldn't have anything to do with the overly intimidating cock you're wielding at my lady bits."

A chuckle rolls through his chest. "I think you're going to be surprised when you soon discover we're made for each other."

I want to believe that, but as he slowly nudges the tip in, I don't see how this is going to end in any way other than Nathan being thoroughly disappointed by my hostile vagina. She's so tense, it's like she's slammed the door on this potential sexual encounter and put up a *Closed for Business* sign.

"Open up to me, Quinn."

He's not just talking about my girly parts. The look on Nathan's face begs for the trust I so want to give him. That I need to give him. He presses in a little further and I wince.

"I've got another idea." He backs off, but it doesn't provide the relief I expect. Something withers within me. "You're going to ride me."

Okay. Done withering.

I perk up immediately. "Yeah?"

"Yeah. Then you'll be in the driver's seat and can take full control. You set the pace and gear up to whatever you're comfortable with at your own speed."

Alright. *That*, I can do.

I climb out from beneath him and wait for Nathan to get situated on his back before I swing a leg over to straddle his strong thighs.

"Here." He grabs onto my hips and slides me forward. "Use me to get yourself ready."

Yep. I can do that, too. When I rub over his solid length, my eyes roll back. "Oh."

He guides me gently, moving me along his erection. I grip his shoulders and rock my hips as I let out a breathy moan. Already, I feel my apprehension filter away and feel myself getting wetter with each friction-filled glide over his bare cock.

Yep. I'm ready.

I raise onto my knees and take him into my hand.

There's an open look of anticipation on Nathan's face when I lower myself, just a little at first, but then gradually working up to accommodate more. His hand reaches to my breast and squeezes as I nestle him in, inch by inch.

"See? You can take me. Almost there," he utters in a hoarse voice. "God, Quinn. You're so fucking tight."

"I'm sorry." I clench my teeth and push past the resistance caused by the slight sting of pain.

"Don't you dare apologize. That's a good thing."

Letting go of my insecurity, I finally sheath him all the way, sinking fully onto him. My muscles involuntarily clamp, and he lets out a groan that borders on animalistic.

"Such a good thing." He shudders an open-mouthed breath. "Now do you see what I mean?" He holds me in place. "Perfect fit."

He's right. Now that he's all the way inside, I'm stretched in a way that no longer bites with discomfort but is gloriously filling. He's buried to the hilt.

I almost don't want to risk losing this blissful sensation, but I can't just sit on the guy. I lift up. His hands suddenly grip my waist to halt the action.

"Wait." Nathan shuts his eyes. "Let me focus for a second. I want to remember the way you feel around me like this. Bare, with nothing between us."

Something deep within me tightens.

"Shit, Quinn. Do that again."

Can I? I'm not even sure what caused that response.

"Grip my dick with your sweet little pussy again."

Okay, apparently, it's the dirty talk that does it, because I feel something in my core clench around him as soon as the command falls from his lips.

"Fuck, yes. That feels so good." His hands release me, a sign that it's go-time.

I keep my hold on his shoulders as I push up, then settle back down until he bottoms out. I do that a few more times, making sure to clamp around him with each drawn-out stroke.

I imagine even with a condom this would be pure heaven, but feeling every ridge, every part of Nathan, is otherworldly. Skin on fevered skin.

I move faster.

My breasts are heavy to the point of aching. My fingers need to find purchase on something as I jockey up and down on his swollen cock. I claw into his shoulders. He likes that. There's a devilish grin developing on his mouth, and when I rake my nails down his chest, leaving a fresh mark, his hips buck.

"Claiming your territory, huh? I fucking like it." He thrusts again and somehow his body meets right where it needs to, rubbing me on the outside while his dick continues to hit that treasured point of pleasure deep within.

I let out a little scream. "Oh shit. Right there. Just like that. God, Nathan. That feels amazing."

His hips create a rhythm with mine and suddenly a

memory from our yoga session works its way to the front of my brain. I fail to trap in the snicker it elicits.

"What are you laughing at up there?" He continues pumping his hips in time with my movements.

"I was just thinking about yoga."

"Fuck yoga," he groans, adding a little smack to my ass that I wouldn't think I would enjoy, but absolutely do.

"I was just remembering the time I implied you didn't know how to use this particular part of your body." My breaths are shallow, words choppy from all the thrusting.

"And what do you think now?" His fingers spear the flesh on my backside as he pummels into me.

"I've never been so happy to be so wrong."

Just as I say it, Nathan slinks his arm around my middle and rolls us together until he's suddenly on top.

"What are you doing?" I ask, not because I mind the change in position, but because I want to prepare for what's coming. (Hopefully me, followed by him. And maybe me again).

"I'm going to make love to you, Quinn. Just like you asked me to." His knuckles brush back a damp strand of hair from my eyes and he stares into what feels like the very essence of my being, somewhere no one else has ever reached. "Just like I *need* to."

I'm one hundred percent on board with that.

There's a changeup in the roll of his hips that differs vastly from the thrusting drives from earlier. I grind against him, taking him deep and slow. Passion builds between us, a cresting wave that ebbs and retreats before coming back in for more.

Nathan's mouth seals over mine in a kiss, paralleling this

new and intentionally unhurried tempo of our bodies. Our tongues chase back and forth. Our hips meet and release. I pull out of our kiss and look down at where we're joined, in awe of how sensual, how arousing, and how fucking beautiful the sight is.

Nathan braces above me, motionless for a moment I can only measure in breaths and beating hearts. Maybe it's pain, but there's a tug in the center between his brows. Not a frown, but almost like he's thinking through something so sincerely, it takes all of his concentration. Then, as if a realization hits him, his features go lax and he blinks.

"I love you." He's said it before but hearing it now when we're as close as two people can be, it registers differently. I feel it in my body, in my brain, heart and soul. "I'm so in love with you, Quinn. So damn in love."

"I'm in love with you, too, Nathan."

Something shifts, those words setting us in motion. Nathan's hips pick up speed, jacking into me harder, fuller, but still totally controlled.

I huff out a breath with each thrust. My breasts bounce, an invitation for Nathan's hand and mouth to cover them. His lips pull over a nipple and suck. My body has always responded to his attention so effortlessly, but in this moment, there's more going on than just a physical reaction. There's something building within me, a sensation that doesn't just wash over my skin, but hits bone deep. Like he's somehow gotten into my very marrow.

I'm cherished. Protected. Valued and adored in every way possible. I've never understood how a woman could cry during sex—I mean, talk about a total buzzkill—but the water that lines my eyelashes stems from the overwhelming, indisputable newfound love I have for this man. And the love I feel from him in return. I can barely keep it contained.

He makes me want to hand over everything I am and ever will be. I'm not sure how to do that, but this is a good start.

"Nathan," I moan as he continues to slide in and out. "I've never felt like this before."

Our bodies draw together, our sweat-slick skin pressing against each other and the mattress. "Me neither."

We're in complete unison.

Our patterned breathing picks up, gasps matching in increased quickness. He clasps his hands around mine to anchor me in place.

"Look at me," he says when my eyelids flutter closed.

I do. I open my eyes to meet his vulnerable stare.

"I want to come with you," he whispers in a raspy tone that just might get the job done all on its own. "And I'm close."

"I am, too."

Each snap of our hips, each rock of our bodies, each stroke against me has us climbing closer to a place where I'm so tense, the only thing left to do is completely unravel.

He uses his cock like it was made for me and only me. I yelp when he suddenly releases one hand and shoves it in between us, moving his expert fingers to rub while he buries into me.

"Oh, God." I start to quiver. "I love it when you touch me like that."

His teeth nip at my chin; his words are hot against my skin. "I can't tell what you like better." His fingers continue their unyieldingly sweet torture. "My fingers, my tongue, or my cock."

"The whole package," I utter in an unsteady voice that trembles with my body. "D. All the above."

He licks up my neck and sucks my earlobe between his lips. Having his mouth so close to the shell of my ear that he has to whisper makes his commands that much more intense. "Quinn, you better find something to hold on to."

I jut my hand up toward the headboard, thankful for the wooden slats that allow me to stay tethered because I know I'm about to leave my body.

It's a chase toward the finish line filled with cries and moans, skin and sweat.

Nathan's "Just like that, baby," is met with jumbled, unintelligible sounds because real words take too much effort. And right now, all of my effort is focused between my legs where I feel Nathan's erection stiffen even more with each push.

"I'm...right...there," he grinds out between erratic gasps. His voice is low, commanding, and sinfully sexy when he utters, "Say you're mine when I'm inside you."

"I'm yours," I pant against his mouth. "Always and only yours."

I make my pussy pulse around him, tightening as I draw out one long stroke after the other.

He rams into me, his fingers flying over my clit.

"Nathan, I'm...I can't...So close..."

My neck arches, shoving my breasts up toward his face. A single flutter of his tongue over a beaded nipple is all it takes. Like the building crescendo of a song we've been writing with our bodies, I reach that highest peak with a breathless shout before falling back to earth, writhing and wringing out every ounce of pleasure as Nathan spills over the edge of ecstasy with me.

"Quinn, oh God, yes." He collapses onto me, pulsing within me, and kisses me fiercely. Then he looks me in the eye when he says, "Fucking perfect."

And it was. He is. We are.

I'm never going to come back from this, and for the first time, I let myself bask in the reassurance that I won't even have to.

epilogue

Six Months Later
Quinn

I WAKE up to the sound of a saw ripping through the walls.

Sunlight stretches across the mattress in a thin, bright line, peeking through the parted curtains that flutter from the ocean breeze. I twist both hands into my eye sockets, the filmy blur of sleep still coating them. It's early. Too early.

The power tool revs up again, and with it, the memory of Nathan's plan comes barreling back.

He's installing a cat door today that will allow Peeve to move easily between our two places, because let's face it, the cat is more mine than his. I mean, the guy named the poor kitten Peeve just so he could say, "Hey, this is my new pet, Peeve."

Turns out, he's still warming up to the whole idea of having, or even liking, a cat.

But I absolutely love the little feline, so in turn, Nathan puts up with him.

We've become really good at that over the last few months: learning to like the things the other loves. Hell, I've even discovered a new appreciation for middle school math since I've started helping Nathan grade papers for his new class.

We've found our groove in nearly everything. Well, minus the fact that I value sleep and Nathan is a notoriously early riser.

I slip out from beneath the covers and blindly find my slippers with my feet. A yawn chases another groan when the saw rattles and rips through the sheetrock.

My hair is wild. My large t-shirt hangs off my shoulder. And my face likely doesn't hide the grimace created by this loud and early wake-up call. I pad out of my bedroom, my blinks labored, sluggish.

At first, I think I'm seeing things. A swipe of my hands over my eyes proves I'm not.

Standing there in my living room, framed by a door-sized cutout between our two condos, is my boyfriend, all bright smiles and white, chalky dust from the destruction.

"Nathan?"

"I made it a little too big." He lowers the power saw to my coffee table.

"What's going on?" My mouth is tacky, my words muddled.

"We agreed to install a cat door, remember?" He collects my hands and sweeps his thumbs over the backs of them. 'And that was the original plan, but as I started, I got to thinking that maybe it would be nice for more than just Peeve to be able to go back and forth."

My heart flutters. Is this his way of asking me to move in with him? Granted, we've spent so much time within each other's homes that his condo already feels like mine. But this open wall? This opening up of every square inch of our lives? This is new.

"Nathan."

"You're upset." His smile falls into a flat line. "God. I'm sorry. I probably should have asked you first—"

My lips crush his, my arms thrown around his solid shoulders. His body melds against me with the relief I provide through a kiss so deep I see stars shoot across my eyelids. Once I've thoroughly kissed him senseless and need to come up for air, I draw back.

"So, does that mean you're good with this?" His arms curl low around my waist, and he swivels us as one unit to look at the big, busted up hole.

"So good."

"I'll obviously frame it out and make the transition between our two places a bit more seamless—"

"I say knock down the whole damn wall," I interrupt again.

His dark eyebrows pop up. "Yeah? It might be load bearing, so not sure if that's really feasible."

"If it can be done, go for it. I want to merge everything with you, Nathan. You're a great next-door neighbor, but I'm dying to finally have you as my roommate."

Joy-filled relief washes over him.

"What did I ever do to deserve you? Deserve this?" He tugs me close, pressing those rhetorical words against my skin before leaving a chaste kiss on my cheek. "I never imagined the day I dumped a crib on the sidewalk that it would bring someone like you into my life. I knew I took that useless piece of furniture with me for a reason."

"Who knows? Maybe someday, one of those won't be so useless."

"You're not...?" He chokes on a cough caught in his throat.

"No!" I didn't think that statement all the way through. "I'm not pregnant. But I do want it all with you, Nathan. Someday. I want the ring and the vows and the family. I want to make a life with you, in our own time."

"I think we're already making one."

As if Peeve understands our conversation, he trots over to weave through our legs. His long, striped tail curls around us like a little, fuzzy hug.

"Just look at us, two broken hearts learning to love again," I say, running my palms over Nathan's chest. I push onto my toes to deposit a kiss along his scruff-covered jaw.

"Well, that's the flip side of heartbreak, right? You get to choose how you're going to piece yourself back together." He binds me in his arms, keeping me so close I feel his heartbeat mix with mine like we're one. I think maybe we are. "Quinn, you not only helped me piece my heart back together, but you were the missing piece. I love you with all my heart because you've *become* my heart."

We stand in my living room, a cat at our feet, a hole in the wall, and a future filled with endless possibility on the horizon. A future I cannot wait to step into with the person who keeps surprising me, treasuring me, and showing me what selflessness looks like with every word he says, thing he does, and way he loves.

It's a future brighter than anything I could have written for myself, and it's everything I've ever wanted. Just like the man I'm building it with.

———

Keep reading for info on Jace's story in The Other Side of Ever After

the other side of ever after

Follow Jace's story in The Other Side of Ever After

I don't bring my work home with me.

When I hang up my crown after a shift at Ever After amusement park, I'm no longer the prince I have to be while I'm on the clock. Far, far from it.

It's never been a problem until I stupidly answer my one night stand's front door and her ex is there to hand off their kid for the weekend.

Even without my costume, the little girl recognizes me. Now she thinks I'm her mom's knight-in-shining-armor, and I'm stuck faking a relationship and staying in character longer than I've ever had to.

But as time passes, faking doesn't feel so forced. This woman is sunshine and sweetness and gives me serious true love vibes, even though I know it's all a fantasy. Plus, as a single mom who runs her own preschool, she's an expert on playing pretend.

When her ex suddenly wants back in the picture, I feel the need to protect what's mine, even if it's all make-believe. *Even* if it turns me into the villain.

We've played out the whole fairytale thing. I'm just hoping we'll get the chance to see what's on the other side of ever after.

Stay in touch and learn about new releases, giveaways, and opportunities for advanced copies by signing up for my newsletter.

about meg bradley

For the last eleven years, I've written romance under a pen name, publishing over twenty books both traditionally and independently. And while I enjoy a give-you-a-toothache, sugary-sweet story, I've always wanted to give my characters more. More emotion. More angst. More kisses and *definitely* more spice.

The books written under Meg Bradley are a perfect blend of romantic comedy and contemporary romance. Every novel has a guaranteed HEA, both in the bedroom and in the love story.

facebook.com/authormegbradley

amazon.com/stores/Meg-Bradley/author/B0BZGG9Y2S